PIVOT

COURTING LOVE - A COLLEGE SPORTS SERIES

SIERRA HILL

Much love,
Sierra Hill

TEN28 PUBLISHING LLC

❀ Created with Vellum

REVIEWS FOR COURTING LOVE SERIES

Southern Vixens Book Obsessions:

I literally read this book cover to cover in just a few hours. The characters were real, sweet, intriguing and so heartfelt. Hill can also write one hell of a love scene. Hill effortlessly captured my attention with her story.

Summer's Smexy Book Reviews

This is the first book by Sierra that I have read...It's amazing!!! I can't wait to read the next book in the series. I know books have to end at some point but this is definitely one I didn't want to end!

Books Laid Bare

It took me on a journey with them both that covered the full range of emotions, it was full to the brim with not only love and passion but also heartbreak and anger.

The Power of Three Readers

Sierra Hill has a very talented writing style that's so addictive, that I devour the story in one sitting, no matter how late it is.

Phenomenal Reviews book blog

Sierra Hill has provided a great mixture of sweet and saucy all in one. I read the whole book in one day and looked forward to finding out how the story ended! I am looking forward to reading the continuing stories in this series!

"Where we love is home, home that our feet may leave, but not
our hearts…"
Oliver Wendell Holmes

PROLOGUE

Logan - Seventeen-Years-Old

My stomach is a knotted nerves, mess of excitement, and raging teenage hormones.

I look down at my phone, hidden underneath the covers of my bunk, for the thousandth time in the last hour. Lights out and bed check were twenty minutes ago, and I've been anxiously waiting for Carver's text.

He's my first love. The only guy I've thought about since the first time I met him three summers ago. At the time, we were both fifteen, and it was my first summer attending Camp Cheakamus Adventure in British Columbia.

My phone lights up, illuminating the little pup tent I've created under my sheets, and my heart thinks it's just ran a race.

All clear. 10:30 @ the lake

The text holds so much meaning that I nearly weep with eagerness.

Tonight's the night.

I never thought about sex or what it would mean to lose my

virginity until the first time I kissed Carver. Everything from that moment on has been leading up to this point. We've waited. We've hungered. We've lusted. We've done almost everything together in our previous make-out sessions. But we've never done *it*.

I wasn't ready until now. And Carver could have easily given into temptation and gotten the job done elsewhere way before now. But he didn't. He never pressured me and was always patient, even when I put on the brakes. Frustrated, maybe, but always patient.

Tonight, though, my brain and my body are finally ready. And I can't wait.

On this star-filled, clear July night in the middle of the Garibaldi Ranges between Whistler and Blackcomb mountains, I am going to become a woman with the help of the only boy I've ever loved. The most beautiful, sweet, thoughtful boy in the entire world.

Carver Edwards.

He is my everything.

Over the last hour, I've wiggled anxiously in my bed, unable to tamp down the nerves that flit through me like lightning bugs. A restless desire of what awaits me down by the lake drives me to the brink of insanity. I've thrown off my covers five times in the last ten minutes, my body a constant strobe of electricity, like one of those crazy static electricity balls at the Science Museum.

I'm amped, charged and will probably go off the minute he touches me.

I think I'm more nervous because this isn't a spur-of-the-moment decision, nor an act of impulsiveness. No, it's been a slow brew of teenage hormones over the last three years, since our first kiss at the lake. That's a moment I will never forget. That list of firsts with Carver will expand once again tonight.

I hear my bunkmate, Emma, snoring softly above me. She's the only one whom I've confided in about my plans with Carver.

She listened attentively as I mapped out our secret rendezvous for the big event. Emma isn't a virgin – lost it the winter of her sophomore year – so she was more than willing to give me pointers and is excited to hear all about it.

I squirm in my bed, flopping over to my stomach as I flick my phone on once again, the bright LCD light nearly blinding me as my eyes readjust to focus. It's now ten-fifteen. Even a sighting of Sasquatch can't keep me confined to this bed any longer. I can't wait another damn minute.

Slowly and carefully, I peel back the covers and quietly plant my bare feet on the cabin floor. My toes search for my flip-flops that I left on the side of my bed. The moment I slip them on, I second-guess the decision to wear them on my trek toward my escape, so I pick them up to carry outside until I'm in the clear. No sense making any noise on my way out to my secret rendezvous.

I creep to the door, where before bed I'd placed some gum in the hinges to keep my unauthorized escape from being detected. I hold my breath as I press on the frame ever-so-gently and breathe a sigh of relief as I step out onto the porch, holding on to the handle until it closes behind me with a *snick*. Sealing my fate.

I bolt off the porch and run through the darkened, tree-lined path down to the lake.

I know this trail like the back of my palm, as I stop only momentarily to brush off the needles of the Silver Fir and Western hemlock trees that gathered on my feet during my run. Slipping my flip-flops back on, I continue my sprint down to the shore, the only light coming from the stars above and my phone flashlight.

Whether I'm out of breath from the run or the anticipation of what's to come, I bend forward for a second and rest my hands on my knees, looking to gain my equilibrium and steady my heart rate. Which is impossible, really, since I know it will only grow more rapid from here on out.

A second later, my waist is captured from behind by strong, assured hands. Although I instinctively know it's Carver, I jolt at the firm touch, a tiny fissure of fear that dissolves as soon as he plants his lips at the base of my neck.

"Hey, baby." He whispers in my ear, his warm breath lingering like a warm breeze. I shiver at the soft touch and the low reverberation of his voice.

His hand snakes around my middle, toying with the hem of my tank that sits just below my belly button. The need that's been simmering all day is now roaring to life like the black bears that inhabit the Coast Mountain ranges.

I lean into him, enjoying the heat from his body. The top of my head doesn't even reach the bottom of his chin. Carver is a tall, lean basketball player and just had another growth spurt this year. It surprised me when I saw him again at the beginning of camp two weeks ago. It's like someone sprinkled Miracle Grow on top of his head because he's now a foot taller than me.

The thing is, I don't see Carver outside of camp. Our hometowns are more than an hour from one another in Washington state. We could see each other if I allowed it. But it was my decision early on, and Carver agreed to it, that we leave things at camp and not allow it to continue through the school year.

The reason is simple: I never wanted Carver to see me in my natural habitat. I live in a white-trash, poor farming community in Skagit Valley. He lives in the prestigious area of Mercer Island, a wealthy suburb overlooking Seattle and Lake Washington. His father is some hi-tech millionaire. So, it became clear from the start that outside of our camp existence, Carver and I had nothing in common and wouldn't fit together in the real world.

He has no idea what my life is like back home, and he doesn't even know I'm here on an academic scholarship, too poor to ever attend a program like this without financial aid.

But during these few short weeks every summer, I am his and he is mine. And what we will share tonight will bind us together like nothing else ever could. The most intimate act two people can experience. It will be perfect.

Carver's deep voice reminds me of how quiet it is out here in the British Columbia wilderness. He speaks softly, but it echoes across the water and through the sky above us.

"Are you still okay with this, Lo?" His thumb strums across the flesh of my abdominals, having found its way underneath my shirt.

I turn to face him, tilting my head back and reaching up on my tiptoes to place a kiss on his chin. His nose. And then his lips, which immediately succumb to my demands. There is nothing better than kissing Carver. It doesn't matter that we are apart for entire school years. His kisses were always like coming home again. And I keep those embers burning the remaining nine months of the year.

"I'm more than okay, Carver. I've been waiting for this my entire life." I feel his smile against my lip as he takes another taste.

The stillness of the lake only enhances the possibility that we are alone out here. The only life amongst us are the nocturnal forest creatures hiding or foraging around in the dark.

The thought thrills me. We're alone. No one else around to disrupt our night. We can do whatever we want without the concern of being caught. We haven't kept our relationship hidden, but the camp director, Stellan, is constantly on us about our habitual PDA. I've caught him staring at us on more than one occasion, his eyes displaying an emotion I can't quite name. I've mentioned it to Carver, but he just laughs it off, suggesting that Stellan's just jealous of what we have.

Carver clasps my hand and tugs me toward the left of where we're standing.

"Good," he says, pulling me behind him as we swiftly walk toward a clump of trees. "Cause your palace awaits."

We walk along the edge of the shore for a few minutes, his flashlight illuminating the way across logs, stones and fallen pine cones. And then, just as we skirt around the base of a large hemlock, I see the small camp that Carver set up.

I gasp in awe. It's the most romantic gesture ever. It couldn't be any more perfect than this.

"Oh my God, Carver. When did you do this?" My eyes flit between the small tent to Carver. The grin across his face is both charming and devilish.

He shrugs but doesn't answer my question. Instead, he asks timidly, very unlike Carver. "Do you like it?"

There are no words to describe how I feel. My mouth goes dry and I bite my quivering lip to keep my tears from falling.

This boy owns my heart and soul. And he'll very soon take ownership of my body.

"I love it," I respond, following him through the open flap of the tent, which is lit with flashlights. Once seated, I lean in to wrap my arms around his neck, pulling him into my chest. "And I love you, Carver. More than anything."

Anyone in close proximity to our tent might have assumed it was a grizzly nearby, based on the loud growl that rumbles from Carver's chest when my hand lands on the bulge at his crotch. He was already hard before I touched him. I continue rubbing him until he pushes my hand away and rolls on top of me.

Our bodies are aligned so I can feel his hard length in the spot where he'll soon be without any barriers. We've had our fair share of dry-humping over the past summers and have touched each other pretty much everywhere. He's given me orgasms with his fingers and taken me to the top of the world with his tongue and mouth. And I've done the same to him.

No one ever told me how incredible it is, and how much joy you can experience, to make a boy come with your mouth.

"I brought a condom, in case you changed your mind." He says, lifting his head from where it's been buried in the crook of my neck.

I shake my head, sifting my fingers through his tousled hair.

We'd discussed this already. I'd been on the Pill since I was fourteen to regulate my heavy periods. Since we are both each other's firsts, and both of us are clean, I wanted to avoid any awkwardness of fumbling around with a condom.

I am totally okay with this and tell him so, but I appreciate that he is thoughtful enough to bring one just in case. I figured I'd experience pain either way, so at least this way I'd be able to feel all of him. And vice versa.

"No, I'm good if you are. I promise."

Carver cups my cheek and kisses me. His eyes stare at me with love, hope and earnestness.

"I just want it to be good for you."

I can't help the nervous sarcasm that comes out of my mouth. "Well maybe you should stop talking about it, then, and just get on with it."

I giggle when he bites down on my earlobe playfully. But his lips and teeth quickly turn serious, working their way down my neck, his fingers inching the strap of my tank off my shoulder, exposing my breast.

My hands have a mind of their own as they mold around the muscular globes of his ass and squeeze. He groans, sucking on the sensitive flesh just above my breast, thrusting his lower half into mine. I arch into him as his lips hover over my nipple, his tongue lashing at the tip. I hum in response and wonder how loud we are and if anyone can hear us outside the tent.

What if someone happens upon our tent? What if Stellan is doing a bed check and finds ours empty, sending out a search party to locate us and take us back?

No sooner have I thought of every possible worst-case-scenario, I look down and realize Carver has already divested us both of our clothing. Now I'm fully naked, lying next to a fully naked Carver. His hands and fingers touch me everywhere, and with each touch the ache between my legs grows bolder and stronger.

Carver hovers above me, his broad shoulders and muscular biceps holding him over me. His lower body urges my legs open, his hard shaft gliding effortlessly between my folds. I'm already wet and ready, from just that small amount of friction. I let out a wanton moan, the sensation so unique, yet foreign.

My legs automatically stiffen when I feel the tip of his cock probe at my entrance.

"God, Lo...I'm sorry. I can't hold out any longer."

Carver's restraint disappears, his body tight as a crossbow at target practice. Our gazes lock in the dark as he trembles above me, the delicious weight of his body covering me with untapped desire.

"Okay." I whisper huskily.

I should be nervous as his hand moves between us, as he aligns himself up in just the precise spot. But I'm not. I'm turned on and ready for what's coming.

Oh my God, this is really happening.

I see our past. I feel the present. I hope for our future.

A quick push, a slight sting and then I feel the fullness of Carver. He's inside me. I instinctively bring my knees up toward my chest, allowing him more room, as he rocks above me. His biceps strain and his forehead creases as he slides in and out of me. Aside from the pinch at the onset, I now just feel a low-grade burn.

My breath hitches every time he slides out and then pushes back in. It's like the waves of the lake - the rhythmic cycle, licking at the shore, pressing across the smooth rocks of the beach. Each time he pushes deeper, I know he's leaving an indelible memory in my heart.

His grunts grow louder and the movements faster, as the motion of his body becomes more jerky – along with his breaths. And then with one final push, his strong body stiffens unbelievably tighter as he stills above me. Carver groans so deep, I swear the earth below moves with the rumble of his bellow.

He buries his head in the crook of my neck as I stroke the back of his head; his neck; and down his spine, loving the slick feel of his muscular shoulders.

A few moments pass and he still hasn't moved. I know he's still awake because I can feel his eyelashes flutter against the skin of my neck.

And then he says the words that remind me there is nothing that will ever separate us, because we are now one.

"I love you, Logan. You and me forever."

But I will soon learn that Carver's a liar.

And forever doesn't exist.

CHAPTER 1

LOGAN – MARCH FIVE YEARS LATER

"YOUR TEN-THIRTY PATIENT HAS ARRIVED, *LOGAN.*"

And then Bethany adds under her breath, "*If you can manage to tell time, that is.*"

I nod at her as I walk by her desk. She's Dr. Connell's front desk receptionist and office administrator, and has only been here two months longer than I have. Even so, she demonstrates an air of superiority over me, along with an underlying hostility that she only displays when no one else is around. Like now.

The hallway behind the desk is empty and Bethany knows when the doctor isn't around and when she has liberty to shoot these little barbs at me. I honestly don't get it. I've been nothing but nice to her since the moment I walked in to complete my new hire paperwork. I'd joined the dental assistant team right out of school and it wasn't my intention to make any waves with any of my colleagues. I normally get along with everyone, but I have no clue what I've done to make her despise me so much.

It's not terribly important that I make best friends with those

I work with, but it sure makes it better. With Bethany's cold shoulder always on the ready, I've tried my best to suck it up and deal with her rude attitude. My motto has always been *"get along and get 'er done."* I may have stolen that from my father. A family heirloom, of sorts. Possibly the only thing he'd ever given me since the age of thirteen.

That's because nothing free was ever given to the youngest of four from my poor farming family living in one of the poorest farming communities in Washington state. I was lucky to get hand-me-down shoes from the Goodwill by the time I was born. As the only girl in a household of three older brothers, I had to earn my way and keep up – or get beat up. I was not treated like a princess in some fairy tale. There was no slacking or using the *"I'm just a girl"* excuse, because none of them gave a rat's ass that I was their baby sister. In fact, it only made them want to beat on me more.

I suppose I should thank them for teaching me how to survive by growing thick skin. Now I'm able to deal with the likes of the Bethanys of the world, and her snotty attitude toward me. While I don't think I deserve her spite, I'm not about to get my panties in a wad and go tattle on her to my new boss, Dr. Connell.

Her like or dislike of me will not affect my job as the newest dental assistant in one of Seattle's best oral surgery and dentistry practices. My entire goal is to become indispensable to the doctor, so he'll consider me an asset to him. So I won't be tossed away like garbage. Thrown away without a glance back like others have done in my life.

So far, Dr. Connell seems to like me. Perhaps a little *too* much. Since I started six months ago, Dr. Connell has asked me out twice. And in the age of office sexual harassment lawsuits, you'd think an up-and-coming dentist like him would avoid that conduct.

He isn't a slime ball, or creepy, or anything like that. It's not like he's lurking around me trying to get fresh or cop a feel. Apart from him asking me out, Dr. Connell has been careful never to do anything untoward. He's a good teacher and mild-mannered boss, and I enjoy working for him.

I've politely declined each time he's asked me out. He's a decent looking man, probably mid-thirties, and a little geeky but sweet. I'm sure he's quite a catch – but I'm not interested.

Perhaps that's why Bethany dislikes me so vehemently. Maybe she's jealous. I don't really care what bee's up her butt. I shouldn't have to bend over backwards just to win her over. My time is better spent elsewhere.

Picking up the client folder from the slot on the counter, I quickly glance at the folder and scheduled appointment. It's Friday and we generally have scheduled appointments until noon, leaving the afternoon open for any emergency walk-ins and weekly paperwork.

I open the door to the waiting room area and flash a smile to the middle-aged man in the lobby.

"Mr. Arnold. Come on back. We're all ready for you now."

There's something unnerving about him as he brushes past me, walking with an air of confidence, his deep brown eyes scanning me from head to toe. "We'll be in room B today."

Mr. Arnold strides ahead, his navy-blue suit wrinkle-free and screaming *"I'm the shit."* Mary Ann, one of the other dental assistants, warned me that Mr. Arnold is some bigwig lawyer and one of our select clients.

Well, la-tee-da. I treat all my patients the same. No matter what race or wallet size, they all have the same oral care requirements. I will not bow down to anyone just because of their social status.

Even rich people's breath can stink.

"Any changes to your medical history since the last time you were in, Mr. Arnold?"

I take a seat in the rolling chair next to his reclining figure, reviewing his medical information tab on my open computer screen.

The leering snide of his voice has my head snapping toward him, my eyebrows creasing with question.

"In fact, yes, there is…I'm in much better shape now that I'm divorced."

He chuckles with a lecherous undertone, even adding on a wink. "And my stamina is better now than it was in my twenties."

I want to gag up my breakfast.

Growing up with three older brothers, I've heard every sexual innuendo there is and I rarely bat an eye at it. But there's a time and a place for it. Not in my workplace when I'm about to use very sharp metal instruments in your mouth. That's just plain stupid. This guy is obviously not as smart as his thousand-dollar suit implies.

I bite the inside of my cheek and let out a polite laugh at his annoying comment. Although I should shut him down.

Turning back to my computer, I decide to ignore his comment.

"Mm-hm. Let's see here. On your last visit, we were watching the amalgam on your bilateral bicuspids. You were wearing them down quite a bit and the doctor wanted to review it this time to see if a bite guard is necessary."

Mr. Arnold makes another mocking sound, but I refrain from giving him my attention. Behind me he says, "Now that I'm not sleeping with my bitch of an ex, my grinding has stopped."

Douche.

"Well, we'll have Dr. Connell confirm where things are at. Is there anything else we should review?"

There's a short pause and I can't help but swivel around. I find Mr. Arnold blatantly staring at me.

"Now that you mention it, I do have some sensitivity in the back tooth."

He opens his mouth wide and points toward one of the upper molars.

I slip on my latex gloves, covering my mouth and nose with my mask, and lean in. Using the mirror and periodontal probe, I investigate the location he's indicated where the pain stems from. I'm going about my business as his left arm swings up and his hand lightly brushes across my right breast.

I jerk back with a sharp intake of breath. Since I can't be sure he did it on purpose, I'll let it go. This time. But if it happens again, I won't refrain from admonishing him. Fool me once and all that.

His excuse is immediate but lacking sincerity in the apology, as evidenced by the expression on his face. He wears a pathetically smarmy smile. "I'm so sorry. You just startled me."

Mm-hmm. I'm sure that was it.

One of the areas that has come a long way in the dental assistant field is that we no longer have to be subjected to sexual harassment. No woman, in any profession, should tolerate the sliminess that some men seem to wear. Dr. Connell's office harassment policy is very clear that it extends to patients and not just management. This type of occurrence happens more than it should when men feel at liberty to cop a feel.

If I wanted, I could stand-up right now, walk into the doctor's office and call Mr. Arnold out for his indecent groping.

But I won't. It's not necessary. I'll handle it on my own. Just like I've done with everything since I was seventeen.

I tilt my head to the side, my eyes pinned to him with an assessing stare, showing him that I won't back down. I won't cower. I have the upper hand here.

"Mr. Arnold. You should really be more careful. It's very important that I keep a steady hand while I have sharp instruments in your mouth. I'd hate for you to *accidentally* bump me again. That could cause quite the severe outcome." I clear my throat, looking over my shoulder at the computer and then back to him. "And according to your chart, you're quite prone to being *extra* sensitive to dental cleanings."

What I don't mention is that his records indicated that during his last dental procedure, Mr. Arnold cried like a little baby – a simple filling. I have to stifle my laugh when I see his face turn ghost white and he grips the arm rests more tightly from the threat in my response. He knows it and I know it.

Don't mess with me again, otherwise you'll be sorry.

"Now then, if you're ready to proceed, I think the sensitivity in that area could be from the trauma caused by the bruxism." I continue to explain the damage could be extensive, smiling as I do. "We'll get some bitewing x-rays and have a look."

IT'S after one in the afternoon and time for lunch. I'm exhausted from a long morning and an even longer week. My lower back aches from being hunched over my last patient during her root canal and my dogs are barking like ferocious Pit Bulls. As in, my feet hurt like hell.

I'm in the small kitchenette breakroom when Dr. Connell comes in, lunch bag in hand.

"Mind if I join you, Logan?" He asks sweetly, his smile high-lighting the bright white of his perfectly aligned teeth.

Motioning to the chair next to me, I slide my sandwich container over to allow him room at the table.

"Thanks."

I finish chewing my sandwich and close the book I've been reading. One from the James Patterson collection. I've had it in my possession for weeks now and can't seem to get through it very fast. My roommate, Alison, however, is a book whore and speed reader. Our apartment is littered with piles of books, which she calls 'research'.

There's a short pause before Dr. Connell – or Jeff, as he has asked me to call him on more than one occasion – speaks again.

"How was your week? You seemed a little off kilter earlier today."

It's surprising that he picked up on that. I'm usually good at wearing my poker face and keeping my feelings hidden. Lessons learned as a young girl, when I was picked on mercilessly for showing any type of emotion.

I give him a half-hearted shrug and pick up an apple slice from my lunchbox.

"Oh, I'm fine. Thanks for asking. I'm just tired today."

He takes a moment to consider this, nodding his head and pursing his lips.

"Are you feeling okay? Maybe you're coming down with something. Is there anything I can do for you?"

Not likely. I'm the picture of perfect health. I just haven't been sleeping well. It's the time of year where the memories keep me awake at night, revisiting my past decisions. Nothing my boss can do anything about.

"No, I'm feeling great. Work is going well – things are good." I say this with as much enthusiasm as I can muster, hoping to placate him so he'll lay off the twenty questions. It's making me more uncomfortable than Mr. Arnold's wandering hands.

"I'm so glad to hear that. You're doing an amazing job, Logan. I know the patients adore you. As do I."

My eyes slide to his when he says this. Oh, shit. His expression is filled with genuine warmth and affection. I know what this means. I hold my breath and count to ten, uncertain how to proceed.

Dr. Connell – *Jeff* – is a very nice guy. Obviously kind and thoughtful. He reminds me of the character Bill Pullman played in *Sleepless in Seattle*. A little straight-laced for my taste and pretty goofy. I guess he's good-looking, in a dull sort of way. He has neatly trimmed dark hair that's turning a shade of salt-and-pepper at his temples. I could certainly do worse.

But I don't want to do *anything*. I'm not interested in dating or developing a serious relationship with anyone right now. And I fear Jeff is looking for exactly that thing.

He clears his throat, a blush creeping up his neck. "Logan," he begins nervously, "I really like you. You are a terrific employee. I know you're apprehensive about dating...but I guess I'm a glutton for punishment and want to ask you one more time...just in case...in the event you might reconsider."

His hands fiddle nervously with the bottle of Kombucha tea in front of him, and it just makes me feel sorry for him.

He continues, "Would you consider just dinner with me? Only dinner. We could even do the early bird special and I'd have you home by eight."

I can't help but giggle at his offer. Any other girl would be lucky to date him. For me, though, I'm damaged goods. My life isn't the same as most other's my age. I still have too much work to do on myself before I'd ever be ready for what he's hoping for.

I'll give him one thing. The man is certainly persistent. Maybe if I just said yes to one date, he'd get it out of his system. It's just one date.

"Dr. Connell-"

"Jeff, please." He interrupts softly.

I straighten my spine and turn toward him.

"Okay, Jeff. Just dinner. That's all I can commit to. I think it's a horrible idea, though – dating the boss. That's why no-fraternizing policies exist in employee handbooks."

The look on his face is utter glee. Oh geez. He's like a five-year-old boy on Christmas morning. Excited. Hopeful. Happy. Apparently, I'm the life-size present Santa brought him this year.

Jeff's clammy palm lands on top of my hand resting on the table. I want to pull it back, but don't want to reject him, so I keep it there. I see a flash of movement over Jeff's shoulder as Bethany walks by, her eyes glaring with contempt.

Oh, great. Just another reason for her to hate me.

"We don't have that policy in our handbook." His voice rises two octaves higher, snapping my attention back to him.

"I'm so happy. You've made my day." He rambles eagerly, "Is tomorrow night too soon?"

I search my brain for an excuse, but all I have planned is finishing this book.

"Um…well, I'll have to check."

Jeff has already pulled up his phone calendar, perusing the dates on his schedule.

"Do you enjoy college basketball?"

Huh?

I give him a perplexed tilt of my head. *"College basketball?"*

He nods his head and waves his hand in excitement. "Yes! I totally forgot. My buddy from UW works at the arena and invited me to use his VIP tickets for tomorrow night's Regional playoffs. We could go watch the game and then have dinner afterward. What do you say?"

So much for just dinner and home by eight. I don't want to let him down, but college basketball isn't exactly my thing. I've only known one basketball player in my life and he left me without a backward glance. So, no, I can't say I like basketball.

The lunch in my stomach swishes and sloshes around like piranhas in a pool of bodies. But I feel like I'll be the one eaten alive.

Against my better judgment, because of his excitement, I offer up my response.

"Sure, that sounds great."

CHAPTER 2

CARVER

IT'S weird being back home in Seattle.

I can't say it feels like home anymore, because my home has been Phoenix for the last four years where I've attended college. Seattle is simply the place I grew up.

Mercer Island, specifically. That's where my parents live. It's the home to the rich and relatively famous of the Seattle dot-commers and tech-giants. My father is one of those people. He made it big before I was born when he developed a veritable, one-of-a-kind software program and sold it to an off-shoot of Microsoft in the early nineties. Needless to say I grew up in a very influential area.

Looking back, I had a great childhood. I went to the most prestigious of schools, was afforded opportunities to play on elite high school basketball leagues, and attended the best summer enrichment programs and camps that money can buy. My parents loved me and doted on me as their only child.

But that was then and this is now. And my father and I don't talk any longer. Not after he made a decision that affected my future without consulting me. I will never forgive him for it.

Since then, I've limited my trips back home to a handful of holidays. I can't recall the last time we had a civilized conversation that didn't erupt in a shouting match. Or just silence. My mother, God bless her, is amazing, and I feel bad she's been caught in the middle of our war.

It's not with some regret that I chose not to invite my parents to come watch me play in the championship games this week. As captain of the ASU men's basketball team, I received four tickets that I could dole out to my family or friends. I elected to give them to my high school buddies. Call me an asshole or whatever. If my dad wants to come see me play, he has the funds to fork out to purchase tickets. In fact, it wouldn't surprise me to find out he bought a box suite at the stadium.

It's nine a.m. Saturday morning and the team is arriving down in the hotel lobby to catch our bus over to the arena. We're scheduled to play number two, Gonzaga, tonight. We'd just beaten the Huskies at Thursday night's game and barely squeaked out a win. As a single elimination tourney, we're now bracketed against the Zags. One of the toughest teams in the Pac-12.

All our sights are set on winning this Regional game, so we can move on to the Sweet 16. If we do, we'll play next weekend in Houston. If we don't, this will be my last college game of my career. Come May, I'll be graduating from ASU and then entering the NBA draft in June.

Everything is looking up and I'm exactly where I wanted to be in life right now. On the precipice of greatness.

I make my way down the narrow aisle of the bus and take a seat next to Lance Britton, my roommate and one of my best friends. He has his Beats earphones on and his phone in his hand.

I intentionally bump his shoulder when I plop down on the seat next to him. He looks up and glares.

"Mm. Someone didn't eat their Wheaties today, huh dude?" I snicker, knowing that I'll get under his skin with my annoying comment. "Either that, or that chick you were with last night didn't finish the job?"

I love giving the guys a hard time. That's just how I roll. I talk trash on and off the court.

"Eh, fuck you, Edwards. I'm trying to get into the zone here."

I take in Lance's appearance. Even though he's dressed in a suit, just like the rest of the players on the bus, he seems disheveled, like he had an all-night bender. Which may not be too far off the mark. Although we are forced to tone down our drinking during the season, we did party the previous night in celebration of our win against UW.

I left the party around eleven, with a chick in tow, who was eager and ready to get it on. But I lost track of Lance, and don't know where he ended up. He's a great guy – loved by all – one of my best friends. But he has some demons lurking in his soul. Dark ones, that even as his best friend, I still don't know about.

For the last year, it's become more and more noticeable. His regular drinking. Blackouts. Erratic behavior. Sullen attitude. Constant highs and crashing lows. Whatever his problems, they seem to be eating away at his psyche.

Maybe that's true for all of us. I don't know. Maybe I should have gone into psychology instead of business. And maybe it's time for an intervention. But not today.

Today we are going to fucking stomp on our competitors and I'm not going to let Lance get away with being in a pissy mood.

"And what zone is that, exactly? The Danger Zone? The Twilight Zone? The Eastern Time Zone? cause seriously dude, you look like death warmed over. What's your deal?"

Lance turns his head away to gaze out the window, like he's suddenly interested in what's happening out on the street, but he's really just avoiding my direct question.

I've apparently hit the mark. He does look like shit. Dark

circles under his eyes. His skin tone has taken on an ashy-gray hue. And his eyes, which are usually bright and full of mischief, now seem dull and lackluster.

"Nothing. I'm fine," he mumbles unconvincingly.

"Sure, dude. If that's how you wanna play it, that's cool. But if you need to talk to someone, you know I'm here for you, bruh. And so is Coach. You just have to say the word."

As the captain of the team this year, it's been my responsibility to deliver frequent pep talks to other players. One guy came to me about his pregnant girl-on-the-side, asking for my advice on what to do and if he should tell his actual girlfriend. Fuck, what kind of advice was I supposed to give on that topic? I also counseled a red-shirted freshman on overcoming the nerves and stage fright when playing in front of thousands of fans and TV viewers.

Although I'm normally a sarcastic ball-puncher, I've taken my team captaincy seriously because I care about my team. I only wish I could take some of my own advice.

I may look like I have it all together – and for the most part I do – but there are some secrets that no one else knows about. Memories I've kept buried deep beneath the surface – that have left an indelible impression on me. Experiences that shaped who I am and who I've become.

The team bus rolls to a stop in front of the stadium and I lean over Lance's shoulder to get a closer look at all the fans waiting our arrival. A lot of young boys and their dads, hoping for an autograph from their favorite NCAA player. And throngs of college girls looking for a lot more than an autograph from a ball player.

We have affectionately named these girls hoops hunnies, because they love their players and are sweet as fucking honey.

I give Lance a nudge, stabbing my finger toward two leggy chicks standing outside the bus holding handmade signs for us to see.

One says, "I BOUNCE FOR BRITTON", while the other reads, "I ~~COME~~ CAME FOR CARVER."

Not too difficult to read the sexual innuendo there. These girls are DTF.

"Check it out, bruh. No matter what happens tonight on the court, we are both getting laid." I give them a wave out the window and see them both giggle and flaunt their bodies. Lance snickers as we stand to grab our gym bags from overhead, heading off the bus and into the arena.

The excitement over travelling for away games hasn't grown old. I love being on the road and can't wait for my chance as an NBA player. Although the draft isn't until June, I've had my fair share of informal discussions with scouts from the pro teams. Since I've already declared my intentions, my agent has assured me I have a spot on one of the best teams. I'd love to play on one of the coasts – either East or West - but life doesn't always give you what you want. I've learned that lesson the hard way.

As we're getting settled in the locker room, Coach Welby enters and stands in the center of the team. The room goes silent as all sixteen of the squad cop a squat on a bench or stand in formation, all eyes on him.

"All right men, tonight's the night. You've worked your asses off this season, overcoming your share of obstacles and losses. You deserve to be here. This is your moment, and I expect nothing less than giving everything you got out there."

We all know the obstacles he's referring to include Cade Griffin's suspension at the beginning of the season, and losing one of our junior starters to a drug-related offense. It was a tough way to start the year, but it didn't stop our team from pulling together to find a rhythm, making us strong contenders.

Coach continues, "I want to thank you all for delivering strong performances this season. For pushing farther than you thought possible. Some of you will be leaving us soon. You should be proud of what you've accomplished on this team, for yourselves, your families, your classmates. Your school and fans. I'm proud of all of you. As you know, in less than six hours, we will be taking on Gonzaga. But before we do, we're obligated to meet with members of the media to discuss our game day prep. I'm going to hand it over to Jacqueline to walk you through the rules once again on how to handle yourself appropriately and maturely out there."

This gains widespread snickers and grunts from the guys. Dealing with the sports media is part of the process when you play ball. Aside from a few times when they asked stupid questions and deserved to get respective stupid answers, I don't mind being on camera. As my Media Relations and Communications professor, Lori, once told me, "the camera loves my natural charm".

Ironically, she'd said that to me right after we'd recorded our fuck session together.

Yep, I slept with one of my professors. What can I say? I have a healthy sexual appetite and I'm not about to say no to an offer to sleep with a hot female professor. I'm a twenty-two-year-old captain of my college basketball team and virility oozes from my pores.

It's the reason I've never locked myself down to just one girl. I'd done that once before and have the scars to prove it. I'd given her my heart, my fidelity and my soul – and she fucked me over. Without so much as a goodbye.

So, fuck that shit. I'll take the hoops hunnies in constant supply over a girlfriend anytime. I'll continue to accept and enjoy the perks that my position as a player affords me. I'll ride this train right through graduation, and then into my professional career.

It doesn't get any better than this.

My eyes scan the room to watch the faces of my teammates as Jacqueline give her spiel. I'm going to miss these guys. I see Cade Griffin, my other friend and roommate. He's come through some turbulent times but has landed on his feet – dodging a nasty bullet with some legal trouble he recently experienced. Things have settled down for him, now that he's in love with his girl, Ainsley. He won't be following me into the draft because he plans on becoming an engineer after graduation. He's even talked about proposing to Ainsley.

Then there's Van Gerard, one of our power forwards who stands erect at six-foot-six, his long hair pulled back into a neat man-bun. We've had our challenges recently, mostly due to his secret crush on Kylah Griffin, Cade's younger sister. Van and I have had it out a few times this season, mainly because he's been playing like a thug, which is not okay on my team. But also, because I'm hella protective of Kylah. She's like my own little sister and I don't want to see her getting hurt.

I'm lost in thought when Christian Lancaster thumps me on the back, jarring me back to the present.

"Yo, everything okay there, Cap?"

Christian's a decent guy, if not dumber than a box of rocks. But he's our center and stands the tallest of all of us, nearly six-eleven. He gives us the defense we need against tough teams like Gonzaga.

I shake my head free of the cobwebs. "Yeah, thanks man. All good here. Just thinking about the strategy for tonight's game."

"I hear ya. I think we have a fucking damn good shot, man. We just need to keep the eye on the prize and play good ball. 'Cause there ain't no 'I' in losing."

My jaw drops as I laugh loudly, my head falling back to look up at him. Like I said, dumb as a box of rocks.

"Uh, I think you mean 'there ain't no 'I' in team'. Because there *is* an 'I' in losing."

Christian gives a deep resounding guffaw and quirks an eyebrow, patting my shoulder like I'm the idiot. "Yeah, sure, C. Whatever."

I watch him walk off, shaking my head at his lumbering

idiocy, and know right then and there that he'll be a fifth-year senior.

THE ERUPTION of loud cheers and fan excitement has my adrenaline pumping as we run out onto the court to take our spots on the sideline seats. It's like no other drug in the world – the sounds of the crowd roaring to a deafening decibel. It's my addiction of choice. I never want to give this up.

The announcer calls out our starting line-up as the arena lights go off, the spotlight waving over us as our names are called individually.

"Starting tonight, from the Arizona Sun Devils, at forward, a six-six senior from Tucson, Arizona, number five, Donovan Gerard."

The strobe lights flicker, the fans go wild, and I watch from my seat, my knees bouncing with anticipation, as Van walks through the tunnel of team players on each side of him, slapping hands and bumping fists as he steps onto the court.

The next three starters are announced, including Lance, Cade and Scott Wagner. And then the lights dim a fraction of an inch more, and the crowd suddenly grows unnervingly quiet.

"And now, at guard, a six-three senior captain from Mercer Island, Washington, number sixteen, Carver Edwards Jr."

I jump from my chair and whip off my warm-up pants, tossing them to the floor and head out to join my teammates. The thirty-five thousand fans are cheering and screaming, chanting my name like I'm a rock star. I'm not immune to the accolades and fan worship, giving myself a fleeting moment to feed off the love and vibes coming from the stands.

I make my way into center court, where my boys stand waiting for me, and we raise our arms up to form a teepee structure, our team chant slowly growing louder.

"Let's go. Let's show. Let's roll." We repeat three times in unison until we break with a final shout.

The chant and team comradery has me a bit emotional, knowing this could be the last time we all say it together. All of us are seniors, except Wagner, so if we are defeated tonight in this single-elimination game, we'll be heading home with not only a loss, but the last game of our college career. Bittersweet.

We line up at mid-court, waiting anxiously for the opening tip; Van is our center/power forward and is in the middle against the Gonzaga center, the ref in between them with the ball in his hand. I'm behind Van, waiting to receive the tip.

The game begins, with Gonzaga in possession, as I take off after the Zag's point guard, Dillon Chambers.

We play strong for the first twelve minutes, taking the lead early on and sustaining it as we continue dribbling, passing, shooting and blocking against the Zags. I'm feeling good about how the team is playing, all zeroed in on the same goal of winning so we can move to the Sweet 16 in Houston.

We set up for one of our trick plays, as I cross the mid-court line and make a quick, behind-the-back pass down the perimeter, over to where Wagner catches the ball and takes a three-point shot, a hook from the corner. He sinks it and the crowd grows wild, as the other team inbounds and we all head the opposite direction back down the court.

I guard Chambers, the offensive point guard. I follow the ball as he dishes it off to another player. It's then that my gaze lands on the Zag's player near the sideline, where I notice a woman taking a seat in the front row. It's just a fleeting glimpse of long, honey blonde hair. Silky strands that are born of my memories, long held in my dreams at night.

The woman turns back to the court, brushing the hair out of her face, and our eyes connect.

This is not just any blonde-haired woman.

My gaze is locked with the most beautiful blue eyes I've ever seen.

The eyes of the only woman who owned my heart, took it and never gave it back.

The woman who single-handedly broke my heart. Who turned me off to the possibility of ever having another relationship again.

Logan Shaw.

I stare at her for less than two seconds – but it feels like two hours. I take in everything about her in one flashbulb moment.

The soft curve of her hips, the tight skinny jeans clinging snugly around shapely thighs, her legs fitted with knee-high boots. The green sweater that tapers at her waist, tugging across her perfectly palm-sized breasts, emphasizing the weight and volume a man can get lost in.

She quickly looks away, and takes her seat, clearly unaffected by my appearance. Where as I, on the other hand, am now a fucking mess.

I hear my name called and my head snaps to the left just in time to see the ball flying at me with the speed of a bullet. I catch it on reflex and begin dribbling it down the court, calling out the Zebra play. I look to the right, and fake left before passing it to Cade, who tries posting up, but the man-to-man coverage is too tight. He dishes it back to me and I see an opening. So I take it.

I fake a dish to my left, a spin on the balls of my feet as I skirt around the defender, and take a leap up for a layup, using the backboard as my accomplice. The ball goes in, scoring two points, but not before I'm elbowed hard in the face by the Zag's beastly center.

There's a loud crunch as the connection is made, followed by a sharp pain that explodes at the bridge of my nose. I tumble to the hardwood, sliding on my ass as the taste of copper floods my mouth. Blood flows down my chin as I try to stand. But then my vision goes blurry. The lights of the arena dim.

I wobble, my legs losing their balance and I fall backward across the boards again. My ass hits the floor behind me, one hand reaching out to catch my fall, the other instinctively covering my mouth. My eyes sting from the excruciating burn that's ripping through my head. I glance up through watery eyes to see Cade and Lance hovering over me, their wild bewilderment simultaneously telling me this can't be good.

And then everything goes black.

CHAPTER 3

LOGAN

MY DATE with Jeff hasn't been as bad as I had anticipated. Better than I'd expected, actually. Even though I'm still a reluctant participant, I can't complain because he's treated me with the utmost respect, better than any other guy in recent history.

He's a perfect gentleman. Attentive to my needs and courteous in every way. He hasn't even tried to touch me, except for a gentle press of his hand to guide me into the arena, which I appreciated. I don't like it when men feel they have the right to paw me. The few guys I have dated assume that because I'm voluptuous, they have an automatic right to touch me without permission. Some scrambled Neanderthal-brain thing. See boobs. Touch boobs.

Uhga-uhga-uhga.

But Jeff has kept a respectful distance. He was even good-humored when I asked him to meet me at the office instead of picking me up at home. I didn't want the end of the date awkwardness where he felt obliged to kiss me at my doorstep. He simply agreed with my request and bashfully handed me a bouquet of flowers when I got out of my car in the parking lot.

From there, we stopped by a bar for a drink and some appetizers before we left for the arena. We engaged in a rather interesting conversation over travel and global warming while I finished my glass of wine. By the time we finally left to head for the game, traffic around the arena was congested, getting us there and into our seats well into the first half.

I'd never been court side at any game before. That kind of special treatment is usually reserved for the rich or famous. His college friend really did him a solid and hooked us up. We entered through a special VIP area of the arena, where there was even a hospitality room with finger foods and an open bar. I picked up a beer and some popcorn before we were led to our seats by an employee in a purple and gold jacket.

Now as we proceed to our seats, Jeff apologizes to everyone we pass for unintentionally obstructing their views. I'm almost annoyed with him by the time we get to our seats because he's so damn polite, but I'm too excited when I see where we're sitting.

I honestly have no idea who's playing tonight. All I know is what Jeff told me about the game, which is that it is a local Washington team playing against another top-ranked team, vying to move ahead in the tournament.

With my hands occupied with my beer and popcorn, I clumsily maneuver myself around my seat before I can sit down, trying not to spill on myself or anyone else. I turn at my waist and place my things on the floor next to my feet before turning back to face the court. As I do, I lift my gaze to find a *very* tall and *very* familiar face staring straight at me.

I blink twice.

When my eyes adjust again, my heart bottoms out in my stomach, the wine I drank earlier sloshing around like it's inside a barrel tipped on its side.

I feel dizzy.

Dazed and confused.

My jaw goes slack, mouth agape in horror at who is less than fifteen-feet from where I sit. It feels like I'm in that scene in *Star Wars*, where Princes Leia is held immobile by the Storm Troopers and their stun-guns. If Seattle had an earthquake right this minute, I wouldn't even feel it because I'm so shaken by the man who stands on the court.

Staring right at me as if I'm a ghost.

Holy shit.

The only boy I've ever loved.

The only boy who meant everything to me.

The only boy who threw me away and wasn't there when I needed him most.

Jeff leans over and whispers in my ear, startling me so bad that I jump in my seat like it's on fire.

"Do you know that player?"

My hands tighten into fists in my lap.

"No, I don't think so," I lie, glancing away from the action on the court. Away from Carver's penetrating stare.

I have no idea what happens over the course of the next few minutes. All I hear is a rush of noise swirling in my head. Players run up and down the court and back again in front of me, shooting and dribbling – but it's all a blur. Plays are called out, coaches yell at their teams to hustle on the court. Refs blow their whistles indicating fouls. I watch in a daze while trying to regulate my breathing.

Breathe.

You can handle this.

I'm now fully aware that the Washington team, Gonzaga, is playing against ASU. Carver's team. I try to keep up with the game, pretending to act normal and not at all freaked out that I just laid eyes on the guy I've worked so hard to forget.

How is this even possible that Carver is here? I mean, I knew he played college basketball and that he attended ASU, but the odds of him playing here? Tonight? Playing in the only game I've ever watched live and in person?

Carver is at the far end of the court. He accepts an inbound pass from one of his teammates. My mind reels, my eyes glued to his movements, as he agilely handles the ball, effortlessly hurling it off toward another player. He runs down toward the goal post, weaving in and out of other players, receiving and passing the ball smoothly – confidently – taking it to the basket.

And then all hell breaks loose.

My brain can't keep up with the fast-paced action. One minute Carver is ten feet in the air, the ball hitting the backboard and swooshing in the net, and the next, he's sprawled out on the floor beneath the basket holding his mouth.

Loud gasps of air can be heard amongst the crowd; shouting, whistles blaring, players and fans craning their necks to see what's going on at the far end of the court.

"Carver." I whisper under my breath, as I slap at my hand over my mouth to keep myself from shouting his name out loud.

The game clock has stopped, music is being pumped through the arena speakers, and a time out has been called.

"What's happening down there?" I ask Jeff, trying to sound calm and unaffected by what I've witnessed.

My eyes go wide, as I look down at my knee where Jeff's hand has landed. "I think that player got elbowed in the face. These things happen all the time in sports. It's just part of the game. He'll probably be back at it in a few minutes."

His callous tone, coupled with his touch, has me ready to jump up and deck him.

Memories of Carver and I bombard me all at once, hurling at me in a frenzied cyclone, like a busy day on the New York Stock Exchange floor.

The first kiss we shared after hiking to the top of Panorama Ridge overlooking Singing Creek. The first time he told me he loved me, with my hand held tightly in his as we rode the chairlift up to the top of Blackcomb Mountain. The thrill of cliff diving into the lake and swimming in waterfalls together, our wet bodies clinging to one another – holding on for dear life.

My chest tightens with an emotion I can't name. Bittersweet loss of something once so beautiful that's turned into a dusty memory.

My summer memories are packed full with Carver Edwards.

Those thoughts are sidelined as I see the team's trainer and the medics carrying out a stretcher, as they hover over him, assessing his injuries. He's surrounded by people, as his teammates watch in silence. It must be a scary proposition for them, wondering if he's seriously hurt, or maybe concussed. There's movement from the crew, and then the men depart as Carver is lifted and carted off down the long corridor with deafening applause.

The game continues for the next five minutes, the crowd noise amplified in my muddled brain, as my thoughts are back in the locker room, wondering what's going on with Carver. Suddenly I become aware of a man standing in front of Jeff and me, wearing a polo shirt and khakis.

The man speaks directly to Jeff, as Jeff rises with a broad smile and shakes his hand. "Jeff, so glad you could make it tonight."

"Hey, Thomas. Thanks for the tickets. It's an amazing experience to watch from court side." He looks over his shoulder at me and motions. "By the way, let me introduce you to Logan Shaw."

He extends his hand down to help me stand and I take it without a second thought.

"Logan, this is my pal Thomas Coleman. We went to school together. He's the arena physician who gave us the tickets tonight."

Ah, that makes sense. "Nice to meet you, Thomas. Thank you so much for the seats. I'm having a lot of fun," I reply on autopilot, sounding much like a Cyborg.

The man turns back to Jeff and leans in so that no one else around us can hear what he's about to say.

"Listen, Jeff. I need your help. The kid they just brought back – Carver Edwards. Looks like his nose is broken, which I'm able to reset. But he also knocked out one of his teeth. I don't know the extent of the damage, but he might need some emergency oral surgery."

He stops for a moment and glances around, one hand on his chin, brow scrunched in concern. "I really hate asking this of you, since you're here on fun and not on business, but I don't know anyone else on emergency call tonight and your practice is relatively close. Would you mind coming back and having a look at the kid? See if it's something you could do? I'd owe you big time."

My heart thuds so loudly I'm worried it can be heard over the thumping pop music being played from the arena speakers. I feel dangerously close to puking. Or fainting. Or maybe both.

Jeff gives me a weary glance, and then bends his head forward as if resigned to the fact that our date just got cut short. I know Jeff. He'd never walk away from a patient in need of his care. It's one of his many admirable qualities.

He places a gentle hand around my shoulder and pulls me in toward him, giving a guarded smile back to his friend. I'm as stiff as a starched shirt. "Lucky for you – and Carver Edwards – I have the finest dental assistant with me tonight. He'll be in good hands."

Jeff has no idea what kind of problem this will cause. How difficult it will be on me. How uncomfortable the locker room will be when I walk in and talk with Carver for the first time in four years.

No matter what happened between us, I can't shirk my professional responsibilities or say no to my boss, given that he's the reason I'm even here tonight. But I'm under no illusion that our patient will be happy to see me or to receive my help.

"Do you mind?" Jeff asks, his puppy dog eyes pleading with me for my support.

"Of course not."

Thomas blows out a breath in relief. "Great. Follow me then."

Picking up my purse, leaving behind my unfinished beer and popcorn, we follow Thomas down the long corridor into the bowels of the arena. We're stopped by a security guard, who motions us through when Thomas flashes his ID badge.

Sucking in a deep breath, I work to steady myself – giving myself a secret pep talk that I desperately need before facing the guy I never expected to see again. Trepidation single-handedly sends me into a panicked frenzy. From the outside, I probably look icy calm and assured.

On the inside, my tummy flutters with nerves. Butterflies have made way for a flock of angry birds that have set up residence, their wings flapping in spastic patterns. That pukey feeling from earlier has returned.

I stand behind the two men as we enter the locker room, my eyes scanning around in search of a trashcan. There's a distinct possibility I just might hurl.

Beside me, Thomas is giving Jeff a quick assessment of the situation, most of which I've tuned out because my attention is on the low, agonized moans coming from an anterior room toward the back. Hushed whispers circulate through the sweat permeated room. Considering this is the first time I've been on the inside of a men's locker room, I'm impressed with my first observations. It's very luxurious, with wood paneled lockers and soft lighting overhead. But décor aside, there are distinct odors that still linger, not easily covered by bleach and Febreeze spray.

Inhaling through my mouth, I bring my perfume-spritzed wrist up to my nose to mask the obnoxious scent of mildew, stinky feet and B.O.

A pained wail penetrates the room, dragging my attention away from the odor. My body instinctively jolts and tightens in recognition of Carver's sounds of agony. I've only heard that loud shrill once before, during our second summer at camp.

We'd been screwing around down by the lake dock, swimming and diving off the edge into the water. I don't know how it'd gone unnoticed before, but there was a rusty nail protruding from the wooden ladder we'd been using all day. Carver was climbing up the rungs, clowning around, his head thrown over his shoulder laughing at something I said, when suddenly I heard his scream ripple across the water.

His left hand had been punctured by the nail at the base of his index finger. Blood gushed everywhere and he'd turned sheet-white. His friend Brandon and I had helped him up on the dock and I ran to the get the camp nurse, while Carver nearly passed out from the agony.

That's the exact sound I now hear coming from the other room, although his groans are much deeper than they were so long ago. I cringe in advance of what we're about to see, knowing it won't be a pretty sight.

Jeff walks in front of me but turns back suddenly when he notices I haven't moved from my spot.

He cocks his head. "You doing okay, Logan?"

I shake my head, clearing the memory, nodding as I follow him past the shower stalls and to a doorway marked Medical. Taking another deep breath before we step in, I resolve to stay in control of my thoughts and facial expression. I will not cower or collapse. And I certainly won't vomit.

But nothing can prepare me for what I see.

The door swings open with Jeff and Thomas partially blocking my view. All I can see is a pair of very long, sweat-drenched legs, sticking off the end of the exam table. One of the black Nike basketball shoes he wears has been kicked off, exposing the red sports socks. I used to tease him about his big feet. They were enormous, and too big for him. Like a puppy dog's paws, who has yet to grow into them.

When I get a look at the rest of his body, it's obvious he finally grew into his size thirteen sneakers. Up close like this, he looks massive. A writhing, angry giant.

Unable to see his face yet, I brace myself against the door frame, not really listening to Thomas introduce us. But then Thomas turns toward me, allowing me an unobstructed view of Carver, and he of me.

"I'm sorry, remind me of your name again?"

I realize Thomas is speaking to me, but it takes a gentle nudge from Jeff for me to speak. "Oh...uh, it's Logan."

"Ah, yes. Carver, this is Dr. Connell's assistant, Logan."

Thomas looks at me again, presumably for more of an introduction.

I chime in, "Shaw. Logan Shaw." I try to force a natural smile, but I'm sure it looks more like a crazed clown.

I've never been a fearful girl. My brothers cured me of that when I was a kid. That will happen when a seven-year-old finds a snake in your bed or dog shit strategically placed in your shoes. Yeah, my brothers were assholes. Still are.

But right now, in this instant, my limbs quiver nervously. I have no idea how Carver is going to react to seeing me. Will he hate me? Scream at me to leave? Call me despicable names in front of my boss and his friend? I should just turn and leave on my own accord so I don't create a scene.

I close my eyes and wait for it, ready for the attack. But nothing comes. If Carver does have a reaction, it's covered in a mask of pain. He just stares at me with blank eyes, looking right past me. His eyes flutter closed, his long lashes fanning across his cheeks that are splattered with caked and dried blood.

Then he goes limp on the table.

Thomas turns with an amused look. "I guess the pain meds just kicked in."

There's another aid in the room, who moves from the counter and hands Thomas a small towel. Thomas hovers over Carver's head. He then places his hands on the bridge of his nose, takes a loud breath and then does some twist of the wrist, snapping Carver's nose back into place. The sound reverberates through the small room and Carver's head jerks off the pillow – his expression clearly dazed and confused, the sound of his guttural groan reaching inside me all the way down to my toes.

The sound of that gasp transports me back to the first time he entered my body. It's the same masculine sound, but in a very different context.

I move out of the way to the end of the table at Carver's feet, keeping my distance until I'm needed. I watch Thomas and Jeff as they hover over Carver's head and examine his injuries, Carver floating in and out of consciousness. My eyes take in his long, muscular form lying on the table, twitching in pain.

Carver's head pops up again, his chin pointing down to his chest. He stares right at me. The words come out in a garbled, mumbled sound.

"Whatareyoudoinghere?"

My eyes grow wide and they jump to Thomas and Jeff, who are staring at me in question. Because Carver's question is clearly steeped in accusation.

Jeff pipes in, completely unaware of the personal reasons for Carver's inquiry.

"Carver, this is my assistant, Logan Shaw. She'll be assisting me tonight as we determine the severity of your oral injuries and devise a plan to fix the tooth that's been knocked out."

As if Carver has completely forgotten the reason he ended up in here, he slowly raises his hand to touch his mouth, but not before Jeff intercepts it.

"Your nose was broken, Carver. And your tooth knocked out from the blow you sustained. But we're doing everything we can to get you back on your feet, with minimal downtime."

Carver's thoughts seem to rally as he tries to rise up on his elbows, shifting his legs to dangle off the table.

"I gotta get out there," he slurs, either from the mouth full of saliva and blood, or the pain medication causing his speech impediment. "We gotta beat the Zags."

Carver surges forward, but Thomas grabs his shoulders, gently prying Carver back onto the table, laying him down and placing his head onto the pillow.

"Don't worry, son. Your team is doing an admirable job out there. Let's just work on getting you patched back up so you can move on to the next round. First though, we're going to need your consent to take you offsite to Dr. Connell's clinic. Are you able to sign for yourself, or would you like us to call someone for you?"

I'm about to blurt out his father's name, but Carver interrupts.

"No, I'll sign it. Just do what you have to do to get me back out there."

Jeff and Thomas give each other inquisitive looks, sympathy on their faces. We all know that Carver won't be playing again tonight. Not only is he high as a kite, but they can't risk him going back out on the court and potentially bleeding again. He may also have a concussion and has to be watched carefully.

Jeff clears his throat and speaks to Carver, his voice soft and reassuring, "We'll do our best, Carver. You just lie back now and let us do our job."

"Will you stay with me, Lo?" Carver mumbles, his eyes penetrating my gaze with so much emotion I have to look away for fear of breaking down.

Once again, the doctors look at me as if I've just grown two heads.

I shrug my shoulders, pretending that I'm just as clueless over Carver's question as they are.

"Sure, Carver. I'll stick around."

He gives me a drugged-out, stupid grin. "Okay. Thanks, babe. Love you."

And then he falls asleep.

I cringe, my cheeks burning with embarrassment. I hope and pray Jeff and Thomas don't think twice about what Carver just said in his drug-induced delirium.

Because if not for the drugs, I know without a doubt, Carver wouldn't be calling me babe or spouting his love for me. Not after all that happened.

CHAPTER 4

CARVER – FIFTEEN YEARS OLD

SWIMMING when you have a boner is problematic.

It's not only uncomfortable, but it requires that you remain in the water much longer than necessary – effectively turning into a prune. And in this case, no matter how much I want to get out of the water, I can't leave until she does.

She's the one who put me in this state of physical discomfort to begin with.

I've been at Camp Cheakamus Adventure for two full days now and I think I've had an erection for the past forty-six hours straight. And Logan Shaw is to blame for my condition.

I initially laid eyes on Logan at dinner the first night of camp. I was in line waiting to get my grub when I noticed her stand up from a table and walk over to the milk dispenser. My friend, Brandon, had to shove me in the back to get me to move forward because my feet were literally glued to the floor. I just stood there immobile and dumbly stared at her filling up her milk.

I ask Brandon over my shoulder, "Who the hell is that?"

Brandon follows my eyes and land on the girl. She was laughing at something her friend said to her.

"Logan something," he says, annoyed with my immobility, impatiently cutting ahead of me in line. "Kind of a stupid name for a girl, isn't it? It's a boy's name."

I shuffle forward, slopping some fries on my plate and look back to find her returning to her table. Good, there's two seats next to her and her friend. Exactly where Brandon and I will sit for the next two weeks if we're lucky.

"I think it's a beautiful name." I whisper softly, mainly to myself because Brandon is already way ahead of me in line.

We maneuver through the cafeteria, Brandon heading over toward the table where our friends are already sitting when I casually steer him in the opposite direction.

He snarls at me. "What the fuck, dude? What are you doing?"

"Hopefully getting us laid this summer, bro."

It may have been an overly confident statement, but I have no other ammunition with Brandon. He's just like any other fifteen-year-old boy – horny-as-fuck and motivated by any way he can get in a girl's pants.

Reluctantly he follows me toward the table where Logan and the other chick sat. I set my tray down next to Logan, as both her and her friend's heads popped up to find us standing there, towering above them.

"Hey." I say, because at fifteen, I have no brilliant pick-up lines in my arsenal.

The girl across from Logan shrieks, as if she's just seen a mouse scurry across the cafeteria floor. "Hi!"

Logan rolls her eyes, saying nothing in return.

"Can Brandon and I sit with you guys?"

Logan's friend bobs her head furiously, giggling and playing with her hair. Logan just shrugs and mumbles, "Have at it. It's a free country."

I give Brandon a nod, motioning him across the table to giggly-girl, as I throw my legs over the bench to slide in next to Logan.

"I'm Carver Edwards. This is Brandon Penske." I say by way of

introduction. Logan just gives me a huff and continues noshing on a potato chip, seemingly uninterested in anything the two of us can offer.

Hmm. Tough crowd.

Then out of nowhere, Logan jerks back suddenly, screeching out an "Ow!" I notice her friend is smirking at her, like she's kicked her under the table. My gaze slides between them both, finally landing back on her friend.

Giggly-girl smiles coyly. "I'm Emma and this is Logan. She's not normally this bitchy." I barely understand her through her annoying giggles.

I direct my comment to Logan, shifting next to her so I can look at her when I speak. "Cool name, Logan. I like it."

Truthfully, I expected to get a smile or something from her, but I get nothing.

"Where are you guys from?"

Because this is a camp run up in the wilds of Canada, most of the campers are from the local areas or at least somewhere in British Colombia. That's where Emma is from.

"I'm from Burnaby. This is my second year here." She smiles broadly, showing off her brace-covered teeth, but I barely spare her a glance. Instead, I continue staring at the pretty girl next to me.

The prettiest girl I'd ever seen.

She has this silky, golden blonde hair that's pulled up in knot on top of her head. I lean over the table, reaching for a napkin and catchimg a whiff of her perfume. It's powdery-soft and makes me salivate for some reason. It also makes me wonder if she smells like that everywhere. And yep, just like that, I have an erection.

I don't have a lot of experience with girls yet. I'd made out with a few from school and my neighbor, Trendil, from down the street. Got to first base with her when her parents weren't home. I was hoping for a blow job, but she said she wouldn't do that, even though I heard from Michael Daugherty that she sucked him off the summer before.

I must be invading Logan's comfort zone because she leans to her left, giving me a sidelong glance.

"Ever heard of personal space, Carver Edwards?"

Oh fuck, the sound of her voice saying my name has me nearly running back out to the latrines to rub one out. It has this kind of a raspy-quality, but maple syrupy at the same time.

It's then that I realize I'm hovering a little too close so I sit back, allowing her to resume an upright sitting posture. But when she does straighten, it makes her boobs stick out even farther. And now all I'm picturing is her great rack in a bikini.

"So where are you from, Logan?"

She sighs heavily. "If I tell you, will you leave me alone?"

I laugh. Fat chance of that happening. "Why would I want to do that? I just got here. And the scenery at this table is awesome."

I take a bite of my hamburger and grin – the one I know girls like, and the smile that the old ladies at my church always swoon over, pinching my cheeks hard with fervor.

Emma giggles (again) and I hear Brandon let out an expletive. "Jesus, he's a fucking sap." *More giggles escape Emma's mouth.*

Logan turns to face me and gives me the once over. I'm wearing a Washington Husky basketball jersey, backward baseball cap, and light-weight basketball shorts. Casual camp attire.

When her blue eyes finally make their way to my face, I give her my brightest smile. The one I know brings out my dimple on my left cheek. For some reason, girls go nuts over my single-dimple. And sure enough, I see a flicker of interest, but then it's doused just as quickly.

Another sigh. "I'm from Skagit Valley. Live on a farm. There. Are you satisfied now?"

Wow. For being such a hot chick, she had a tremendously big chip on her shoulder. Don't know what that's about. But I am going to make it my goal this summer to break it off and make her mine. I have no other alternative. She is by far the hottest girl I've ever met, and with that 'don't fuck with me attitude,' – I have to have her.

"Cool. You're not too far from me. I live in Mer-" *I'm about to divulge where I live, because we both live in Washington, but I don't want to tip the scales on her animosity toward me. Knowing that she's* from a small farming town, I don't want her to get the wrong impression about me. My parents may be rich, but I'm not about to flaunt it in front of her. I may use it as an advantage to get things I want in other situations, but I can already tell she'd be turned off by it.

I decide to go with something less identifying to keep our conversation alive. "I live on the eastside. We're practically neighbors." I smile again, wiggling my eyebrows and clinking my plastic cup against hers. She rolls her eyes like I'm the stupidest boy she's ever met.

And that's how I was first introduced to Logan Shaw. My dream girl.

Now, after spending two full days of valiantly trying to win her affections, I'm finally able to chisel away a little of the ice that seems to cover her pretty exterior. The four of us had gone hiking this morning and ended up on the cliffs at Panorama Ridge overlooking Singing Creek. The creek is at least twenty-feet deep in this section, where the mountain snow runoffs end up gathering in early spring, creating a deep basin watering hole in the summer.

Perfect for cliff diving. After I'd made that suggestion to the crew, both Brandon and Emma declined, no matter how many names I called them over their pussing-out. They thought it looked too dangerous.

But not Logan. She was all in. In fact, we argued over who would jump in first. I tried to contend that as the guy, I should go first to ensure it was safe. She concluded that girls should go first. So instead, we compromised and jumped together.

Hand in hand. Screaming at the tops of our lungs as we crashed into the water below.

Best thrill of my life.

And now for the last two hours, we've been swimming, laughing and talking under the heat of the sun. She's so beautiful with her long, wet hair, shining with wet droplets of water. It just accentuates her dewy tanned skin that glistens in the creek's reflection.

Fuck, I want to touch her so badly.

I want to kiss her even more, but I'm afraid she'll resist. I've been working hard to keep my distance in the water, aside from the head dunking competition we have going between us. At one point, my hands were clasped at the top of her head, as I pushed her down underwater, her nose brushing up against cock. I turned hard in an instant, my thoughts going to what it would be like if her lips touched my dick.

I freeze as she comes up sputtering, calling me every dirty name in the book, but I can't move or think. I watch the water droplets cascading down her face and into her open mouth.

Fuck me, this is hard.

Literally. My dick is so hard I think it might crack like marble under the pressure of the blood pumping furiously down there. I might go off like a geyser.

I can't stand it any longer. I have to kiss her.

My toes touch the pebbled bottom of the slippery creek and I move forward an inch, reducing the space between us so that when she finally blinks the water out of her eyes and opens them, she gasps at how close we are. Our noses nearly touch.

I've kissed girls before. Countless girls starting in the sixth grade. Yet I know instinctively that kissing Logan will be different. It will change me. I don't know how, but I feel it through every pore and every cell of my body.

Logan's lids close slightly, eyelashes wet with mountain spring water. I bend forward, zeroing in on her dewy lips. I feel her warm breath against my face and then I close the remaining distance, my arm capturing her waist and yanking her into my body.

It's incredible. The feel of her slick, tight body against my chest. Heaven.

My mouth latches onto hers in the briefest of touches, really just to test the waters. She hasn't budged or swam away, so I know she wants this too. I open my eyes for a peek at her and notice how serene her face looks, her eyelashes fanning across her cheeks, the pink of her cheekbones adding even more color to her already tanned face.

I slide both hands down her back, until I'm cupping her butt, and hike her up into my arms. She gasps a tiny intake of air, but it doesn't linger because I'm sucking it up with my mouth. This time, it's a solid, hot kiss that goes on forever. My tongue invades her mouth, taking possession of what's mine. She's hesitant at first, flicking her tongue sweetly over mine. My hands have a mind of their own, squeezing and caressing her ass, which is only covered by a flimsy bikini bottom.

Her skin is so warm and her body soft and pliable. I glide one hand up her back to her neck and I feel the goosebumps scatter over her skin. She lets out a sexy whimper and the dam bursts open as Logan lets go of her inhibitions. It hits me like ecstasy, like the cascading fall of the water above us rushing through the open waters, drenching us in a deluge of lust.

She begins rocking her hips into my stomach, hitting the tip of my cock with enough pressure and friction that I'm sure as fuck going to come. We groan wildly together – probably loud enough to scare away any forest creatures in the area.

My fingers are just about to skim between her legs when we hear shouts from the shore. Brandon and Emma stand on the bank of the river calling after us.

"Hey Carver! Hate to break up your make-out session, but we gotta get back before old man Stellan makes an example out of us for being late and gives us kitchen duty."

Fucking Stellan and fucking Brandon for interrupting us. Stellan's the Camp Director and already seems to have it out for me. He's like thirty, and acts like a perv, always finding ways to flirt with the girls at camp. There's a rumor going around already that he likes his girls young and virgin.

I'm about to wave Brandon on ahead so I can continue kissing Logan – damn the consequences - when she wiggles out of my arms and swims to shore, leaving me in waist deep water with a raging hard-on. I've got about five-seconds before I need to get out, so I try to conjure up any and all boner-killer thoughts to alleviate the pressure. Basketball stats. My Aunt Carla's saggy cankles. Jabba the Hut from Star Wars.

Yet at the same time, counteracting my intentions, my eyes veer toward the beach as Logan steps out of the water, her incredible ass and *long legs on full display. She's wet and sexy, and I now know what her body feels like. Every other thought flies out of my brain.*

Logan Shaw is going to be mine.

I WAKE from a dream that I can't quite place.

It made me feel warm. Tingly. Contented.

But now my brain feels fuzzy. My mouth is dry as the Sahara and tastes like I've just eaten cat litter. There's a whirring sound in the background and a weird vibrating, suctioning noise. I can't feel my face.

But holy fuck, I think there's a jackhammer beating on my skull.

Prying my eyes open, I blink several times to clear my vision. There's a light shining above me and something covering my eyes to shield me from the brightness. I can hear voices on both sides of me in stereo, but I can't turn my head to see anything.

My jaw is throbbing, propped open with some sort of rubber block. I'm not afraid to admit that I'm a little freaked out, uncertain about what's going on, so my body does what comes naturally. I instinctively try to get up. To move. To escape this weird reality.

And then I hear it. The sultry, angelic voice from my past that reminds me of sweet summer nights under star-filled skies.

"Carver, hang tight. We're almost done here and then we'll explain what's going on."

I turn my head to the side as far as it goes to find the beautiful face attached to that melodic voice.

Logan.

The one person I should hate with every fiber of my being, yet can't seem to truly rid from my thoughts.

She embodies everything that I've ever loved and lost.

CHAPTER 5

Logan

It's well after nine p.m. when Dr. Connell and I finish up with the placement of Carver's temporary tooth. I haven't had a date in a long time, but I can almost guarantee this isn't how they end up – having to do emergency oral surgery on your ex-boyfriend, whom you haven't seen or heard from in over four years.

It's a little unnerving.

Carver has been so doped up on whatever pain medication they'd given him at the arena, that he was out for the entirety of the procedure. We still had to numb him up, though, before we began, since the tooth root was exposed. I know he's going to be in a ton of pain for the next few days, as the nerve is super sensitive after procedures like this.

I'll be honest. Even in my darkest hours, when I cursed Carver's name for leaving me high and dry, I'd never wish this type of pain on him. I know he's a tough college basketball player and all but this kind of oral trauma can leave even the strongest man lying in a weeping mess on the floor.

Dr. Connell is back in his office to finish up his medical charting and procedural notes, as I remain behind in the exam room with Carver. I've been desperately trying to keep my focus on the small tasks associated with after-surgery protocol, but my attention continues to veer over to the beautiful man lying in the dental chair.

The air around me ripples with a strange sort of energy. It's kinetic – filtering through the small alcove room, zapping me with awareness of Carver. The rise and fall of his chest as he inhales and exhales the same air I breathe. The scent of him – musky, masculine; powerful but not overpowering. I'm overcome with flashes of images – memories I've shoved in the back of my mind that are now clawing their way out.

And when Carver speaks for the first time since he's been in the chair, my body sizzles with heat. His voice blankets me with its deep tone. Warm and comforting. Although, it's kind of hard to keep a straight face when he talks, with his tongue and mouth still numb, causing him to slur his words like a drunk.

But I do my best impersonation of a dental professional and avoid laughing at him.

"*Whas hathaned thu me?*" I think he means, 'what happened to me?'

My back was to him, so I turn toward him, just enough so I can see him in my periphery vision as I answer. His unfocused eyes wear a confused expression.

"Someone clocked you good in the face. Broke your nose and knocked out your front tooth. We extracted the bone fragment and put in a temporary bridge. Once you heal, you'll need to return for a permanent replacement."

He groans and goes silent for a second, before asking, "Why are you here?"

I've been preparing for this question, but still don't know what to say. Or know where to begin. It's such an unusual situation and I'm still digesting how this all came about.

I take a long breath and exhale before I swivel in my chair to face him.

His hair is matted to his head, and I still have the napkin bib tied around his neck. His nose is swollen and he's already turning a deep black and blue underneath his eyes from inflammation.

He looks downright horrible. Like he got beat up.

Even so, he still looks good. Better than good.

Carver Edwards was a good-looking teenager - cute in a mischievous way. But now he's just downright hot. An unbelievably gorgeous man.

Sexy, tattooed biceps are on full display in front of me, which I was ogling while he was under anesthesia. There's tribal ink, a devil and a pitchfork, and some other tats that I don't recognize. There were no tattoos on his body the last time I saw him.

Just another realization that our lives have changed in that time and so much has happened since we last met.

I straighten my spine as I look down on his imposing figure.

"To answer your question, I work here. And by a weird twist of fate, Dr. Connell and I just happened to be at your game tonight because Jeff knows the arena physician, who enlisted our help when you got hit. Does that clear things up? Are you in any pain?"

Carver blinks and shakes his head.

"Are you a thenis?"

A giggle inadvertently slips past my lips because when he says this, spittle launches from Carver's mouth and lands on his arm. I use his bib to wipe it off at the same time he reaches for it too.

It's the briefest of touches, but it creates a flare of friction. He quickly retreats, allowing me to finish cleaning him up. I'm slammed with memories of his touch, but they dissipate in a flash.

Shifting in my seat, I shake my head. "No, I'm Dr. Connell's assistant."

I'm about to explain further – how I bypassed college and had to work for a few years before getting my dental assistant training at a community college. Really, Carver doesn't need any of that background. It would serve no purpose and wouldn't change anything between us. He's going to leave tonight and never look back.

"Ambithus." Again, it's slurred and pronounced with the lisp of a toddler, adding a 'th' at the end.

I wave off his ambitious comment. "Nah. Just had to earn a living."

What I don't offer up is the reason. Why I had to learn how to survive on my own at a young age. I've been doing it now for the last five years. From the moment my dad booted me out of his house.

I clear my throat of the sudden emotion pricking at my tear ducts, returning my attention to the after-care instructions I need to provide him.

I've done my best to place him in the back of my mind, in a special spot reserved for happiness, joy and bittersweet memories. If I think of him too often, I'll be overcome with hopelessness and resentment. For the cards that fate dealt me and the way that life can leave you alone and abandoned.

I lower the chair down by depressing the foot lever, bringing Carver to a sitting position so he can get up. He twists to the side, his feet hitting the floor slowly and our knees bump together. I scoot back to allow him room.

Reaching for the small prescription note on the counter, I hand it to Carver who glances at it for a second and returns his gaze to me.

The warm chocolate of his eyes has always been my undoing. Melts me. Makes me fall in love with him.

I give myself an internal *tsk*. Move along, sister. Don't even go there.

Carver's soul-searching stare tells me everything. Confusion. Bitterness. Loss. Hope. Disgust.

I don't blame him. And yet, I do.

He left me when I needed him most.

"Dr. Connell has written you prescriptions for a pain med and an antibiotic. You can get them filled at the 24-hour pharmacy down the street and need to start taking them right away tonight. Don't wait, because you don't want to get an infection. You don't have an allergy to penicillin, do you?"

I raise my eyebrow and he shakes his head.

"Okay. You've been fitted for a permanent replacement tooth, so you'll have to either schedule a return visit in the next ninety days, or we can work with your local dentist in Phoenix, if that works better for you."

I look away under the scrutiny of his stare. I'm sure there is nothing Carver wants less than to return here for a follow-up visit. Or to ever see me again, based on the intensity of his glare.

Carver turns his head suddenly in the direction of the office door.

"How'd I get here?" He asks out of the blue.

Oh, shit. I forgot that he doesn't have transportation back and has no personal belongings with him. No phone or credit cards. Just the blood-soaked jersey he came in with.

"Um, we brought you here. Do you want me to call someone to come pick you up?"

He continues to stare at me. I honestly don't know what he's thinking. I assume his parents must have been at the game and worried sick about him. Who knows? Or maybe there's a girl-friend or fiancée waiting to hear from him? That thought is like a thousand pin pricks to my heart.

"Your parents?" I ask tentatively.

Carver sighs deeply, like it's a ridiculous question I've just asked him.

"No. My *theam* is proly sill playing. Can you *thrive* me back?" He's still talking funny. Had this been five years ago, we'd both be laughing hysterically right now.

But we aren't those people any more. And the situation isn't at all funny.

This is such a weird predicament. Considering Carver has no other alternative of getting back to his hotel, unless I put him in a cab with a twenty-dollar bill, he's reliant on the doctor or myself to transport him. My car is parked outside in our employee parking ramp, where I left it prior to my date, but it feels strange to offer to drive him.

If it were anyone else, would I offer to drive them home? Is it something I'd do for any other patient?

"Wait right here. I'll go check with Dr. Connell about the protocol. Liability and all." I shrug, using this as a means of momentarily escaping his presence.

I practically sprint down the hallway and slam smack into Jeff as I enter his office, who halts my forward movement with his hands on my shoulders.

"Whoa, there," he chuckles good naturedly. "Everything okay out there?"

I must look a mess. To say this evening has been more than unexpected is an understatement. I'm a jumble of nerves and anxiety, my mind playing tricks on me over the complex emotions evoked over seeing Carver again out of the blue.

"Oh, I'm not sure what to do. Carver needs a ride back to the arena. I'm heading that way on my way home, but I don't know what you want me to do? I can drop him off. I know you have some paperwork to finish up here."

We both glance over his shoulder at his cluttered desk, the piles of patient records and paperwork strewn everywhere. Jeff turns back to face me, a flush of embarrassment taking residence across his cheeks. He is wonderful dentist and a great mentor and boss, but as unorganized as they come.

"Do you mind?" His forehead and nose scrunch in question. "If it's not an imposition?"

While the thought of spending more time with Carver tonight

has my nerves strung tight, I really don't have any excuse not to take him, since he is right on my way home. Even though being alone with him seriously messes with my head and will open old wounds that have tried to heal.

I fiddle with the edge of my sleeve, as I bite my lip in a nervous pattern. The sooner I can drop him off and get him out of my life once more, the better off I'll be.

"It's no trouble. Shouldn't take me more than five minutes."

I'm about to turn around to head out front when Jeff's hand latches around my wrist, stopping me in my tracks.

"Logan, about tonight. I'm so sorry I screwed up our evening together. I hope you'll consider letting me make it up to you."

He looks so genuinely apologetic and hopeful. I give him an encouraging smile, even though I don't want to go out with him again. "I have to say; I've never had a date end quite like this one did. It certainly was memorable."

No truer words were ever said.

This garners a bashful laugh from him. "Yes, it was."

We stand there awkwardly for moment and I wonder if he's going to try to kiss me. He's looking at my lips like he wants to, but I just can't let it go there. I take a giant step back and turn the opposite direction.

"Well, goodnight then. I'll see you Monday. Don't work too late."

I breathe a sigh of relief that our goodbye wasn't any more awkward than that, and startle when I find Carver sitting in the lobby reading an old copy of *US Weekly*. The one with Brad and Angelina's twins on the cover. It's probably six years old.

"Getting caught up on your celebrity gossip and current events?"

Carver's head pops up and he Frisbee-tosses the gossip mag on the table in front of him.

"Yeah, apparently, a lot has happened since I've been in college."

Isn't that the truth? He lets those words dangle between us, the implication of the underlying meaning weighing heavy on my heart. Then he shakes his head and stands. "Haven't had any time to keep up with anything outside basketball, I guess. And now I hear they're getting a divorce."

Carver towers over me like a downtown high rise. He must be at least six-three or four. A full foot taller than me. Back when we were just teenagers, he was only a few inches taller. He's definitely had a few growth spurts since then.

It's the middle of March in Seattle, where the temps can dip into the low thirties at night with wind and rain pushing springtime into the Puget Sound like the proverbial lion. It's really cold, as I fumble to zip up my coat, and I realize Carver has no jacket with him. I wonder for a second if I should run back in and get him a blanket from the stash we keep for patients, but Carver seems completely oblivious to the chill as we walk out to the parking lot.

I'm scrambling to find my keys at the bottom of my purse, pulling them out and nodding my head toward my car. Just as I round the trunk, my hand brushes against the frame and the keys slip from my grasp, landing on the ground between us. Carver bends down to pick them up and is handing them back to me when he stops.

He tilts his head. "You still have this?"

He's referring to the fuzzy pink heart keychain in his hands. The one that says, '*I Wuv You*' in white script lettering that's rubbed off so much it's barely recognizable.

He doesn't need to read it to know what it says. He's seen it before. It's the same one he gave me after winning it at a carnival game. The one and only time we ever met outside of camp during our junior year in high school.

Back then, Carver and I had made a pact at the end of camp our very first summer. We both agreed that it would be too difficult to see each other during the school year, because we lived over an hour from each other. Neither of us had our license or a car to transport us at the time, so we made the decision to take a break between camp sessions.

This idea was originally mine to keep Carver at a distance. It was clear early on that it would be futile to try and maintain a long-distance relationship as teenagers. No matter how much we meant to each other, we would've failed. We lived two completely incompatible lifestyles. I knew, even back then, that he'd break my heart one day.

I didn't even give him my phone number, and I wouldn't accept his. We didn't friend each other on Facebook or Snapchat. We didn't have each other's home addresses. The only thing we did have at our disposal was our email addresses. We'd promised each other we'd use it sparingly – only for the occasional good news, holidays greetings or special occasions.

I did this to protect myself. Attending Camp Cheakamus was about being surrounded by hundreds of rich and advantaged kids spending two weeks adventuring and exploring the great outdoors in the lap of luxury.

No one else knew it, but I was a scholarship kid. The only way I could afford to attend a camp like that was through scholarships I received from the VFW and Eagle's charity, which my father, a retired Army man, was affiliated with.

I feared that if Carver found out where I lived, or knew of my life outside of camp, he would have turned right around and never spoken to me again.

But on that late fall weekend, a month after camp ended that year, Carver sent me email after email, begging me to meet up with him at the carnival. It was midway between our hometowns. He begged and pleaded with me, saying that it was his only birthday wish – his upcoming seventeenth - to see me one more time before school started. Before we were relegated back to our normal lives, where we'd never fit together in reality.

I broke down and met him at the fair. It was, and still is, one of the greatest nights of my life. It seems that any night I ever spent with Carver happened to fall into that category. He made me feel special. Like I was the only one on Earth that he adored and loved. It was on top of a rickety old Ferris wheel that night that he told me he loved me.

Not puppy love. Not the passing fancy or fickle crush of a teenager. The type of love that you know will never leave you because it's sewed in every fiber and thread of your being.

I yank the keys out of Carver's hand with a growl, hastily unlocking my door and sliding into the driver's seat. I reach over the console and unlock his car door, as my beat-up late eighties model-Volvo doesn't have automatic locks.

My hands grip the steering wheel tightly, as I turn down the arterial road heading back to the arena, and an uncomfortable silence descends us. Out of my peripheral vision, I see Carver staring out the passenger window. I try to stop myself from wondering about what he could possibly be thinking about, even though a part of me wants desperately to ask him.

It's none of my business, I scold myself. We mean nothing to each other any longer. We're practically strangers; who once shared the beauty of first love, but now live completely different lives.

As the car idols at a red light, I see the top of the Space Needle, which is an ever-present fixture in the cityscape. Carver startles me with his confession, his voice low and deep.

"I've thought about you for years, Lo. I've wondered how you were doing."

My head snaps to him, his eyes holding a soft expression. Why can't he hate me? Why does he have to be so Goddamn nice?

I blink back the sting of my tears, turning back to the front window, concentrating on the light ahead. I have no desire to walk down memory lane with him tonight, so we need to keep things short and brief. No time for sweet nostalgia. Or sad endings.

My throat is tight as I swallow the sharp edge of pain, the prickle in my voice harsh and cold. "Well, as you can see, I'm doing just fine."

"I can see that."

I turn into the stadium entrance and flash the VIP ticket from earlier as the guard nods me in. Before we left, I asked Carver if he was sure he just didn't want me to drive him to his hotel. There was no way he was playing again tonight, and in fact, the game would likely be over already. But he assured me, he wanted to be back with the team.

I drive slowly through the coned-off areas toward the doors where Carver will enter, as he once again leaves my life as quickly as he entered it.

Shifting my clunker sedan into park, I feel a chill run through my body like the cold water of Singing Creek.

"Lo." He uses my nickname and I practically crumble under its weight.

I dare a glance and regret it instantly.

His face is etched with pain, and not the physical kind. "Was it a boy or a girl?"

Oh, shit. Not that question. Anything besides that.

I'm not ready for it. I will never be ready for it. The answer to that seemingly simple question will haunt me the rest of the days of my life.

I swallow the lump in my throat and wish I could just turn invisible and fly away – leaving that question unanswered. It hurts too much to say it out loud. But maybe if I do, I'll never have to say another word to him again. Maybe it'll absolve our guilt, our pain and our shame forever.

"It was boy. We had a boy, Carver."

CHAPTER 6

Carver

It's been a week since the game that ended my college ball career.

Seven days since we've returned from Seattle and hung our heads in defeat after the traumatic outcome of that fateful night and everything that transpired post-game. Honestly, it feels like I'm still in a drug-induced haze. Like whatever they did to my tooth has muddled my brain.

Or maybe that's just from seeing Logan.

If some of the guys have noticed my surly-ass mood since we've returned, no one's mentioned it. Likely for the fact that all the guys are in a similar stupor over our humiliating loss to Gonzaga. I've been wrapped up in guilt knowing my injury left them all high and dry when they needed me most. I'm not being overly arrogant about my impact to the team, but I was the team captain and point guard – so leaving them when the stakes were so high was a devastating blow. I mean, they had to bring in LeQuan Williams as backup point guard, a fucking freshman who hasn't even gotten his dick wet yet, much less the skills to bring in a victory.

My mood is seriously going from bad to worse as I sit at the kitchen table, reading through all the messages left on my social media accounts. Some are words of encouragement, but others are just downright nasty jabs, which piss me off even more. I'm reading a particularly harsh comment on Twitter when Cade comes stumbling into the kitchen.

I glance up, noticing his disheveled hair, lack of shirt and wrinkled boxers.

"Late night or early morning?" I ask casually, my attention dropping back to my phone. "I didn't hear the Screamer last night, so you must've been at her place."

I laugh at my reference to Cade's girlfriend, Ainsley. I've been giving them shit about her loud antics in the bedroom ever since they hooked up earlier in the school year.

Let's just say it's very noticeable when they're at our place, because Ainsley is not a quiet girl in the sack. Christ, that girl has a pair of lungs on her. I'll admit, hearing her scream that she's coming has gotten me horny and hard many times when I'm alone in bed. Call me a perv, or whatever, but shit. When you hear porn-star moaning in the bedroom right next to yours, it's gonna get you worked up. I've had to make a few late-night booty calls on more than one occasion from my ever-growing list of hoops hunnies, just to get the edge off.

Cade grunts, turning his back to pour himself a cup of coffee. He also flips me off from behind his back, making me chuckle even harder.

"Fuck you, Edwards. Like you've ever been quiet with any of your conquests. If it's not a threesome, I swear I can hear you spanking girls. Do you have a paddle or something in there?"

I chortle, because yeah, I do. What can I say? It's my brand of kink. I enjoy spanking the bare ass of the girls I fuck, but I prefer to use my own hand. I like to feel the biting sting on my hand. To relish in the red mark that I leave behind, which I know gets them wet. I guess I have some sort of fetish with spanking.

And, threesomes? Well yeah, I've had them. What single guy in their right mind would say no when two girls want to get it on with him? Not this guy.

Letting his comment linger, I pick up my empty cereal bowl and head to the sink. Out of the three of us, I'm the only one who ever puts my dishes in the dishwasher. Cade will remember to do it when Ainsley's around, but Lance never does it. Half of our dishware seems to end up in his bedroom closet, under his bed or on his desk. The guy is a fucking pig. And I swear, I'm like the naggy-wife in our relationship, always harping on him to clean his shit up.

The dishwasher closes with a thud, and I pull out the OJ from the fridge and take a big swig from the bottle.

"So, were you over at Ainsley's last night?" I ask, figuring he stayed the night there.

"Yeah. We had to go see her little sister's school performance and then I crashed there."

"How are things going with her, by the way? I mean, with her mom skipping town and all."

I'll admit, I have mad respect for Cade's girl. She went through hell and back with a crazy-ass mom who left her and her fifteen-year-old sister to fend for themselves. Who the fuck does that?

You, asshole.

While the circumstances are completely different, I guess the same could be said about me. I left Logan alone to deal with her pregnancy by herself. I abandoned the mother of my child and listened to my own fucking father's advice.

"She's just a money-hungry gold digger. Don't let her fool you into thinking you need to raise a child with her. She's going to ruin your college and future NBA career, son. Let me handle it for you."

So I did. I let my dad take matters into his own hands and deal with it while I was out partying like a rock star in college.

Well, actually, I wasn't even aware about the pregnancy right way. I found out much later and by then, it was too late. The problem had been solved. But I knew I'd made a mistake and I'd tried reaching out to find Logan. To explain.

But she never responded to any of my emails – not one single one. Even after I'd sent dozens.

And then one day, they just came back Sender Error. I was left with no other way of locating her. I didn't have her number. I didn't have her address. I didn't even know where she wound up going to school – or even if she did. Damn her for making me agree to her no contact rule. It could have changed the course of our life.

Begging my father to help me find Logan was of no use. He remained tight-lipped and wouldn't allow me access to any information. Said it was for my best interest to just drop it and forget about her.

What the hell was I supposed to do? I was a freshman in college, twelve-hundred miles away from her, working my ass off to prove myself for a future ball career in the NBA. I had no other choice but to let her go.

The guilt I felt turned me into a man possessed. I became obsessed with two things: becoming the best college point guard I could be, and adding as many notches on my bedpost as I could. And let me tell you. When I set out to accomplish a goal, I damn well do it with gusto. There was no stopping me.

Now as a senior, I'm so close to the NBA draft in June that I can taste it. And I've had more than my share of hoops hunnies along the way. So I'd say I did a pretty damn good job of achieving my goals.

It was the only way I could release her from my thoughts. To get her out of my head and out of my system. Fat lot of good that did me.

The problem with any form of self-medication – drugs, alcohol, food, women - is that it rarely works. I've remained unattached and single my entire college existence because no one could ever measure up to Logan. To her perfection.

I know – no one's perfect. And over the years, my feelings toward her morphed. I began to doubt what we had was ever really that good. Surely it was simply my over-active imagination that remembered her as this unblemished, untouchable woman that really didn't exist.

All those doubts vanished the moment I woke from my semi-conscious state to find her sitting next to me in the dentist chair a week ago.

Logan's thick, blonde hair had been tied in an intricate braid, that swooped over her left shoulder, hanging down low. The tip brushed the top of her round, shapely breast. I'd never been so envious of hair before.

Even with my eyes closed, her soft sweet scent – lavender and powder – transported me back to the summers we spent together. It brought a spark of lust that my body long since remembered.

I wanted to hate her. For ignoring me. Dropping me without so much as a word.

But when she spoke, the whiskey-smooth sound of her voice had my body melting into the chair. I was ready to let go of my simmering anger to spring forward into action, falling at her feet and begging for forgiveness.

I've always been an easy-going guy. Unflappable. While most see me as annoyingly cocky and full of myself (which I admit, I am), I'm also pragmatic. I don't allow my emotions to get me riled up or off course.

It's what made me a good team captain – on and off the court. I've had to talk guys down off the ledge many times over the years. Most recently, when Van struggled with some of his life drama, I had to straighten him out. Set him on the right path. Remind him what was important.

Why was it so hard to do that for myself after being confronted unexpectedly by Logan? My first girlfriend. My first lover. My first everything.

After Logan ditched me, I said fuck it. I wasn't going to put myself through that kind of devastation again. Fool me once, etc. You get the picture.

Cade is still blathering on about something that happened last night with Ainsley's sister when Lance stumbles in, looking like death warmed over.

His voice is gravely, likely wrecked from all the puking I heard last night while he was wasted. Seriously, I think we need to stage an intervention soon.

But I won't say anything this morning. I'm not ready to take on anything that serious right now. I just need to get through the next two months of school, graduate and then get my ass drafted into the pros.

And that means forgetting about Logan Shaw.

Three-Weeks Until NBA Draft

Moving is backbreaking work.

It sucks, especially in the heat of Arizona. So why the hell I offered to help Van move from his dorm and into his new apartment is beyond me.

Graduation was last week. Van, Cade, me and a few of our other teammates all graduated with our degrees. Lance didn't fare so well, so he'll remain behind as a fifth-year senior. Not a biggie, though – a lot of the guys do that if they were redshirted as freshman – which Lance was. It gives them another year of eligibility.

But for the rest of us, we're moving out and moving on. In Van's case, he's going to be shacking up with Cade's little sister, Kylah. Or Ky-Ky, as I've called her for years. It still freaks me out that they're together.

I wasn't surprised they became a couple, because they're a good fit, but I was shocked at the speed in which Van turned it into a serious relationship. Living with a girl? That's a big fucking move.

And then there's Cade. He just got engaged. Holy fuck - to get engaged right after graduation? Fucking stupidity, if you ask me. But nobody did ask me, because I'm a Debbie Downer when it comes to relationships. Guys steer clear of that topic around me.

Van and I have already made a few trips down to the moving van and I'm sweating like a pig. Sweat pours down my back as we carry his couch down the hallway. I'm at one end of the couch walking backward when I notice Van grinning.

"I don't know what the fuck you're smiling about, dude, but we've still got at least three more loads. And then you promised me a twelve-pack."

We slide the couch in the back of the van and he waves me off, heading back up the stairs to his room.

"I was just thinking about everything…you know, what's going on with everybody now. How crazy it seems that Cade's going to be a married man in the next year."

I scoff. "Idiot. Why the fuck is he rushing into something like that? No man should settle down at twenty-two."

Van gives me an eyebrow raise, as if it's the stupidest thing I've ever said. He'll probably be Cade's brother-in-law some day in the future. Hopefully he and Ky will take their time, though. She'll only be a sophomore next year.

Van slows down ahead of me and peers at me over his shoulder. "He wants to settle down. Knows she's the one. I get that.

Unlike you…some of us like having a girlfriend. It's nice to know you'll have someone to sleep with every night."

We enter his dorm, which is clean and tidy, save the boxes strewn about.

I take a swig of water and wipe my brow. "Eh…I can have someone in my bed every night, too. They just don't have to be there in the morning to make me happy." I smirk.

Van laughs, running his hand through his newly shorn hair.

"Yeah, I'm sure you'll have tons of hot women following you around once you go pro."

"Damn straight, I will. Getting pussy anytime I want, in every city I go." I grin, knowing the odds of getting laid by a bevy of hot female fans is a sure bet. I'm getting wood right now just thinking about it.

As we wait for the elevator, his desk resting between us, Van poses another question.

"Now that we're done with school, are you going back home before draft day? Aren't your parents back there?"

I've known Van for four years and he's never asked me about my background or family story. Then again, I've kept that information private and haven't divulged much about my early years. I don't like people knowing about my wealthy upbringing. It turns people into clingers, who only want to become friends because they think you can give them something.

And my feelings toward my father are complicated, at best. If I bring him up or talk about my family, questions always arise about our relationship. And that's uncomfortable territory. My dad and I used to have a solid father-son relationship. He was my biggest fan. Staunchest supporter.

He still is, but I don't reciprocate those feelings. He took away the one thing I'd found, other than basketball, that fulfilled me. I can't forgive him for that.

I try to evade Van's inquisitiveness with my short, smart ass reply. "Maybe. Not sure. Next question."

Van scratches his chin and chuckles, seemingly undeterred by my evasiveness. "What about your tooth replacement?"

"What about it?"

"I thought I remember you saying you had to go back in to get the permanent tooth seated or something like that." He shrugs his shoulders.

When my tooth was knocked out back in March, the dentist replaced it with some sort of temporary bridge. I have a permanent structure waiting – and have received several messages from his office recently - but was waiting until after graduation.

I rub my hand over my jaw, the sweat sticking to my facial stubble. "Technically, I can have the work done anywhere. But yeah, I'll be back up there next week, after Memorial Day weekend."

"So you *are* going back to Seattle. Are you going to see your family?"

Van's digging, and I don't understand why. Maybe it's just to pass the time as we move his shit, or because we'll soon be going our separate ways. Either way, he's never been this interested in my life.

I know Van has a great family dynamic. I've met his parents and his brother, Dougie, on numerous occasions. They are great people and I can tell they are a strong family unit. But that doesn't mean I want to compare stories or discuss my dysfunctional family drama.

The elevator door opens again and we set the desk down, both stretching our backs and necks in the process. I could definitely use that beer right about now.

I tilt my head and roll my eyes at Van, who's casually standing there like nothing is amiss.

"What's your deal? Why so interested in who I'm going to see when I'm back home?"

He shrugs. "I don't know. It just seems like you're hiding something, man. You never talk about your family. I mean, you know everything about mine – even Dougie. But I don't even know if you have siblings or if you're an only child, or what."

Van's got a point. Everyone on the team knows, acknowledges and understands the situation with Van's brother, who has cerebral palsy. But that doesn't mean I'll be an open book like him.

"I don't. So enough of the inquisition."

"Okay. Chill out, bruh. Sorry it's such a touchy subject. But it's clear there's an issue there. Ever since we returned from Seattle, you've acted weird. Different. And it's not because we lost or you got your tooth knocked out. What happened?"

I sigh deeply. "Fuck, man. It's complicated, okay?"

"What's so complicated about it?"

I have to say Van is more perceptive than I've ever given him credit for. Christ, he should go into investigative journalism instead of finance. The guy won't let up.

I rub the back of my neck before we lift the desk again, heading back toward the moving van.

Fine, if he's looking for a salacious bit of gossip, I'll give him that. "It's just weird, okay? I ran into my old girlfriend back in March. It turns out she's a dental assistant, and works for the dentist who did my emergency repair."

Van's lips twist into a smile, his eyes wide. "Wow. That is weird...you had a girlfriend?"

He laughs hysterically and I punch him in the arm to shut him up.

Once he catches his breath, he grins. "Such a small world, ya know? How'd it go with her?"

I give him a sardonic laugh. How the hell can I describe what happened with Logan? Everything about that night is surreal. All the memories it evoked. The uncomfortable tension. The guilt it dredged up. The anger that flooded me for letting her get away and for her not ever responding to me.

I think back to how we left things. She was both sad and angry. I don't blame her.

"I think if she could have, she would've knocked out all my teeth instead of repairing them."

"So, things didn't end well?"

I shrug my shoulders and stare off in the other direction, trying to decide how much I'm willing to divulge. But Van's a trustworthy guy, so I go for it.

"I honestly don't know. One day she was just gone; vanished. And I haven't seen or heard from her until I ended up in the dentist chair."

We're both quiet for a moment, letting the words hang between us like a heavy tree limb. Heavy with the implications. Weighted with the history between Logan and me.

"Whoa." Van acknowledges softly. "Sounds like some kind of star-crossed lovers story."

I huff. "You have no idea."

Van's silent again, which I've always appreciated about him. He doesn't talk to fill air like Lance does. He's thoughtful about his approach. And then he leans into the front cab of the truck and returns with two ice-cold beers, handing me one.

"Sounds to me like it's beer o'clock. And then you can tell me all about her."

CHAPTER 7

LOGAN – MEMORIAL DAY WEEKEND PRESENT

IT'S my roommate's birthday this weekend and I'm baking her cupcakes.

Baking has always been my favorite hobby. Although I'd likely be labeled an 'outdoorsy' type of girl – one who grew up on a farm and didn't mind getting dirty – there is something so homey about baking that appeals to me. I guess it's a way of trying to connect with my late mother. She passed away when I was twelve from ovarian cancer.

Fuck you, cancer, and the horse you rode in on.

My mom made every birthday special by making elaborate birthday cakes for us – my brothers Luke, Landon, Leo and me. The lone girl. The daughter my mother desperately wanted and the girl my father tried to forget.

I still have love for my dad – I really do. He'd tried his best for many years to be there for me after mom died. When I found out about Camp Cheakamus Adventure, he did everything in his power to help me find a way to attend. The cost was too big for a dirt-poor farmer's daughter, but he helped me find the funds through scholarships offered in the community.

Those were my formative years. Puberty sucks in the best of times, but for a motherless girl living in a testosterone-filled home, it was as pleasant as a Vietnamese POW torture cell.

My brothers were hellbent on making my life as difficult as possible. They didn't dote on me like other brothers might with younger sisters. I was like a zebra in the lion's den. They tore me apart every chance they got. If they even heard a sniffle from tears, they'd either make it ten times worse by taunting or picking on me. No emotional support whatsoever.

My dad, on the other hand, gave it his best shot. He just wasn't around enough – working from before sun-up to sunset, and then a part-time job down at the local pub. He did have some intuitive sense to know when things were bad. He'd comfort me when I was sick. Help me when I struggled with my homework. Sit on the sidelines of my soccer games and cheer me on during the games he could attend.

Those encouraging endearments abruptly ended the moment he found out I was pregnant at seventeen. That's when he kicked me out of his life and his home.

It took me years to recover from his rejection. From the humiliation of facing a pregnancy alone, with no one to hold onto when I needed the emotional support of family. Or anyone to love me.

But the pain of rejection was a thousand times worse when I tried contacting Carver – who was by then in his first two months of college. It was weeks after I sent him the initial email, pleading for him to call me. At first I just wrote a "Hi, how are you doing? Please call me." I gave him my cell number, but didn't hear back which thoroughly surprised me, because he'd always begged for me to give him my number.

On the second attempt, I emailed him the entire story – how I was pregnant, didn't have a place to live, didn't know what to do.

I was so scared and terrified about having a baby. I didn't want to ruin his life, or mine, but I needed his help. I wasn't too proud at that point to ask for it.

What I received in response wasn't what I had expected. To this day, I don't know if it was a lifesaving moment or one I'll regret the rest of my life.

Carver Edwards Sr. was the one who reached out to me. He promised me help. He told me Carver had given his consent and asked that his father step in to assist. Based on what I now know from my brief run-in with Carver, I'm not sure that was the case after all.

"Oh my God. It smells so good in here!" Alison's voice squeals from down the hallway of our small apartment on Queen Anne – a neighborhood in walking distance to the Space Needle and Seattle Center - shaking me free from my thoughts.

I look over my shoulder to see her casually stride into the kitchen, throwing her purse down on the table with a *thwap*.

"Did you leave work early? I was hoping to have these ready before you got home."

Ali leans over and snags a big scoop of vanilla cream frosting with her finger, shoving it into her mouth, following it with a long moan of satisfaction.

"Oh hell…it's like an orgasm for my mouth. So good."

I laugh, watching her face morph into an "O" expression, eyes closed and head tipped back in ecstasy. It's almost embarrassing witnessing her porn-like response.

"Geez, Al…get a room, will ya?" I joke.

She snickers. "Yeah, it was a slow day. I gotta go take a quick shower because Troy said he's picking me up at five-thirty for our date."

I cock my eyebrow. She and Troy have been dating a month, but he seems enamored by her, taking her out to some fancy places around town that neither of us could ever afford. He's some sort of lead coder at Amazon and if one of those nerdy dudes who could easily be mistaken for a homeless guy based on how he dresses, but has enough money to buy a small island.

He and Ali met where she tends bar at a trendy spot near the Amazon headquarters. He'd apparently been talking to her for months but never got up the nerve to ask her out, so she finally took it upon herself to do it. I love that about Ali. She's fearless and unconventional.

I wish I were more like her.

"The big turd won't tell me where we're going tonight. He just said to dress 'nice'. What the hell does that even mean? We live in Seattle for fuck's sake, where *nice* is a pair of jeans and a wrinkle-free flannel shirt." She sighs, shaking her head with flummox. "I guess I'll leave the Chucks in the closet and wear the new knee high boots I got on our last shopping trip."

"Ooh – sexy. He'll like that." I affirm, spreading a thick layer of frosting across a cupcake I have in my hand.

She turns to leave the kitchen and then says, "Are you still going to meet us over at Cal's tonight? I think Hari, Joel, Kristof and Lara are all coming by around ten."

Cal's Place is where Ali works, not far from our apartment complex. It's great for late nights when we need to walk off the alcohol in our systems. No driving or Uber's required. Although the climb up to the top of Queen Anne Hill is a killer when you're wearing heels of any kind. The last time we were out, Ali had to practically give me a piggy-back ride, my feet hurt so bad. I was also not in any condition to walk on my own.

"Don't be silly – of course I am. I wouldn't miss your party. I may be a little late, though. I'm going out with Jeff again tonight." I pseudo-whisper that last part. It's still a little hard to choke out.

This will be our third official date since the fateful night in March. I'm actually glad for Jeff's old-fashioned manners. He takes his time with this dating thing. I just couldn't handle it if he pressured me into seeing him outside of work more often than we do.

Don't get me wrong. I like Jeff. He's a decent guy. But I have zero physical attraction to him. He's annoyingly dull and has very squishy lips.

Yes, we've kissed, but that's where it ended. It was on our second date. He'd taken me to the symphony at Benaroya Hall – *yawn*. My forearm was red and sore that night from where I had to keep pinching myself to stay awake.

It's not like I'm so country redneck that I can't enjoy the fine arts. But give me a rocking country band in an old, beat-up tavern and I'm one happy camper.

That's another thing about dating Jeff. We don't share common interests, outside of the dental arts, and there is no passion.

I want sparks. A man that takes control and heats me up from the inside out with his mouth and his hands. A chemistry so strong that there are explosions in my belly every time I'm near him.   Over-the-top-desire.   Can't-get-you-out-of-my-mind daydreaming. Hot, no-holds-barred fucking.

Suddenly, Ali is standing right in front of me, her hands on her hips, glaring at me under her long lashes.

"Remind me again why the hell you haven't ditched Mr. Potato Head yet?"

A burst of laughter escapes my throat and I cover my mouth with my hand, which smells like vanilla icing.

Ali started referring to Jeff with that unflattering nickname a month ago because she thought his personality is so dry and dull, like an over-baked potato.

"Stop calling him that." I swat at her arm. "It's not nice. Jeff is a good guy."

She uses air quotes. "Nice equals boring."

I give her an eye roll. She's not wrong. That's why I've promised myself that I would politely end it with Jeff tonight.

"Logan, you are twenty-two years old. You're daringly gorgeous and guys drop at your feet where ever you go. I swear, every time you walk into the bar, Kristof and Hari stop what they're doing and drool. Lara, too, and she's not even a lesbian."

"Whatever."

"Seriously. Why waste your time on Mr. Dud when you can get a Stud?" She wags her tongue suggestively, rotating her hips in a sultry hula-dance. "I get that the good Doctor might be a catch in some circles – *dead ones*, that is – but you are not dead or desperate, Lo. God, it makes me cringe to think of you ending up with him. Eww." She shudders dramatically.

No, I might not be desperate, but I am dead. *Inside.*

I'm numb, like all the blood and life has been sucked out of me.

How can you possibly feel alive when your heart hasn't beat for years? When it died at the revelation that your only love didn't want anything to do with you and kicked you and your unborn child to the curb without a backward glance?

"Geez, tell me how you really feel. What if I were really into Jeff? Would you be this brutally honest?"

Ali grabs the top of my shoulders and squeezes. "First off, I say what I think. So yes, I'd probably give it to you straight even then, because I know he's not right for you. But I do know you aren't crazy over him. It's like you're dating him out of some sense of obligation, which is just wrong. Just because he's your boss doesn't mean you need to put out. So why postpone the inevitable? You need to find yourself a hot, single man whose gonna bring you to your knees with just the sound of his voice. Not put you to sleep."

Wanting to avoid any further arguments on her birthday, I don't respond to her lecture. Instead, I fold her in my arms for a hug and squeeze the ever-living crap out of her.

Releasing my hold, I shoo her out of the kitchen. "Now go get your stinky ass ready for your big night, birthday girl. And I'll see you later."

She hesitates only momentarily, but then leaves me alone with my kitchen mess and my even messier thoughts of Carver.

Ali is right about one thing.

I do need to learn to live again. The last few years have been tough. I've gone through a bloody mess of emotions, enduring the impossible and thankfully meeting great people like Ali along the way.

So tonight, I plan on letting Jeff down easy and then going out to celebrate my youth and a bright future ahead of me.

And to forget about my past.

CHAPTER 8

Carver

It wasn't my plan to go out clubbing my first night back in town. But my old friend wouldn't take no for an answer.

I've been in town for less than two hours and haven't even told my parents I'm home yet. For all they know, I'm still hanging out down in Tempe. The last time I spoke to them was when they flew in for my graduation ceremony two weeks ago. I know my dad wants to bury the hatchet, but I just can't bring myself to do it.

When I decided to make the trip up to Seattle for the long weekend, I called one of my old friends from high school, Joel, who attends UW. He seemed excited when I told him I'd be visiting and had no qualms about me crashing at his place. Joel already had plans to go out tonight and told me if I didn't come out with him, he'd make me sleep in the hallway, instead of on his couch.

I could've found another place to stay, or paid for a hotel room, but it is Memorial Day weekend. Finding temporary lodging could have proved difficult. I'm only here until Tuesday and plan to leave as soon as my appointment is done. Once that's done, I can return to Phoenix and prepare for the draft.

My agent, Cristopher Markum, has been blowing up my phone over the last week with possibilities of my draft pick selection.

My head swirls in a fog from everything inhabiting my brain recently. It's almost too much for me to handle. I'd never admit that to anyone. Well, maybe Cade, but definitely not Lance. He's too sensitive to deal with losing all of us all at once and I don't want to add to his issues.

So maybe coming out tonight with Joel isn't such a bad idea after all. Have a few drinks. Laugh. Dance. Meet some girls. Maybe get laid. Feel like my old self again.

Now that would be nice.

I guess you could say I've been in a bit of a rut. In the months since the failed championship game, I haven't been laid. And it isn't for lack of interested partners.

My notoriety on campus and nationally, has chicks hanging from me left and right, and practically on top of me twenty-four-by-seven. My old MO is to bang as many as I can and move on to the next batch.

But you know how many chicks I've slept with in the last two months?

Zip.

Zilch.

Absolutely zero.

I've had no interest in fucking random girls. My dick went from getting daily flagpole sitters to a limp dick with the flag hanging half-mast. I think I'm in need of some motherfucking psychotherapy.

It doesn't take a genius to know what my problem is. A shrink would tell me what I already know to be true. I'm stressed over the uncertainty of my future – uncertain where

I'll end up, what team I'll play for – or if I'll even be playing at all.

It's all fucking with my head.

There's also the tiny matter of all the shit that went down between Logan and me, and the unfinished business we've never dealt with properly. All we did was shove it under the rug and forged ahead. Now it's like I'm unpacking the boxes of my life and all that shit's spilled out over the floor, keeping me from getting to the door.

I guess it's true what they say. The past really does have a way of catching up to you, and when it does, it knocks you on your ass.

That's why I've been sitting around like a sullen, angsty sonofabitch, crying in my beer, when I should be living it up and enjoying my freedom. Damn, I should've gotten a degree in Psychology instead of Business - because I'm a freaking Sigmund Freud.

We've been at this little bar downtown for an hour now, and Joel is over at a corner table laughing and joking with a group of school friends. I met a few of them already – they're all cool. Some are recent graduates like me, but others are still in school with Joel, who is studying to become a lawyer. We're here to celebrate a birthday of a girl he used to hook up with. Ali something-or-other. She's over at another table chatting with the guy she came with and a cluster of girls. One of them has been giving me fuck-me eyes for the last twenty minutes, licking her lips like they're covered in sugar and fluffing her hair with her hand.

Classic flirtatious behavior. The same thing I get from a hundred other chicks. I've never had to chase a girl. If not for my basketball prowess, it's because they identify a man in need of solace. I swear girls can smell a brooding man like sharks sniff out blood in the water. There's something about the vibe guys emit when we're off-limits that has girls salivating to get their hands on our dicks.

And let me tell you, if I were in any mood to hook up tonight, I'd be all over that chick in a New York minute, because she's fucking hot.

But her hair isn't the right shade of blonde. Her nose doesn't have the slight bump in it from breaking it when she was sixteen from a fast-flying soccer ball. And her eyes aren't the same shade of sky-blue that I love. The eyes I've missed gazing into the last four years.

Hot girl looks like she's about to make her move. I glance away, swiveling in my bar stool and taking another sip of my beer, hoping to avoid her overt attention. In all honestly, I don't want to try hard with anyone tonight – even with one as hot as she is.

I scan the bar crowd from the mirror above the bar. There's a titter of excitement and energy as people celebrate the start of the long weekend. Aside from tonight, Joel and I made no plans for my visit. He invited me to join in on a camping trip that he's taking with his friends, but I haven't decided yet. Downtime has been lacking for me, as I'd been working like a dog up to graduation in May.

Alone time this weekend, with nothing on my schedule to do and nowhere to go, sounds perfect. I may just hang out and watch Netflix all weekend.

I set my empty glass on the counter and grab Joel's attention, who's looking in my direction but talking to the girl next to him. The girl that's been eying me all night has now moved her attentions elsewhere. Good thing for both of us.

"I'm hitting the head." I mouth to him, motioning my head in the direction of the bathrooms. He nods and turns back to continue his discussion with his female companion.

There's a couple guys at the urinals, and another guy in a stall that sounds like he's taking a dump, so I wait for a few minutes as the others finish up. I run a hand through my hair at the sink as I debate whether to head back to Joel's now or return to the party.

I'm not usually like this. I'm known as the life of the party. Crowned king of the keg.

I give myself a stern lecture as I head out of the bathroom, telling myself to get my head out of my ass and figure out how to have fun again. Life is too short and my youth can't be wasted on regrets.

I've finally reached a decision to stick around when I round the corner and my eyes snag a glimpse of long, honey blonde hair.

It's loud in the bar but in my head it's quiet – like I'm underwater. I blink a few times. It's got to be a hallucination. An apparition. Maybe I'm more drunk than I realize.

My feet don't want to move. Like some mystical vine has risen from the hollows of the scuffed wooden floor and wrapped its steely ropes around my leg, anchoring me to that spot. She's standing over by the table where all of Joel's sit, leaning over some girl, showing her something on her phone. When her head pops up, it turns in my direction and our eyes latch on to each other, and that vine creeps up to my neck and begins choking me.

Now I can't breathe *or* move. Fuck my life.

The only good thing to come from this moment is that Logan appears to be just as freaked out as I am. Her eyes grow wide as the ocean – a very deep, blue ocean- and I can see every ounce of hesitancy in her features.

I don't know what I expected from tonight, but it certainly wasn't this. Running into Logan out of the blue. *Again.*

For one tiny second, I consider finding the nearest exit and getting the hell out of here. This is just a fucked-up twist of fate. It no longer feels like a coincidence. It freaks me out.

As I remain there dumbfounded and debating what to do, Logan whispers something to the girl, and then slowly stands tall. Her friend's head snaps up, catching a glimpse of me at the bar and drops her mouth open. Then she swats Logan on the ass, as Logan walks toward me.

She maneuvers through the crowd toward me at the bar, my focus never leaving her. My mouth is dry and I wish like hell that I'd gotten another beer right away.

She gives a small smile. "Well this is very weird and just a tad bit awkward."

My lips twitch. "You could say that again."

Logan laughs briefly, her eyes twinkling with humor as they move from my face down to my chest, scanning my T-shirt. Her laugh is carefree, and shakes away the tension, as her smile grows broad.

"Nice shirt, Carver."

I look down because I don't remember which one I wore tonight. I'm kind of known for my filthy and foul-mouthed attire. It's good for some laughs and conversation starters. Cheesy fashion pick-up lines.

The one I'm wearing now says, *'All This and a Big Dick too.'* I quirk my eyebrows and give a casual half-shrug, plastering on my signature smirk – the one I know releases my dimple.

"At least it's not false advertising."

Then all hell breaks loose as she doubles over with laughter. Like full-on belly laughs. Luckily, my ego is shatter resistant. And I know my dick is an impressive piece of equipment. She just got the early version of me when we were kids. I've come a long way, and have only gotten better with age.

She guffaws. "Oh shit. When did you become so full of yourself?"

When we ended and I had to overcome my insecurities.

"I'm not conceited," I confess, lifting my chin with indignation. "It's a well-known fact that I have many talents known worldwide. I'm a damn-hot commodity, if you don't know. I learned a lot in college."

She stares at me blankly, her smile fading, and now I feel like an asshole. Logan glances off to the left, sucking in her bottom lip between her teeth, as if concentrating on some difficult task.

Maybe I shouldn't have said that. I don't know. She's messing with my head. This is not my normal mojo. I'm usually smooth, charming and a lady killer. Not a bumbling idiot ex who has to extol his own virtues.

She seems to recover, her beautiful eyes sparkling and her smile returning, as her fingers slip a strand of golden-hair behind an ear. "I bet you did. Smart college boy."

Nodding, I motion us over to the edge of the bar where someone just vacated. "I'm going to grab a beer. Can I get you something to drink?"

I've only been drunk with Logan once before. It was our last summer together – before we lost our virginities to each other. Back then, as a student athlete, I avoided hard alcohol and always stuck with beer. But that night, when our friend came back with a bottle of Canadian whiskey and marshmallows to roast, we all got trashed. Wound up puking our guts out down by the lake well into the night. To this day, if I get a whiff of that sweet marshmallow scent, I gag.

"Oh, thanks," she pauses for a second, tapping her index finger against her lips. The action draws my attention to the glistening moisture lining her heart-shaped mouth. I swallow and flag down the bartender.

"How about a Long Island Iced tea?" She says.

"You got it."

We stand quietly next to each other as a wiry, handlebar-mustached hipster saunters over to us and takes our order. When his eyes remain on Logan a moment too long, I want to reach over and snap the stupid suspenders he's wearing. He leaves with our order and I turn toward Logan, who's forced to stand shoulder-to-shoulder with me due to the crowd I can see she's not wearing any make-up to hide her unflawed complexion.

We lapse into silence. It's weighted with so many questions. Accusations. Guilt.

We open our mouths to speak at the same time.

I laugh, gesturing for her to go ahead.

"What are you doing here?" It's with genuine surprise and interest that she asks this. Said in a way that sounds like she's pleased to see an old friend versus bitter or irritated that I'm here. I take this as a good sign to proceed.

The bar noise and music overhead make it difficult to speak in a normal tone. So unless I want to shout at her, I have to lean down to speak directly into her ear.

I'm suddenly enveloped in her scent. Warmth travels the length of my body and I inhale a deep intoxicating breath.

"I'm staying the weekend with Joel Davis. He's a friend of mine from high school."

I point behind her where the group is congregated and Joel is slamming a shot with the others at the table.

"Small world. Joel and my roommate, Ali, used to hang out a lot. She bartends here and that's where they met. He's a nice guy. Smart, too."

I nod. "Yeah, the fucker's a good guy. But doesn't know his limits." I give her the universal sign of drinking, tipping my hand up to my mouth. "But he is smart, I'll give him that. I wish I had that brain of his."

She takes a sip of her drink that was just delivered, giving me a sidelong glance. "I don't know, you're not giving yourself enough credit. I mean, look at you. You could've drafted early and never finished school, but you stuck it out and got your degree. That says you're smart enough to consider your future and have something to fall back on later in life. That's admirable."

I'm stunned by her compliment. It's unexpected, considering she could hate me for ruining her life.

Which makes me wonder about her life since…well, over the last four years. All I know is she's a dental assistant. Does she have a boyfriend? She mentioned already that Ali's her room-mate, so that tells me she doesn't live with a guy.

"What made you decide to become a dental technician? Or

assistant. Or whatever you call what you do." I feel dumb because I don't know exactly what she does.

Logan chuckles, a smile curving her lips that are currently wrapped around a straw. My dick starts to perk up at the enticing picture. It's pretty hot, and she'd probably smack me if she knew what I was thinking about doing with those lips.

"Dental Assistant," she corrects me sweetly. "I didn't go to a traditional four-year college...I got certified through a community college program."

I swallow my drink. "What? I thought you were going to attend Western U? You'd already submitted your application and everything that summer. You were so excited about it."

Her fingers toy with the straw, swirling it around the glass, avoiding my gaze. I realize my mistake as soon as I see the flash in her eyes. Logan is a year younger than me, at least in school years. She was about to start her senior year when I started college. And that's when...*shit*. I'm an asshole.

"Fuck me...I'm sorry, Lo. I wasn't thinking."

I place my hand on the back of her head, her silky hair slipping through my fingers, as I drop my forehead to touch hers. It's intimate and comforting. "I'm so sorry. I didn't realize it... changed your plans for college."

She pulls away from me, sharply turning her ahead and sucking down the rest of her drink.

The easy connection we just had is now lost.

"It's okay, Carver. The world didn't end just because I didn't go to college. I made a career for myself. I'm good. And I can always go back at some point to get a sociology degree. I'm in no hurry."

There's more to the story that she's not telling me. I just know it. But it's obvious she doesn't want to go into the details, so I let it slide for now. In the meantime, I'm enjoying the truce between us, and just being in her presence.

It's both familiar yet new and different. There's so much I

remember about the younger version of Logan, and so many things I don't know about her as a woman.

The party seems to be picking up speed, as I hear someone call for another round of shots. I raise an eyebrow at Logan to see if she's going to partake. She just shakes her head and smiles.

And then I say the stupidest thing. I can't control it – the words just slip out of my mouth unbidden.

"Do you want to get out of here?"

Her eyes grow wide with skepticism.

"I mean, maybe head over to 13 Coins for pancakes? I haven't been there for years."

The smile she gives me is radiant, like a hundred-watt bulb, and it makes me feel like a lottery winner. Her smile is every loser's lucky day.

"That's a nice idea, but I really should stay and celebrate Ali's birthday. You only turn twenty-three once, right?" She flicks her thumb back toward the group.

"Oh, sure. Yeah, you're right."

Shit, I've already forgotten the reason I'm here tonight. I've been so wrapped up in our conversation. In being around her, that I didn't want that to end. My hopes of spending more time with her are dashed when she turns back to the group and sighs.

She's about to say something else, but then stops. The chewing of her lip resumes. I wonder if she's nervous.

Nah, not Logan. She's one badass girl. Was always tough and handled everything that came at her like a prize fighter.

"But maybe…" She hesitates, her hands clasping and unclasping in front of her. "Do you have plans for the weekend?"

Well, fuck me up the river. I'm not sure where she's going with this, but I'm in. Whatever she has in mind, I'm on board one-hundred percent.

I give her a noncommittal shrug.

"Nothing that I can't change. What'd you have in mind?"

She speaks with more confidence now. "This weekend the

National Parks are free for day hikers. I'm already planning a hike in the Cascades with Ali, but my guess is the birthday girl isn't going to be feeling up to the trek after tonight's activities. So…um…would you want to go with me?"

I've never been at a loss for words. I'm the epitome of cool under pressure. But Logan's invite has me almost tongue-tied. But there's no fucking way I'd ever turn down her request.

I try to joke, even though excitement hits me in the pit of my stomach. "You asking me out, Lo?"

I give my one-dimpled smirk.

The affect is funny. Exactly how I knew she'd respond.

"Fuck you, Edwards."

She slaps me hard on the chest, but I'm quick and grab her wrist, tugging her into me.

"Just so you know, I don't put out on the first date."

Our faces are an inch apart, our bodies pressed together to barely allow space to breathe. I brush my thumb over the pressure point on the soft underside of her wrist. I can feel the rapid heart rate beating under the skin.

Her gasp is loud and quick and it makes me insanely hot. I want to hear that same gasp when I bury myself deep inside her again someday.

"I'm just messing with you, Lo. I'd love to go hiking with you. It's been a long time since I've done something outdoors just for the fun of it."

I kiss the tip of her nose for good measure.

Tomorrow morning can't come soon enough.

CHAPTER 9

LOGAN

WHAT THE HELL was I thinking inviting Carver Edwards, the man I had no intention of ever seeing again, to join me on an all-day hike? In an isolated area in the Cascades?

Was I that drunk after one Long Island?

I'm kicking myself over my absolute stupidity, and over the fact that I actually enjoyed myself with him last night. He's even funnier than I remember, and is an extreme flirt.

And let's not forget incredibly gorgeous. Every single woman in that bar had him in her sights.

Carver and I continued talking and joking with the rest of the group for another hour after I opened my big mouth and offered up the invitation to hike. A highly inadvisable decision, but something I couldn't take back once I said it. Now as I drive through the steep hills of Seattle toward Joel's Green Lake rental house, I consider a thousand different excuses for cancelling on him last minute.

Emergency appendectomy? Nah, he might come to the hospital to visit me.

Flat tire? Nope, he'd come to my rescue and figure out a way to get it fixed.

Twenty-four-hour flu bug? Hm. That one's no good, either, because then I'd have to stay at home all day and pretend to be sick. And the point of today was to get out and stretch my legs.

Despite my discomfort, I couldn't get up the nerve to lie to him. Maybe we can use this time together today to find some resolution and tie up the history between us in a nice, tidy package. Perhaps even forgive each other for the hurt and damage we caused – intentional or otherwise.

Even if none of that happened, at least we'd enjoy a beautiful day out in the North Cascades. And there's nothing more beautiful and serene as that.

Because being out in the great outdoors with Carver, surrounded by mountains and lakes, won't do anything, whatsoever, to bring back the memories of our summers together.

Did I mention how stupid I am?

I make a right turn at the corner and drive slowly down the tree and car-lined street, looking for the address Carver had texted me last night. Out of nowhere, he materializes in front of me before I can even notice the house number from the street.

Carver is waiting out front, two coffee cups in hand, dressed in comfortable hiking attire.

And damn, he looks fine.

Carver Edwards has only grown more handsome. And holy Lord – filled out.

Although he's wearing a light jacket, the long Lycra sleeves hug against his clearly defined biceps. Like the rolling hills of the farm country where I grew up – his muscles are beautiful. I see tufts of his golden-brown hair peeking out from under his baseball cap. Such a guy move – wake up and throw on a hat and still look sexy.

Although, I can't condemn him, since I only pulled my hair up into a messy bun the moment I got out of the shower. While the temps are tricky in the mountains this time of year, a lot cooler than the city, you can work up a good sweat while hiking. I like to keep my hair off my neck so I don't get all sticky and sweaty from the excursion. Dressing in layers is a necessity, because an hour in, I start shedding clothes.

Pulling up to the curb, I lean over and open the door to a way-too-chipper Carver, who drops his ass into the bucket seat of my Volvo with a flop, holding the cups in front of him – being careful not to the spill the hot liquid.

"Morning," he chirps, handing me a steaming cup of liquid fortification.

I accept the gift and place it in the cup holder between us. "Thanks."

When I glance back up at him, his brows are creased in a frown.

"What?" I ask with skepticism. I run a hand over my mouth, in case I have a glob of toothpaste still on my lips. "Do I have something on my face?"

He shuts his eyes for a second, a disgruntled chuckle leaving his throat. He opens them again and stares at me with an intensity that draws a wave of heat up my chest. I look away to avoid the penetrating gaze.

"No, you're good. I just realized that after all these years, I have no idea if you even drink coffee."

A laugh escapes my lips. Here I thought it was something more serious than that.

"I'm a Seattleite, doofus. Have you been away from home so long that you've forgotten we can't breathe without the comforts of our hot liquid addiction?"

He mumbles his response before taking a long sip from his cup. "It feels like I've been gone an eternity."

There's something there that I don't want to delve into, so I let it go.

"I guess hot coffee isn't a basic life necessity in Arizona."

"Nope."

We drive in silence as I merge onto I-5 and head north, the start of our hour-long drive up to the mountains. I grew up in the shadow of the Cascades. The Skagit Valley countryside, complete with tulip fields, dairy farms and orchards. My dad's farm was small and he worked hard, with the help of family, to make a living – but it never seemed to get us out of poverty. There were times I recall during the harsh, unproductive winters that we relied on foodbanks for staples to keep us fed.

It's been a long time since I've been near my hometown. My dad died two years ago, and I only heard from my brother Leo. They didn't have a service for him, so I stayed put. I didn't miss my brothers and they didn't care to see me.

But I did miss the area. I craved being outside – surrounded by the beauty of the Sound and the mountain ranges. To the west is the Olympics, and the north and east, the Cascade Range. It doesn't get any more beautiful than this.

That's why the scholarship to camp those three summers was so important to me. It gave me a tiny respite from the hard labor I endured the rest of the season at home.

I never understood the appeal for Carver and how he ended up in Whistler, when he could've been off gallivanting in Switzerland or Peru.

"Out of curiosity, how did you end up at Camp Cheakamus?"

I keep my gaze set on the road, but I can feel Carver's eyes staring at me. It feels good, but also slightly unnerving.

"Really? That's what you want to know after all this time? That's the question you're going to ask me to start this reunion discussion?"

It's not derisive, per se. But there's a sting in his response.

I give him a sidelong glance. "You got a better question?"

He scoffs. "Yeah. I have lots."

Without warning, the atmosphere in the car shifts and it fills with the weight of all that was left unsaid between us. Tension seeps in and curls between us, grabbing my heart in a tight fist.

"Lots, huh?" I unintentionally press down on the accelerator so the car's speedometer spikes up to just under eighty-miles-per-hour. Racing just like my thoughts.

"Well, let's hear them."

"Hmm. Okay...how about 'why'?"

"Why, what?"

His gaze shifts forward to stare out the front window. Cars pass. The scenery changes. But we're still stuck in the past. Unable to move forward.

"Why didn't you ever respond back to me?"

I dare a glance at him. The truth is in his eyes. He's hurt. But I don't know why.

"What do you mean? *When?*"

He lets out a harsh laugh. "Come on, Lo. Don't play dumb. I emailed you at least a dozen times after I found out...you never responded."

My gasp can probably be heard all the way up to the Canadian border. My fingers tighten on the steering wheel. I'm filled with both a distinct sadness and shock.

"Carver, I don't know what you're talking about. I shut down that email account after...well, after I'd met up with your dad. He, um...he suggested that it would be the best thing for everybody."

The sound of his hand hitting the dashboard startles me. "That motherfucker." He spews so vehemently that I flinch.

I'm just as angry. That memory is so clear in my mind – like it was just yesterday. The day I met his dad. After he'd responded to my email, he offered me money to have an abortion. When I declined and told him I was going to have the baby, he gave me the name and number of an attorney that he'd pay for and who'd help me with the adoption.

And then there was the gut-wrenching heartbreak I endured when Mr. Edwards told me that Carver never wanted to hear from me again, so I should just cut the ties and move on.

Maybe that wasn't the case after all. Maybe both Carver and I are victims in this story.

I reach out and place a calming hand on Carver's bicep and I feel the muscles relax against my touch.

"My father," Carver says with harsh distain, "Interfered where he didn't belong. He made decisions about our baby without my consent. I didn't know. Had I known, Logan…"

He pauses and my brain begins to click backward in time. To when I first contacted Carver about my predicament.

"Oh my God. So, what you're saying is…"

He interrupts. "Yeah. I never got any of your emails and I didn't know you were pregnant. Not in the beginning. My dad monitored all my email and social media accounts as a means of keeping track of me and keeping me out of trouble. He wanted me to focus on school and basketball, in that order, and nothing else. No other distractions. So he intercepted my emails, met with you and never told me anything. I was none the wiser."

This changes everything. Well, almost everything.

All these years, I thought Carver didn't want anything to do with me. I was just the white-trash, knocked up girlfriend who was now tarnished and damaged goods. Carver had a bright future ahead of him and didn't want a girlfriend and baby to screw up his good times. I always assumed he asked his dad to handle it on his behalf. The way kids in seventh grade handle break-ups. Using someone else to do their dirty work.

"Wait…but you obviously found out at some point that I was pregnant. When did that happen?"

The anger and resentment from Carver is palpable. "When I came home for Christmas break that year. I was searching my dad's office for tape to wrap my mom's present and I opened one of his desk drawers and came across a file labeled

L. Shaw. I was curious why the hell my dad would have a file with your name on it. He had all these email print-outs, and legal documents pertaining to your pregnancy. And the subsequent adoption. Apparently, he wanted to ensure he had everything in writing in case you ever came back to extort us."

Carver looks at me with sorrowful eyes. "The minute I read those emails, I confronted him. And then I tried to call you. And email you. God, Lo. I tried everything to track you down."

"Oh."

Carver's voice is raspy. "He called you horrible names, Logan. He made up awful lies about your intention. I'll never forgive him for that, Lo."

The sting still hurts, knowing that someone could think such awful things about me. I'm surprised when I glance to my thigh to find Carver's large hand resting on the top of my leg. His warmth radiates through my yoga pants and my tummy does a nervous flip.

"I've been called far worse. It's no big deal."

Which is true. My dad, brothers and friends at school called me so many variations of the word whore after finding out about my pregnancy that I'd become immune to it. It hurt, but I always knew the truth about who I was. I wasn't who they proclaimed me to be. I didn't sleep around, hook up randomly for attention, or get knocked up by some stranger. And I certainly didn't get pregnant and give up my future scholarships in order to trick a guy for money.

I was in love with my baby's daddy.

"I confronted him right away, Lo. I fought for you. For us. But my dad told me it was too late. Things had already been handled and that I should just let you go. Move forward with the plans for my NBA career. He told me I'd soon forget about you and that you'd do the same."

He runs his hand roughly through his hair, shifting the hat on top of his head. His voice is gravely and full of emotion. Tortured.

How can I not forgive this boy? This man who stood up for me. Who hadn't left me behind on purpose.

Pushing the cap back down over his head, so most of his face is hidden, he continues.

"In the early days, the thought of you moving on with another guy drove me fucking crazy. I tried to contact you. But after so long, after never hearing back, I just stopped. It was useless."

My heart lights up with joy knowing that long ago, the boy I loved tried to find me. Tried to track me down to be there for me. In my darkest hours, I had always hoped and prayed that he would find his way back to me. That he could come rescue me like a Knight in Shining Armor to whisk my baby and me away.

But then my heart plummets, remembering the reality of how desperately alone I truly was. No family. No boyfriend. No support. The only thing I had was the staff at Grace Homes, the home for pregnant teens where I lived for just under a year. Until my child was born and I gave him up – as planned – for adoption.

"I wish things had been different." I whisper. "I'm sorry it happened that way."

Silence descends upon us again as I pull off the highway toward the North Cascades National Forest. We drive a few more miles until I park at the ranger station in Verlot, where we register for our hike.

As we walk back to the car, Carver stops me by gently grabbing hold of my wrist, the warmth of his touch breaking the remaining ice left around my heart.

"I'm the one who's sorry, Lo. I wish I could turn back the clock. I'd have worked hard to have found you sooner. We've missed so much. Time I can never get back with you. I would have handled it differently. *Everything* would be different now."

CHAPTER 10

Carver

WHETHER IT'S from the confessions in the car on our way here, or just being outdoors and surrounded by the stillness of nature, I feel like a completely different person then I was eight hours ago.

Or four years ago.

Logan and I have been hiking up the damp, mossy trail leading up to Lake 22 for the last forty-five minutes. It's a five-and-a-half-mile round trip, with an elevation gain of thirteen hundred fifty feet. We've been making the steady climb up the rocky shale paths, crossing rickety wood bridges over flowing creeks bursting with melted-snow run-off. It's beautiful and makes me remember how much I've missed the Pacific Northwest. The desert of Arizona is beautiful, but nothing compares to the thick undergrowth of the rain forest at the base of Mount Pilchuck.

The smell of the woods alone is like breathing life into your lungs. It fills you with a peaceful serenity where everything is washed clean. Like there's no problem too big that can't be solved out here. It brings to mind one of Henry David Thoreau's poems, where you should treat this time as a blessing in your day.

My boots are muddy and wet, and my breathing ragged, as we continue our assent. Sweat drips down the center of my back from excursion. As an athlete, I'm in damn good shape. I work out six days a week and take good care of my body.

It's not the exercise that's the problem. It's not what has my heart chugging like a freight train as I follow behind Logan up the trail. The real reason for my shortness of breath is walking four feet ahead of me.

Her ass in tight black yoga pants.

I'm not sure how much longer I can handle watching her ass swish and sway with every step. I might just break down, fall on my knees behind her and roughly grab a handful of ass cheek, begging her to stop the torment. It's driving me out of my fucking mind.

Something has shifted between us since our car conversation. It was cathartic. The burden that once weighed me down like an anchor was lifted and I finally feel free. On top of the world. Ready for something...anything...

Logan's demeanor toward me has changed, as well. She's been laughing with me – or at me. She smiles more. I've also caught her staring at me when she thinks I'm not looking. And it makes me want to wrap my arms around her and never let go.

Logan stops so abruptly at a curve in a switchback, I have to place my hands on the back of her shoulders to avoid plowing into her. She jumps and then seems to relax under my touch. I let go just as quickly to avoid any unnecessary touching, but not before I feel how small she is underneath my hands. Delicate as a petal, yet strong as a hemlock limb. She's feminine, yet toned. She feels fan-fucking-tastic under my touch.

I've always loved that about her. Logan Shaw was a force to be reckoned with back in our teens, and drew me in with her unwavering confidence and lack of bullshit. She wasn't one of those vapid teenage girls who fussed over her hair and make-up. Every part of her personality was bright, beautiful and buoyant. Even a sky full of stars couldn't outshine her on even her worst day.

"Whoa," I manage to say as I catch a whiff of her sweet, fragrant scent. "Is something wrong?"

Logan bends down at her hips, giving me an amazing view of her ass. Oh fuck. I want to pull down those pants and spank her bare ass so we both light up from the burn. I manage to fold my hands into fists, commanding them to stay at my sides.

She trudges up a bit further, but not before I notice she's limping. She finds a spot to sit down on a large rock in the side of the hill.

"I'm okay. I just have a Charlie horse cramp. I just need to stretch it out for a second."

Squatting down in front of her, I grab underneath the leg she has stretched out and I gently shove away her hands from her calf and begin massaging the tense muscle. It's knotted tight, so I know she must be in pain. She moans – either from the pain or maybe from my touch. I hope it's the latter.

"Is this okay?" I ask, not wanting to spook her with the intimacy of my touch. But it feels amazing. She feels amazing.

As a teenager, Logan was incredibly athletic and beautiful. Lean, limber and full of endless energy. Not much has changed, it seems. Her body is spectacularly toned.

"Do you get these often?"

She nods her head.

"Yes. I'm probably just dehydrated from drinking too much last night, and not enough water." She smiles with a remorseful glint in her eye. "I suppose you've had your fair share of sports injuries out on the court."

This is the first time she's ever brought up anything related to my basketball career. Usually when I'm with a girl, that's the only thing they want to talk about. Like I'm nothing more than just a ball player. A commodity.

Logan has never really known me in that aspect of my life. Our relationship was so compartmentalized – there was our life at camp and our lives outside of camp. We lived in a bubble.

"I've been lucky," I smirk, squeezing a spot on her leg that she seems to like, if her gasp of breath is any indication. "Until recently with the tooth and nose break. But I haven't broken anything else."

My fingers dig deeper into the knotted tissue and it begins to release under my ministrations. I move my hands a little further up her leg, just underneath her knee – maybe testing how much latitude she's going to give me.

I like this connection we have and I don't want to let it go. It's like we're in our own little universe under the canopy of the Alderwoods and Red Cedars. Cocooned in a place where it's just the two of us and no one else. No history. No past. Just the here and now.

Logan fixes her gaze on my mouth and the corners of my mouth edge up into a smile.

"God, I feel awful for not asking, but how is your tooth doing?" She asks.

I release her foot and place it on the ground, leaning in so that I'm now crouching between her legs.

"I'll let you examine it if you want."

I'm getting all up in her space, using my flirtatious line to see how far it gets me. I place my hands on the top of her thighs, and allow my fingers to spider-crawl up to her hips. My fingers find purchase in the softness at her rear and dig in as I jerk her forward to bring her in to me. Her sharp intake of air has my dick turning as hard as the rock she's occupying.

Her eyes go wide, but close on a moan as I press my lips into hers for a taste.

She tastes of mint, dewy rain and mountain air. Everything I love and have missed since I've been away.

My mouth aligns with hers and I search for any reason I

should stop, but come up empty. I bring one hand up to the back of her head, tilting her face to the side, as I take deeper possession of her mouth. I close my eyes, allowing my tongue to slide through her soft, wet lips and delve into her mouth. She meets me there, her tongue sweeping over and tangling with mine.

It's like memories of camp fires.

Of dark summer nights.

Of rushing waterfalls.

It's like coming home.

The kisses I've shared with other girls since Logan can't hold a candle to this feeling. There's no comparison. When we kiss, it's like dynamite. Explosive and detonating. It's like the bite and sting of the waterfall across my back, covering me from head to toe in tingling exhilaration.

The trail has been mostly deserted in the last hour, save for a few groups of hikers, but somewhere in the not-so-far-off distance, we hear the sounds of laughter and voices getting closer. They could be just around the bend. It doesn't worry me in the slightest, but Logan breaks the kiss.

She leans back, her breath choppy. I blink a few times, watching her chest heave and her eyes morph from a hazy heat to cold, alert awareness.

I don't want to lose the physical contact with her, so I glide my hand down her arm to grasp her hand. As I stand, I pull her up alongside me. She appears unsteady and a little weary as she glances down the trail for any sign of oncoming hikers.

"They aren't too close." I explain, reading her thoughts. She shakes out her leg, stretches it and continues her climb once again without a word.

I have to say, I'm a bit stunned by her reaction. The aloofness is a sudden departure from what we've been sharing thus far. Before she gets too far, I reach for her hand, threading my fingers through hers to stop her progression. Her head wrenches behind her, capturing my gaze with hers.

"Why'd you stop?"

"We've still got a ways to go if we want to summit the top before lunch."

I could care less about breaking any speed records on this hike, I want to get back to more kissing.

"I want more of that," I say, and I know she understands I mean her kiss.

Her expression is a mix of weariness and hope.

She shrugs nonchalantly and grins. "Maybe. We'll see."

Then off she sprints up the hill, leaving me behind to run after her.

Just like our summer four years ago.

I've never chased after a girl before. She's the only one. And this isn't the first time I've had to run after her.

This time I resolve to chase her until I can pin her down for good.

"HEY, WAIT UP!" I yell after Logan, as she takes the rickety steps up to the top with grace only granted to gazelles.

She stops for a second, turns her head and grins.

"Can't keep up with a girl? That's just sad, Edwards." She taunts.

It's exactly the ammunition I need to push forward with lightning-fast speed that I only reserve for the basketball court. In under two-seconds I've reached the precipice, grabbing her around the waist and spinning her around as she screams in joy.

"What were you saying about my manhood, Miss Shaw?"

My hand is on her hip as she slides down my body. I know she must feel my bulge. It's not exactly easy to hide in my nylon running shorts. Logan places her feet on the ground and turns back to me.

Without a word, she leans in and kisses me solidly on the mouth. She clasps her hands behind my neck, as they feather into my hair. My own hands graze lazily down her back and grasp her ass, which is the most perfectly heart-shaped ass I've ever felt. Much less seen. She arches her back and presses firmly into my cock, which twitches upon contact. Begging for friction.

We continue to kiss, sampling each other's lust, swallowing the other's moans. The sun is high in the sky overhead, burning holes into the tops of our heads, intensifying the heat that already exists between us.

Logan pulls back with a gasp.

"No one else is around." She whispers conspiratorially – equal parts mischievousness and shyness, her bright blue gaze never wavering.

I confirm the truth by scanning the top of the plateau overlooking the lake. It's quiet and serene from this vantage point. There's no one else around, as all the other campers are off doing their extra-curricular activities elsewhere, whereas we snuck off to be alone.

I raise my eyebrow. "Oh, yeah? What did you have in mind?"

She giggles and shrugs her shoulders, blushing as red as the beak on the Red Nosed Pecker.

"I want...to do something."

Ah, hell. I'm praying I know what she's interested in doing, but I don't want to get my hopes up.

In my dreams, we've done everything under the sun sexually; but in reality I've only gotten to second base with her. Our camp schedules are typically chocked full of activities and chaperones, leaving us little alone time. And at night, our bunks are heavily watched for any illicit goings on between the young, horny teenagers looking to cop a feel out in the woods.

This is our second summer together. We're both still virgins. She's told me she doesn't have a boyfriend at home – which I find impossible to believe. I've hung out with girls during the school year, but I'm not interested in dating. None of my high school buddies know anything about Logan. She's my secret. Not because I'm embarrassed by her. I just don't want anyone to know how whipped I am over a girl I barely know and only see two-weeks a year.

But the moment we reunited a week ago, after nine long months *apart, we picked up right where we left off. I wish I could describe the feeling. Logan just burns me up from the inside.*

Truthfully, I hate the arrangement she made me agree to at the end of last summer. She said it would be too difficult to commit to a long-distance relationship during the school year; we're free to date or mess around with anyone we want without feeling guilty.

I thought things would change between us after that much time apart. But the minute we saw each other again, it was like no time had passed and the previous nine months didn't exist.

"What is it that you want to do?" I ask hesitantly, praying that she wants the same thing I do.

She bites her lower lip as I grab hold of her hand and walk her over to a patchy area for us to sit. We place our backpacks on the ground, as I pull the water bottle out and take a swig, offering her one. She accepts, taking a long swallow as I watch her throat bob up and down. It gives me way too may dirty thoughts.

She recaps the thermos and looks down at her feet. "I want to touch you."

I try to swallow, but it gets stuck in my throat. The water spills out of my mouth as I turn to stare at her wide-eyed.

I mean, fuck yes. I want her to touch me, too. Duh. But did I accidentally misinterpret what she meant?

"Um, exactly what part of me do you want to touch, Lo?" I whisper, careful not to choke on the words.

"You know..." she acknowledges, drawing out the O and tilting her head down to my lap.

I try to remember how to breathe. In. Out. Inhale. Exhale. I have a choice to make. It's a fork in the proverbial trail.

What if she just wants to touch me once? Like at a petting zoo when they take out the boa constrictor and the kids get to feel it. They think it's cool and scary, and want to be brave, but then as soon as their fingers touch the scaly skin, they turn and run screaming.

If that happens once Logan touches my boner, I'd be screwed. I'm a sixteen-year-old boy who'd be left with a killer boner that I'd have no way to relieve. Would she even understand the amount of pain I'd be in? Forget about hiking down the mountain.

On the other hand – fuck yeah. If she wants to do this, I'm all in. As long as she lets me touch her, too. It might just get us both what we want.

"Only if I get to touch you. It's only fair."

She blanches slightly, then thinks about it for less than a second before she agrees. "Okay."

I practically jump up, flinging stuff out of my backpack to find something to lay on the ground beneath us. This garners a low chuckle from Logan, but I don't care. Because in a minute, I hope she won't be laughing at all. I hope she'll be so turned on, all I'll hear is her soft moans of satisfaction.

We end up laying out our towels side-by-side, making a small bed upon the moist, pine-scented earth. We lay on our sides facing one another and begin kissing. Slow pecks at first, which grow into longer, lingering kisses, as my hand finds the curve of her hip, playing a little back-and-forth against her skin.

Making out with a beautiful girl has got to be the best thing in the whole fucking world. My lips have now migrated to her neck, which I suck on for a while. She seems to like it a lot, as her body squirms against me, her pelvis moving in a sexy rhythm. She allows my hand to burrow underneath her T-shirt, my fingers tracing a pattern of circles up, up, up until I reach the underside of her boob.

My dick twitches in anticipation, knowing I'm going to touch what I've coveted for so long. They were the first thing I noticed about Logan after our nine-month absence between last summer and now. Her boobs had seriously grown another cup size since last summer and were practically busting out of her bra. I heard one of the other boys say something about the way they bounced when she ran and I was about to punch him in the face, but thought twice about it, since I didn't want to get kicked out of camp – the only two weeks a year I spent with Logan.

My hand leisurely roams the soft swell, as I test out the sounds she makes. I think it's torture for both of us. I don't want to move too fast, *but so far things seem to be going really well. I like that Logan's giving me the latitude I want and not playing games.*

My fingers inch their way up to the center of her bra and I find that there's a snap there. I fumble a little and then get it to unlatch. Her chest rises and falls, faster now, as I slip the material away from her skin. My thumb skims across the hardened nipple and she flinches and gasps simultaneously. And it's the sweetest, sexiest sound I've ever heard in all my life. She exhales a moan as she presses her breast into my palm.

My cock grows harder and pushes into her side, as I begin dry-humping her leg. The magical thing is that she doesn't seem to mind.

"Mm." She moans and I couldn't agree more.

Lifting the edge of her shirt, I expose the beauty of her creamy skin. The perfectly smooth and unblemished flesh normally hidden underneath her bikini top, and the area of sun-kissed tan that's seen endless hours under the hot summer sun.

My lips take possession of her nipple, sucking her taste into my mouth for the very first time. I feed on her like a starving man, sucking and nibbling at her perfectly taut breast. My lower half instinctively grinds against her looking for relief from the pain and pressure that's been building to a boiling point.

That pain is momentarily extinguished as Logan's hand tentatively skims down between us to slide over the material of my shorts. I groan a desperate, dying noise and her hand pulls back like she's been burned. We both stop and she recoils.

Her expression is worry-laden. "Oh my God. Did I hurt you?"

I laugh at her outrageous question and she blinks, embarrassed by my reaction.

I grab hold of her hand and place it back on my dick, instructing her kinetically how to make it hurt so much more.

"God, no. That feels good. Keep doing that, okay?"

She nods, her tongue peeking out between her lips in concentration. I want to be selfish and just lay back on the mossy ground and let her have at me. But I also want to make her feel good, too.

Returning my hand to the waistband of her jean shorts, I begin to unbutton her fly, but first get her approval through eye contact. She nods and we continue kissing, getting lost in each other and in the moment. My concentration flits back and forth between wanting to get my hand between her soft, wet center, and relishing in the feel of getting rubbed off by her.

After struggling a little with the shorts, my hand finally lodges within the warmest, softest place in the universe. I'm momentarily dazed when I slide my middle finger through the downy softness of her curls and make my way down to every boy's dreamland. Moving my finger through the valley between her folds, my thumb strokes over the small nub, which draws out a lusty moan from her, as well as a hip thrust. I notice out of the corner of my eye her head moving side to side and I grin.

As I continue my quest to bring on the first orgasm I've ever given a girl, I feel Logan's hand untying the draw string of my shorts and slipping her hand inside. I think I forget how to breathe. The minute I feel the skin-to-skin contact of Logan's small hand against my hardened skin, I'm ready to explode.

I want to tell her to grip it hard with all her might. To stroke and pull it like the way she pulled in that bass the other day at the river. But instead, I show her because the words are stuck in my throat.

Placing my free hand on top of hers, I curl my fingers around her hand and together we begin to stroke me off, as I give her time to adjust to the motion. And then she takes over.

We are out in the wide-open middle of the Canadian wilderness, doing the most natural thing in the world with one another. It's incredible. What dreams are made of.

"Am I doing this right?" she asks breathlessly.

"You're perfect. It's so good."

As I continue to circle her clit, I decide to go big or go home. My fingers inch further south, opening her slick folds, and I penetrate her wet entrance. She bucks against me, stopping her own hand movements, as I enter her body for the first time. My finger plunges into her wet heat and she jolts against me.

"Ah," she whimpers, her hand stilling on top of my dick for a moment, before resuming her grip and pumping.

I feel the explosion growing – it's climbing higher and higher – until I know I'm seconds away from unloading all over her hand.

"Lo," I barely get out just as I begin to come all over my stomach, my head tipped back in glorious release.

I think my climax may have brought out her own orgasm, because within seconds, her body tightens around my finger and she surrenders herself to me underneath the sun-drenched sky.

There's no way either of us will forget this day for as long as we live.

CHAPTER 11

LOGAN

I WANTED to forget about Carver Edwards. Forget he ever existed.

I'd done it for years. Buried that part of my life and moved forward...for *years*.

Now he's somehow back in my life. Larger than life. Worming his way into my heart again just like he did when I was fifteen. Goddamn him.

The thought both thrills and terrifies me. I've come such a long way since those endless summer nights. I'd pushed forward in my life and found a fulfilment living on my own. I don't need anyone – or any man – to come along and mess with my head. Or my heart.

The rest of our hike was a little awkward after the intimate moment we shared. And that kiss. Goddamn that kiss. It had me weak in the knees and wanting for more, even though I did my best to keep my distance the rest of the hike. And he seemed to understand that unspoken message. No more touching. No more making out.

It makes me nuts. I don't want to want him. But the moment he kissed me, it was like a switch was flipped and all my desire was turned back on. My feelings came tumbling out of the cave I'd kept them hidden in and had me practically floating back down the mountain trail.

The moment his strong, capable hands touched my leg up on that mountain side and he began to massage my calf, I nearly broke down in surrender. The white flag was almost raised in complete and utter defeat. I wouldn't be surprised if my forehead wore a sign that said, TAKE ME, I'M YOURS. I was so ashamed of how easily I gave into his kiss. It brought back every powerful memory we'd ever made together.

When we finally made it to the top of the trail – our destination stretched out before us in a glassy-mirror of icy beauty. The reflections across the water are so incredible it could send artists into a weeping mess.

We stood on the wooden bridge crossing the narrowest part of the water for a good twenty-minutes, just staring in silence. If you believe in an all-powerful God who created all the heavens and the earth, you'd surely see it when surrounded by the magnificence of nature.

I'd brought along some sandwiches and Powerbars to eat for lunch. It felt natural - even though my brain was going a hundred-miles-per-hour, overthinking every little interaction we'd had together. The sexual tension was so strong – so intense - it nearly sent me careening off the bridge overlooking the lake. But Carver seemed unaffected.

It's now late in the day and we've pulled up outside of Joel's house. We'd been talking about our plans for the long weekend on our drive back, and Carver mentioned Joel was on a camping trip.

My car idles on the street because there are absolutely no parking spots available. Street-parking in Seattle neighborhoods is crazy-bad.

I turn to face Carver. "Thanks for going with me. I had fun today."

His tall and muscular body barely fits in the front passenger seat of my car. Even with his seat pushed back as far as it can go, it still looks too compact for him. I have to angle my body to look him in his eyes.

The late afternoon sun shines across the side of his face, highlighting the dark blond scruff on his jaw. His grin is bright. And if I didn't know better, calculating.

"The day's not over yet."

He'd caught me off guard earlier and I'd made the mistake of telling him that I had no plans for tonight, since I'm technically single.

Last night, I broke it off with Jeff. Although it went well and he acted like a grown-up, he still requested that I think about it, and said if I changed my mind, he'd be there. I reluctantly agreed, but now I know for certain that will never happen. Jeff and I don't have that spark.

Nothing like what I have with Carver. If someone walked by us right now and brushed up against my car, they'd likely be electrocuted.

BAM! Sizzle and fade to black.

Carver leans forward, encroaching on my personal space, as I shift backward, my shoulder bumping the steering column.

"I want more time with you."

I swallow thickly. There's no excuse I can give him, even though it would be a futile attempt. He doesn't take no for an answer.

"Um…"

He surprises me then when he wraps both hands on each side of my jawline, holding me still. My heart rate skyrockets and my breathing accelerates. He can feel it. Hear it. See it.

Carver leans in slowly…ever so slowly…

"I want to kiss you again."

My breath stalls. My mind goes blank.

"Do you remember our first kiss?" he asks, softly stroking my cheek with his thumb.

I nod my head.

"It feels the same way now. Only it's more intense."

I nod again.

His lips are just about to brush mine. His breath warm against my mouth. I'm so ready to just give in to him. To let go and enjoy this brand-new thing we've rekindled.

Honk, honk, honk.

Three loud obnoxious blares come from behind my car and startles us both. Carver growls in irritation as he pulls away, snapping his head toward the back window.

"Asshole," he mutters.

I laugh at our situation. I'm blocking the road, leaving no room for the driver behind me to maneuver around because the street is too narrow.

"I've got to move," I say in a panic, more to myself than to Carver. I put the car in drive and accelerate forward a little too hard in my haste, earning a laugh from him. I make a sweep down the street, turning at the roundabout to circle back around to the house.

While I drive, Carver takes out his phone. "What's your number?"

I rattle it off as he enters the digits into his contacts.

"I'll call you later. You can send me your address and I'll pick you up."

"You're being kind of presumptuous, aren't you?"

He's not and he knows it. I'll give in and go out with him and he's that arrogant to know I won't deny him. My guess is no girl in the history of the world has ever denied Carver Edwards anything.

"Let me have a do over and rephrase that. I've never actually asked a girl out on a date before, so that wasn't very eloquent."

I pull to a stop once again and stare at him incredulously. "Wait, you've never dated before?"

Carver lets out a scoffing chuckle. "No, I didn't say that... what I said was that I've never *asked* a girl out. I've never had to." He shrugs like it's no biggie.

I'm very confused. Maybe I'm dense, but I don't understand what he means. He's dated, but he's never had to ask...oh, wait. Now I get it.

"Oh...that's right. Mr. Big College Basketball stud. Silly me. I guess I should just fall down and kiss the ground you walk on."

"If you wish."

His dimpled smile and sarcastic reply have me taking a swing at him for being such a self-centered jerk, but he grabs my forearm before I can lay a palm on his chest.

"Gah – you're so..."

I can't finish that statement because Carver yanks me forward and crushes me with his mouth. My body complies instantly to his demands, free-falling into his touch. I just hope there's a safety-net to catch my fall.

We kiss for a few minutes until I find my resolve and pull away from his warmth. I glance at his lips, which are shiny from my kiss. I can't deny what I'm feeling for him. I do want more, even if it's just for the weekend.

My breath is choppy and I notice the windows are foggy from the steam forming on the inside. Our first kiss in a car. And it was hot.

"I'll call you. Be ready."

Before I can say anything else, Carver is out the door and up the walkway toward the small bungalow house. My eyes can't help but stare after him as he walks away. Tall. Built like a strong, sturdy house. Kind and genuine, yet boastfully arrogant.

There's so much about him that I don't know yet. Things I've missed since he's grown from a strapping teen to a full-fledged man. Did I make a mistake all those years ago shutting off all contact? Perhaps our lives would be different if I'd chosen a different path and not followed his father's orders.

Regardless of the circumstances, I'm here with him now. The world still spins on its axis, using the same gravitational pull that seems to draw me into Carver's world. A fly in a spider's web.

I'm caught and I'm not sure it's even worth fighting.

CHAPTER 12

CARVER

MY PHONE HAS thirteen messages on it when I return to Joel's. I'm half tempted to ignore them all, but most of them are from my sports agent, Cristopher Markum.

I met Crissy two years ago after the NCAA championship game my sophomore year, in which we sadly lost. Seems to be a theme for me.

At the time, I was eligible to declare my intentions to draft, but I'd chosen to remain in school. I've always known I was destined to be a NBA player, but I didn't want to lose out on a regular college life. For my parents, it was my education that I would inevitably need to fall back on someday when I retired from the game. Which for a professional basketball player, can come as soon as you hit thirty.

Sure, there have been numerous NBA players that have outlived their expiration dates out on the court. Namely, Tim Duncan, Kevin Garnett and Vince Carter. They're all pushing forty and still on the court. But for the average player, retirement typically comes in your late twenties. The game is fucking hard on the body. And that's if you aren't sidelined with injuries.

At the time of our initial meeting, Crissy pushed me to draft early, citing all the reasons why I should consider – mainly money. I could have made four million dollars or more by now. Instead, I owe forty-five grand in college tuition. Well, technically my parents paid for my college education. I just had to stay in school for it.

I open the texts on my phone.

Crissy: Need to talk to you

Crissy: Urgently

Crissy: Need your signature on the endorsement contract for that shoe line

Crissy: And we need to consider your options and plans for draft. I'll have Angela schedule your flights

Two weeks from now is the draft. Over the last two days, I've nearly forgotten all about it. I haven't thought about the game or any of the stress that comes with it while I've been filling my time with Logan.

I'm not sure what that means. That's never happened before. For nearly ten years, I've lived and breathed the game. It's all I've ever thought about. My life's ambition.

Now all my thoughts are on Logan.

The future seems blurry. Unfocused. Like the crystal ball is now cloudy and uncertain.

The phone rings and startles me out of my thoughts. I press the button without checking the display, because I assume it's Crissy.

"Yeah?" I answer.

His voice is authoritative. Direct. Father-like. "Why must I hear you're in town from Ken Watson?"

It would be nice to hear a normal greeting from my dad. Would that be too much to ask?

"Don't know why Ken Watson should even know I'm in town.

I haven't seen him." I search my memory over the last few days. Nope, haven't seen him.

"His daughter, Cari, saw you at some party. You know how I feel about you being in public drinking. It's not good for your image."

Ah, yes. My image. My father's only concern. Heaven forbid the media would find out a twenty-two-year-old, recent college graduate and soon-to-be NBA hopeful was out drinking at a bar. Because that never happens. Maybe next time, I'll pull a Charlie Sheen. See how he likes that.

"For the record, I was at a friend's birthday party. There wasn't any debauchery, much to my dismay, and no fist fights. I doubt you'll see any naked photos surfacing, either. But it would've made a helluva story."

My dad and I have a contentious relationship. We've had many heart-to-hearts (aka screaming matches) over this topic. He's tried to get me to see that his intentions are far from malicious, but rather, based on the fatherly need to care for his son's future. To ensure that I don't end up trapped in a life that would ruin me from my true potential.

My thoughts on that subject? He had no fucking right to make a unilateral decision that affected me without my consent. Without my knowledge. And without first learning of the love that I had for Logan.

We were young – I get it. I was heading to college with the doors wide open to possibility. Being saddled with a girlfriend and a baby wouldn't have been ideal. But I know myself. I would've done right by her. If anything, she wouldn't have had to go through it alone.

And I wouldn't have turned into the man I am today.

"Dad," I say, plopping myself down on the frayed and tattered couch in Joel's small living room. It looks like it's seen better days – like back in the 80's. "I'm up here getting away from that scene. Trust me. I needed a break."

Which is true. Everywhere I go in Tempe I'm bombarded with fans. Guys looking to hang with a future NBA star (that's what *SportsTime* said in their article about me earlier in the spring); young kids who look up to me and want my autograph; jersey chasers and hoops hunnies who want to say they slept with an athlete.

Don't get me wrong. I've enjoyed the ride. It's been my pleasure bus – great for my ego and a celebrity cruise for my cock. I've been with loads of girls – sometimes two at a time – and getting my rocks off like I was a king. Believe me, it's good to be king.

Until I ran back into Logan again, I hadn't realized the torment I'd been dealing with. The feelings I'd stuffed down like the material in a Build-a-Bear, the ones that I've chosen to avoid, along with any real connections. It takes a man to acknowledge that he suffered the pain of heartbreak. I was eighteen, and I used that pain to become a nationally ranked college ball player.

But as they also say, it's lonely at the top. My circle of friends was tight – only my teammates and Lance and Cade. Outside of that, no one got close.

My father sighs heavily over the connection. He's probably sitting in his brown leather overstuffed chair in his library office, all my trophies and sports memorabilia mounted across the wood-paneled walls and shelves. If it's one thing my father is, it's proud of my achievements. I do love him for that. It's the way he managed my life without asking me what I wanted that broke our relationship.

"I can appreciate that, son. It just would have been nice to know you were here. Your mother would love to have you home for a while. You're her only child."

Okay, that's unfair. My mom is a good mother and if she finds out I'm in Seattle without calling or visiting, she'll be crushed. Now I feel like a shit.

Picking at the thread of the worn seat cushion, I consider my options.

"Fine. Does she still host Sunday dinners?"

"Of course," he replies, sounding hopeful.

"I'll be there. And have her set an additional plate. I'm bringing...a friend."

Maybe it's a way for me to get back at my father for what he did to Logan and me, but there's a small part of me that can't wait to see his expression when Logan walks through his front door. It's me giving him the middle-finger - a 'fuck you' for trying to keep us apart. But we're still here. We managed to find our way back to each other.

Whether Logan wants to come is another story. She may very well give me the finger and want nothing to do with my parents. Who could blame her?

"Any friend of yours is a friend of ours, son. We'll look forward to it. We'll see you tomorrow night at six o'clock. Until then, stay out of trouble, will ya?"

I chuckle, knowing once he sees Logan, he'll want to eat his words.

Now I just need to get Logan to agree to come with me.

I SPENT the rest of the afternoon following up on the phone calls I owed everyone – including my agent. Then I called Cade. I wanted to find out how his graduation party went last night and if Ainsley accepted his proposal.

He answers on the second ring. "Yo, Edwards!"

"Hey, bruh. You sound awfully chipper, so it seems things went according to plan. Or maybe you went down in flames and realize twenty-two is too young to get suckered into marriage," I cackle, throwing in that punch. I'm just goading him. He knows it.

"Eh, fuck you, C. It was epic. Ainsley had no clue I was going to propose. I was fucking stealthy as hell."

I find this hard to believe. Cade's a loud-mouthed, chatterbox who can't keep a secret to save his life.

"*Riiigght.*" I say with enough sarcasm to sink a boat. "So, how'd it go down?"

Before I left for my trip to Seattle, I apologized profusely to Cade for missing out on his party. I really do feel bad for not being there for my best friend's monumental moment, but I needed time away to clear my head. My life is about to change in a big way in the next few weeks and I needed to prepare for the unknown.

Cade starts prattling off a bunch of details about the party. "I wanted to keep the actual proposal private, ya know? So I asked Ky and Van to get everyone back in the house at five o'clock so it was just Ains and me out on the patio. She honestly didn't even notice because I got her talking about one of her new patients."

I laugh along with him knowing how much Ainsley loves to discuss her work. She's a CNA in an assisted-living facility where she gives her heart and soul to her aging and elderly patients. She's a good catch for Cade.

He continues, "Then I got down on one knee, my hand in my pocket with the ring and she finally notices everyone peering out of the glass doors and windows, watching the scene go down. I gave her my spiel that I'd been practicing for weeks and still wound up fucking it up…but she got the gist of it. Started crying and then I got all choked up and shit. Fuck, man. I think I was more nervous in that moment than I was at any of our championship games! My hands were shaking, dude. I looked like a chump."

"You *are* a chump, Griff. A stupid, fucking, love-struck idiot. But don't leave me hanging. What'd she say?"

Cade laughs at me like I'm the idiot. "Dude, she said yes, of course."

"Uh-huh."

There's no doubt Ainsley's in love with Cade, but she's a very independent and strong chick and has proven she doesn't need a man to take care of her. If anything, it's the other way around. Cade doesn't realize it, but he'd been waiting for someone like Ainsley for a long time.

It makes me wonder about Logan. She's gone through a lot on her own over the years. Even as a fifteen-year-old girl, she knew her own mind and didn't need a guy – especially a guy like me – to prove that she was worthy. She knew – *knows* – herself. Has a confidence that blows me away. Sucks me in to her orbit, like the Earth revolves around the Sun.

"Ainsley was stunned when I popped the question, and there was a second – maybe a nanosecond – that I thought she might say no. But she said yes, bro. I'm getting fucking married!"

Oh Jesus. Here we go. The beginning of the end. My first friend to walk the plank. I love Cade like a brother, but I don't see why he's rushing into this whole life-time commitment thing. It seems insane to me. To tie yourself down when we're this young for the rest of your fucking life? No, thank you.

Instead of voicing all my inner thoughts on the subject, I just say, "Congrats, bro. I'm happy for you and Ainsley. You two are great together. And I can't wait to plan your bachelor party. It'll be off-the-hook."

It hits me then. Maybe my feelings toward Cade's pending marriage vows is exactly how my dad felt about Logan and me. That we were too young to know our own minds or to realize it then, but having a baby that young wasn't the right thing at the time.

The only difference is that he jumped in and took that decision out of my hands without giving me a say. While I disagree with Cade's decision to get married, I still support him and I'm not about to ruin it for him.

Maybe I need to let bygones be bygones and forgive my dad.

Learn to accept that we are where we are because he did what he thought was in my best interest at the time. I consider this for a few minutes. It all depends on how things go tomorrow night at dinner.

Before that happens, though, we have our date.

I say goodbye to Cade and pull up Yelp to figure out where I'll take her tonight.

It's a new feeling for me – this excitement and nervous energy when I think about spending time alone with Logan. She's the most beautiful woman I've ever known, yet she's still nearly a stranger to me. The kisses we shared today only solidified the fact that we still have the chemistry.

I wasn't kidding when I told her I wanted more of that with her. But I also want to get to know everything about her - who she is and what she wants. Where she wants to go in her life.

And hopefully find a way for me to tag along.

CHAPTER 13

LOGAN

I HAVEN'T BEEN this nervous since I took my board exams a year ago.

My palms are clammy, my pits are sweaty and my tummy is churning like the heavy-rinse wash cycle.

My behavior is ridiculous. Although I've remained single, I've been on plenty of dates in the last few years. I've even slept with guys if the feeling struck. I'm not a novice at this. But none of them get to me the way Carver does.

Dissecting my feelings toward him is difficult. It could just be nostalgia – the lingering emotions I hold that stem from first love. Or it could just be the man I've gotten to know in the last forty-eight hours.

Carver's changed so much, yet is still the same boy I knew from our summers. His body is far more muscular and massive than it was at eighteen, that's for sure. I've never felt biceps that big before. They were like giant tree trunks and my two hands couldn't even close around his arm.

After dropping him off earlier, I was so exhausted from our hike, that I crashed for an hour-long nap the minute I got home. Sometime during that hour, I had the most vivid, sexually explicit dream that I'd ever had. I woke-up with an ache between my legs.

The dream was the two of us, holding each other in the lake. His strong arms were wrapped around me, pressing me into his body, and my hands were on the length of his back, sliding up and down the sinewy, wet canvas. The next thing I recall is that we were naked under the waterfall and I was licking drops of water from his naked chest.

My body reacted so strongly – so viscerally – that my hand was already between my legs when I was startled awake. Realizing I was on the living room couch, I had to glance around the empty room to make sure I was alone.

God, how embarrassing would that have been to be caught masturbating in my sleep?

Thankfully, I was alone in my apartment, panties wet from the flood of excitement that passed through me while I slept.

Throwing the blanket from my legs, I decide to get up and shower, ignoring the lingering need tingling through my body to get myself off. It would be easy to just relieve the tension using my own hand or the shower head, but achieving a release as an outcome of a dream about Carver would only solidify my desire for him. And to be honest, I don't know if I want that.

Just because I enjoyed my day with him, and the fact that he's easy to be around, easy on the eyes, and easy to talk to doesn't mean I want to fall for him again. And the closer I get to him, the more likely I'll be to rehash our history together.

I'm not willing to open up and recount all the low points in my life with Carver right now. How it felt to learn about my pregnancy; to be ostracized from my family and home; to have a bastard child and then give him up for adoption without the support of family or friends.

In retrospect, I should have told him that I had plans tonight.

Made up an excuse so I could avoid spending more time with him. There's no reason to continue hanging out with him this weekend. This thing between us is going nowhere.

Carver hasn't mentioned it yet, but I know he's entering the draft in June. All the sports pages are talking about it – and all the local news stations have done stories on Carver because he's a hometown boy. Carver has a future as a big NBA star ahead of him, and will have throngs of groupies following him around. Women who want to get into his bed. It's what Carver wants.

So I should shut this down now, before I get hurt.

Then again, why not just have a fun weekend with him? I have no other plans for the three-day weekend and I don't work on Monday. Ali's gone. Most of my other friends are out of town. I'm an unattached, single girl.

I finish up my shower and wipe away the steam that's accumulated on the bathroom mirror when I hear Ali's voice coming from the front room. She must be talking to Troy because I hear a deep male voice rumble with laughter. Ali is giggling like a schoolgirl, which is rather uncharacteristic of her.

I tuck the corner of the towel a little tighter between my boobs and step out of the bathroom, quietly tiptoeing around the corner to see what's going on.

I'm stunned when my eyes land on a very familiar pair of latte-colored irises. *Holy shit.* Carver is standing in my living room, whooping it up with my roommate. And he's an hour early for our date. What kind of parallel-universe is this?

Forgetting all about my attire, I step into view and clear my throat to gain their attention.

Wrong move.

Carver's head pops up and his eyes slowly rake over me with a look that I can only describe as unfiltered desire. My knees may even wobble a bit. My stomach does an Olympian-sized flip.

Having Carver's lust-filled eyes peruse me from head to toe is unnerving. But makes me feel insanely good. The way he makes me feel is better than chocolate-caramel ice cream. Better than a hot bubble bath on a cold, dreary Seattle night. Just better than anything else I know.

I don't miss the dimple that makes an appearance as the corner of his mouth tips up into a smirk.

I stammer like I'm drunk, "Uh...Carver? Ali? What are you two doing?"

Good one, Lo. Way to get control of the situation.

Ali whips around and smiles a cat-that-ate-the-canary smile. "Hey, Lo. I was just chatting with Carver, here. He happened to be outside our apartment waiting for you when I came home to grab some things. Since I didn't get a chance to meet him last night at my party, we're just getting to know each other."

She prattles this off like it's no big thing that he's here. Then she giggles and covers her mouth with her hand. "Well, according to Carver, we actually did meet last night, but I don't remember. I may have been a teensy-weensy bit drunk."

She pinches her index-finger and thumb together and winks, turning back to Carver and grabbing him by the shirt to drag him over to the couch.

"Carver was just telling me about how you two know each other. Small world, don't ya think? And that he's here to pick you up for your *date*."

I glare at Carver, his grin just growing wider. *Asshole.*

Hot asshole.

Ali's like a little pit bull when she wants to be, and will find a way to uncover any and all information about him. How we know each other. Who he is to me. Why I haven't mentioned him before.

I know my friend. She will persist until she finds out every dirty detail of my former relationship with Carver. By retelling our story, I'll need to decide if I'm going to leave out some critical pieces of information – lies of omission – about our shared history.

For the moment, I go with nonchalant.

"Carver and I met at summer camp when we were kids. I guess you could call us old friends."

Carver crosses one leg over his knee, cocking his head at my declaration. In that instant, I know he's going to blow my cover.

"Old friends, are we?" He says with a hint of battle-ready sarcasm.

Ali's head turns back and forth between us, her eyes growing wide with interest, then lands back on Carver.

"I'd say we're a little more than friends, wouldn't you, Lo?"

I'm still standing there in the middle of the hallway in my towel, wet hair dripping water droplets down my back. Carver's eyes slide over me licentiously and I drop my gaze to the ground in embarrassment, folding the towel in tighter at my breasts.

The need to run and hide in my bedroom – to bury myself underneath a mountain of pillows and blankets – is overwhelming. At the very least, I should go change so I'm decent. But I fear leaving him alone with Ali. I know she'll get the truth, and Carver will go along willingly.

"Oh *really…*" Ali bellows, jumping up and down on her knees on the couch like an excited toddler. "I want to know all about it."

"I'm sure you do." I scowl in protest.

She sticks her tongue out at me, her lips pursing into a bratty duck-lip face, as she shoos me out the room. "You!" she admonishes. "Go get your ass dressed. You're making a slutty spectacle of yourself. In the meantime, Carver will give me all the sordid details."

I watch with a tinge of jealousy as she places her small hands around his forearm, cuddling into him like he's an overstuffed Teddy Bear.

"Hurry up, Lo. Do as she says and we can be on our way. I have a fun night planned for us." He winks at me boldly and returns his attention to Ali.

"She was my childhood crush. Well, actually, Lo was my first love…" he begins and I groan, covering my ears like a child as I stomp off toward my bedroom.

I hesitate in the doorway for a second when I hear the last audible words before I shut the bedroom door behind me.

They knock me off balance. Set me on a course that I'm unfamiliar with and uncertain how to charter. The words leave me adrift and swimming in memories that almost have me in tears.

"Honestly, I'm not sure I ever stopped loving her."

CHAPTER 14

CARVER

A LITTLE OVER A MONTH AGO, my agent asked me to list my top three team choices where I'd hoped to get drafted. At the time, my choices were LA, New York and Miami. All amazing coast locations, with great ball franchises and an overabundance of hot, single women.

That was a month ago. Before I returned home to Seattle and found myself in the company of one very hot and single Logan Shaw.

Now my top choice is the Puget Sound Pilots, the three-year-old expansion team in Seattle.

I have no desire to go anywhere else. Logan just does it for me. She makes my blood burn hot. My skin is licked with flames when I'm with her. And the moment she walked into her living room wearing that skimpy bath towel, I became an incendiary device – ready to detonate on the spot.

Seeing Logan in less-than-nothing shouldn't be a big deal. During the summer, she'd wear bikinis and short shorts every day. Or tiny tank tops that left nothing to the imagination. But that was young, under-developed Logan.

The adult-life-sized version – the one whose legs are long and toned, whose tits and ass are firm and round – is enough to steal my breath and give me wood. Thank God her roommate dragged me over to the couch, otherwise I would've stood there with my boner on display.

And my attraction – and erection – hasn't abated yet in the two hours we've spent together. It's only intensified the longer I'm with her.

After she was dressed and ready, I'd asked her if she minded spending the evening playing tourist with me. It had been years since I'd been downtown and enjoyed the Seattle waterfront. When I was here in March for the tournament, I'd only seen the inside of the arena and the view from a dentist chair.

So tonight – with the weather a balmy sixty-four degrees – we took in all the tourist attractions Seattle offers, starting with Pikes Place Market, making our way through fish-mongers, flower sellers, and tables filled with handmade arts and trinkets by the local hippie community.

We're now sitting on Pier 57 overlooking the Puget Sound on top of the Seattle Great Wheel. My sights, however, are on Logan's legs in the knee-length skirt she wore. They are fucking spectacular.

I want to brush my fingertips over the top of her thigh, to gently caress the soft skin as I hear her breath hitch. I want to kneel in front of her, spread her legs wide and place my mouth at the juncture of her thighs. Inhale deeply and get lost in her feminine scent. Use my tongue and my mouth to make her squirm; watch as she comes undone with the strength of her orgasm before collapsing back against the glass window of the gondola.

"What are you thinking?" she asks innocently, interrupting my very dirty thoughts.

Busted.

This could go one of two ways. If I tell Logan the truth and share my dirty fantasy, she could very well backhand me. Or, she could indulge me, letting me live out my porn-like fantasy.

"You want the truth?"

"Of course. Truth is always best."

"If you insist," I say, taking the opportunity to eliminate the distance between us by scooting closer to her.

Our hips touch as I strategically place my arm around her shoulders, ruffling her hair just slightly. I lean in, placing my lips at her ear, breathing in her scent. She doesn't flinch or move away. This makes me very happy.

"I was thinking very dirty thoughts...about you and me. What I'd like to do to you right now. I bet your voice would sound as stirring as a siren's call as it echoes in this chamber, as you shatter in an orgasm. The one I'd give you with my mouth."

I stop there, the remaining words lodged in my throat. My hoarse voice is thick with desire.

Logan leans to the side, tipping her head sideways to stare at me. Her eyes flash with fascination. The start of a naughty smile takes shape on her mouth, as she licks her lips and then tucks the bottom lip between her teeth.

My brain goes slightly haywire, the neurons firing off in zig-zagging motions – the same feeling I've experienced when I've had a concussion. A little fuzzy and lightheaded.

Taking the opportunity when it's presented, I clutch her chin with my fingers, my thumb stroking roughly over that bottom lip just as I pull her forward to suck on it – moving my thumb out of the way so I can take her entire mouth and lock it with mine. She tastes of cinnamon and sugar from the mini-donuts we just devoured. I flick my tongue against the tip of hers and taste a remnant of sweetness.

If you can ever have a second-chance at a first kiss, this is it. The kisses from earlier today were full of childhood first love memories. This one is made of adult-driven desires. The present tense. The carnal needs of a man and a woman.

I pull back from our kiss and smile when I notice her eyes are still closed in a dreamlike state and her lips glisten. And when she opens her eyes, I see something more than desire. It has shape and color, and a glimmer of possibility.

Her voice is raspy with lust. "What else?"

Logan's question blows me away. She wants more dirty talk. Holy fuck. I could definitely get myself into trouble with this girl.

I don't know anything about her sexual interests or experience, but I like things a little kinky. I like things rough. Not too rough – only to the point my partner allows – but spanking, hair pulling, biting, restraints…yeah, I've got a massive erection right now just imagining Logan laid bare over my knee.

I place my hand between her legs, stroking the soft flesh hidden beneath her skirt. She allows her knees to drop open as my fingers make a journey up to her cleft. They hit pay dirt when they brush against the silky material of her panties and find her wet.

My fingers continue their perusal of her softness, entranced with her reaction as she bites her lip with a moan, her head dropping back against my arm.

"I don't care that the entire city can see us…I'd slide the straps of your dress down your arms and bind your wrists so you couldn't move. Your perfect tits would beg me to touch them. My mouth would take hold of your nipple, sucking it in, wetting it with my tongue. Biting it with my teeth. You'd moan and cry out – asking me to stop – but begging me for more. You'd be at my mercy. And I may or may not let you come. I'd use my fingers and my tongue to bring you to the brink of your orgasm, but I'd stop just before you hit the edge. And then, just when you think you couldn't take anymore, I'd lift you up so you could straddle me. My cock would be so fucking hard and you'd be so wet, just dying to ride me. Your tits would bounce free, and you wouldn't care who could see you."

I motion with a nod of my head at the rows and hills of condos and offices that line the Seattle streets below. Logan's breath has sped up, her chest rising and falling in quick pants. My fantasy, spoken aloud, has turned her on. And I may be going to hell for enjoying that so much.

The ride comes to an abrupt stop as our car sways up at the very top. I'm sure everyone else on this ride has their cameras aimed, taking photographs of the Sound and the mountains, but everything I want to see is right here in this spot. In her state of arousal, Logan's more beautiful than anything else around me.

I continue telling my sensual story, peeling back the edge of her panties and sliding my thumb through the hot, wet seam of her lips.

"And then I'd slam into you, thrusting upward so hard, and so fast, you'd be coming in seconds." I thrust my fingers inside her for emphasis as she gasps in pleasure.

"More," she pants out in a desperate plea.

Whether she wants more of my fantasy or more of my finger fucking, I don't know. But I'll give her both.

I continue pumping, as she scoots her ass down the seat toward the edge, opening herself up to me even more. Fuck, she's so sexy as she rides my hand. The car jerks and jostles us as we begin our downward descent. We're coming toward the end of our ride and I need her to come before we hit the bottom.

Sliding down to my knees, I kneel in front of her – just like in my fantasy. My mouth salivates because I'm about to taste her for the first time. I wanted to so many years ago, but it never happened. She was shy over that intimacy and never let me go down on her.

My eyes flick to her face and I realize any bashful feelings that she may have had then no longer exist, because all I see on her beautiful face is desire.

The ride is going to end soon and I don't want to get busted. It may be considered a felony in Washington. And while that might not be a bad thing for a pro-basketball player's rep, it certainly wouldn't go over well for Logan.

I make quick work of shoving my face between her thighs, inhaling her sweet fragrance. Her skirt is bunched at her hips and covers the top of my head. One hand goes to her inner thigh and pushes outward, the other slides the cotton panel of her panties over to make room for my mouth. And then it's on.

If I had the time, I would spread her out before me, naked as the day she was born, and show her exactly how she makes me feel. I would kiss every inch of her sweet, delicious body and eat her like a six-course meal – going back for seconds to ensure she has multiple orgasms.

In my rush, however, all I can manage is a few flicks of my tongue on the most sensitive part of her body. I know she's close, as her hips begin to thrust against my face. My dick is so jealous of my tongue right now that he's pressing hard against my shorts like he's fighting to get out.

I slide my tongue down her center seam, and it's coated with her essence. She jerks and cries out as I press down on her bundle of nerves just so. And then I pull out all the stops – tunneling two fingers inside her wet channel and sucking her clit into my mouth. Hard.

Her whole body stills for a second before she begins to shake and convulse with what I assume is the start of a powerful orgasm. Logan grabs the hair on the top of my head in a tight fist and holds me there as she lets go of a piercing cry, shattering beautifully underneath me.

And with no time to spare.

I hate wrapping this up with such haste, because I'd prefer to linger, maybe even getting her off a second time, but I notice the car is now making its descent to street-level. I climb back to the seat bench, carefully replacing her skirt across her lap and take a swipe at my mouth with the back of my hand. I taste her everywhere, and it's fucking glorious. I smile smugly when I glance over and take in the expression on Logan's face.

It's a mixture of satiation and bliss. It gives me a cocky sense of pride to know I did that to her. It was risky business – with the potential of serious consequences. Or worse, some gawker could have gotten us on video, exposing our naughty-trip around the wheel. But none of that matters as I watch her pry her heavily-lidded eyes open and see the sexy flush painted across her cheekbones. I know I'd do it all over again in a heartbeat.

Her taste still coats my tongue and I'm sure her musky scent will linger in the carriage as the door automatically opens with a 'whoosh'. The ride attendant assists Logan out by offering his hand, as I climb out behind her.

"Did you enjoy the ride?" he asks Logan, whose eyes flash with naughty mischief. She bites down on her bottom lip to suppress the giggle that's about to break loose.

And then, as if she can't contain the secret anymore, she breaks out into a fit of laughter. I give the attendant a shrug of my shoulder, as if I have no earthly idea what she's laughing about.

"I don't know about her," I say in all seriousness. "But it was the best damn ride I've ever been on."

The older man, uniformed in his Great Wheel shirt, nods his head emphatically.

"You got that right. No better vantage point than up there. It's the ride of your life."

Another giggle tears out of Logan's throat as she walks in front of me a few feet. Reaching for her hand, I wind my fingers through hers, grasping on tight, giving her a quick squeeze.

"What'd you think, Lo? Pretty orgasmic, wasn't it?"

CHAPTER 15

LOGAN

NEVER IN MY adult life have I been this turned on – or allowed my body to lose itself so completely as it did back on that ride.

Carver takes my hand as I nervously glance over my shoulder, surprised no one has rushed out to stop us for our public indecency. I shudder in disbelief. Did I really just let him do that to me in public? Only tramps allow that to happen – and after being called wretched names ad nauseam five years ago – I promised myself I'd never act like one.

Yet one kiss and touch from Carver, and I'm spreading my legs like a bitch in heat.

The steep climb up the brick-lined street to First Avenue has me somewhat winded. Or it could be from losing my breath at the top of the Ferris wheel. I give a sidelong glance to Carver, noticing his easy, calm demeanor. Like he's simply enjoying a leisurely walk in a flower-filled park. Jerk. He's utterly unaffected by what just went down a hundred and fifty-feet in the air.

"Let's get a drink."

Before I have a chance to reply, he's yanking me through the beat-up wood door of an old tavern across from Pike's Market. I haven't been down to this touristy area in a long time, preferring to stay tucked in my quaint little Queen Anne neighborhood with our chic cafes and coffee shops.

My eyes work to adjust to the dim lighting as Carver efficiently maneuvers us around the tables in the room, locating a small, wood-paneled corner spot. The booth is small with crushed red velvet seats that feel buttery soft against the back of my legs as I slide in without prompt.

Dirty thoughts tickle my brain of the sexiness that just occurred ten minutes earlier. Instead of velvet, though, it was Carver's hands touching the backs of my legs, holding me open with strong fingers digging into my flesh so his mouth could plunder my sensitive opening.

I snap to attention when I realize there is a waitress at the end of our table.

"What can I get ya, honey?"

Clearing my thoughts, along with my throat, I ask for a beer, "Whatever IPA you have on tap is good."

Carver holds up two fingers. Oh God, the same two fingers he just had inside me a little while ago. I cringe in embarrassment. Not like the battle-worn barmaid will know what he was just doing with those long digits, but I know. It's both thrilling and disconcerting.

"Make that two, please."

The woman wobbles back to the bar, the sound of her squishy black shoes shuffling against the cement floor. I keep my focus on my hands resting on the table in front of me. Suddenly I'm overcome with an uncomfortable anxiety. I have no idea what the hell I'm doing with Carver.

It was a lifetime ago that we meant anything to each other. And now after all this time and all the pain that still lingers in my heart, I honestly wonder why the hell I'm here next to him. For that matter, what the hell is he doing here with me?

As if reading my mind, Carver swivels toward me, his amber eyes drinking me in. I press my back as far as I can into the back of the booth. I feel like a trapped rabbit, with the sly fox circling me, allowing me my last moments of existence before he pounces.

Carver casually places an arm around the back of the booth, his fingers slipping behind my neck to lock me into place. As if I was going anywhere. As if I have the power to resist him.

His voice is low, his throat moves with the grace of his words. "That back there, Lo, was the hottest thing I've ever done."

He leans in and presses his lips underneath my ear, nipping at the not-so-secret spot that turns all women on. And it does. I clench my thighs together, the ache that had just been dulled with his tongue, now roaring back to life again with the sensuality of his admission.

"I can still fucking taste you on my tongue. You have me so turned on right now, I can't stand it. I want you so bad right now, I'd take you back into that bathroom, push you up against the wall and fuck you like the horny, dirty bastard that I am."

A gasp escapes me as my head drops back against the top of the wood-booth. His admission to being turned on by me is the sexiest truth I've ever heard in my life. This dirty-talking Carver is so different than the one I knew so long ago. He's not the nearly innocent boy I once knew.

He's an experienced player that knows how to get what he wants from a woman. It should turn my stomach to know he's used that naughty mouth on other girls, but it doesn't. I simply want more.

My voice is barely recognizable. "Then why did you drag me in here? My apartment is a half-mile away."

His curse is low and agonized. "*Fuuuuck.*"

And just for giggles, I slide my hand up the thick muscle of his tense thigh and land on the even thicker bulge in his pants. His cock twitches beneath the heat of my palm and I squeeze, watching as his eyelids drop to slits.

His hand brusquely removes mine to stop my groping. I'm disappointed. He's apparently good at dishing it out but can't handle the heat in the kitchen.

"We came in here to give me a chance to cool down. Honestly…if we go back to your apartment right now, Lo, I won't take my time with you." He stares into my eyes and I see the heat flickering in his irises. "Or be gentle."

I swallow the lump in my throat. I don't want gentle. I've had that before and it doesn't do it for me. I want Carver to take me right here in this booth. Just push me on all fours across this bench and fill me fast and furious.

I dart a covert glance around the room, doing a quick scan of the others in the bar to see if anyone is watching. I lick my dry lips, as Carver stares at my mouth with his heated gaze.

"Gentle is for virgins and prissy wives. I'm neither," I state matter-of-factly.

"You have no idea just how gentle I won't be…" he growls.

"No," I admit, shaking my head. "But I want to find out."

The waitress returns with our beers, as Carver takes out his wallet and his phone. She stares at him as he drops a twenty on the scuffed table, types something in his phone, and jumps out of the booth – yanking me with him.

I yelp – not from pain, but from his hasty change of plans.

"What?" I start to ask, but he interrupts.

"Uber. Outside. Now."

"But our drinks…" I stutter, glancing back at the untouched beers we're leaving behind.

His smile is a cross between a snarl and a smirk. Carver takes two steps backward, fists the beers in one hand, and drops them in front of a man sitting at the bar closest to the door.

"Here man," he rumbles as the man's drooping head pops up in surprise. "Enjoy, bro."

My mouth drops open because I can't believe this is happening. Two days ago, I would have never imagined I'd be racing out of a bar with my old flame, zealously anticipating an X-rated evening.

Yet here I am, nearly on fire from the fever that's burning through my veins, with the intense desire to get home as quickly as possible, so I can find out how ungentle Carver will be with me.

We push through the front door and there's a silver Prius stopped at the corner, which Carver descends upon, opening up the door and literally shoving me into the backseat.

His lips and hands are on me the moment the car door closes. He tastes of urgency and wicked things to come. And he also still tastes of me – the tangy essence of my desire. He rolls his tongue over mine, his hand clutching the back of my head to work me closer.

This is not the leisurely kissing from earlier. This is frantic. Unrestrained. Sloppy with intensity.

This is a kiss that means business.

The driver's voice barrels into my consciousness. "Hey. No sex in my car."

I choke out an unladylike sound, pushing against Carver's rock-hard chest to give myself some space. He groans disgruntledly but capitulates with a deep sigh, although his hand remains on my thigh.

I was so lost in the drugging kiss, that I failed to notice we're only a block from my apartment, climbing the steep hill to my neighborhood.

I take a few calming breaths and turn to find Carver's head is laid back against the headrest, his eyes closed. The bastard looks completely unaffected by the heavy make-out session we were just embroiled in.

If it wasn't for the noticeably hard outline of his cock through his jeans, I wouldn't even know he was turned on.

One of his eyes peels open and his one-dimpled smile tells me he caught me staring at his package. I turn away with embarrassment.

"You'll get that soon enough," he mutters, as the car pulls up to the curb. "Just be patient."

"Pfft," I say as we unfold ourselves from the back of the car and head up the walkway to the brick exterior complex.

As I fumble with the keys in the lock, Carver wraps his arm around my waist, his erection poking me in the back, causing an even bigger distraction.

"Hurry up...I need to get inside."

CHAPTER 16

Carver

THIS MAY SOUND like a dick thing to say, but my hope is that once I get inside of Logan, and fuck her to the edge of insanity, it will satisfy my craving.

That this overwhelming feeling of being under her control will vanish and my life will go back to normal. I'll be able to rid my heart of this cruel ache that's been festering since the day she ruined me for all others.

No one else has ever compared to her. I realize that now. I've been trying to compare every girl I've ever been with to Logan. The girl was sheer perfection at seventeen, but she's fucking broke the mold at twenty-two. I know this, because her soon-to-be-naked body stands in front of me right now as I slowly stalk her like a predator. She looks a little edgy as she takes tiny steps backward toward her bedroom. Or at least, I think that's where she's headed.

But fuck that, I can't wait to get to her bed.

I'm taking her right here and now.

She's mid-way through the living room when I pounce, wrapping my arms around her hips and throwing her in a heap on the couch cushions as I fall on top of her. We land with a *"thwomp"* and in a tangle of limbs, her giggle sending a jolt of electricity straight to my cock.

She's on her side pressed up against the couch and one of her legs falls over my hip.

"I'd call this a foul," she comments sassily, spouting her acumen for basketball terminology as I busy myself with my hand at her waist, trying to burrow under her shirt.

Just because I can, I lean in and lick a wet stripe up the bridge of her nose. She gasps in pseudo-outrage.

"I'd call that a flagrant foul. I think I should be sent to the penalty box for my flagrancy."

I give her a few seconds to realize the inaccuracy of my terminology use, since anyone who knows sports knows that there is no penalty box in basketball. It's a hockey term.

She gives me a cute eye roll and a hard shove against my chest, but her hands remain firmly planted there, creating space between us that I refuse to allow. I need to touch all of her. My body craves that connection.

My hand migrates down her hip and onto her ass cheek, where I take the opportunity to squeeze and pull her into me so that our tangled bodies look like a giant pretzel. My dick grows painfully hard, twitching with excitement over being pressed against her soft, feminine middle. He knows what he wants and where he wants to be.

This is no fucking game. There's no going back now and I'm all in. We both win when I'm finally buried deep inside her as she moans my name.

I begin stroking the smooth expanse of flesh where her tank has lifted from her skirt in our acrobatics. I play there awhile as I begin to suckle the spot at her collarbone. That soft indent that's so fucking sexy on a woman. My tongue draws patterns

145

against the hollow of her throat, as my fingers continue inching down around the curve of her ass, landing on the top of her thigh.

She sucks a gulp of air when my fingers find their way under the cotton material of her skirt, lazily approaching their intended destination. I sweep them slowly, methodically skimming along the supple skin of her thigh, toying at the edge of her panties. All the while, I place light, flirty kisses underneath her jawline. Her head lolls back with a soft whimpering and my cock expresses his interest as it twitches against her stomach.

Holding myself together so I don't thrust involuntarily, I slither my body down to the end of the couch, placing kisses along the way. My hand drags under the sweet juncture behind her kneecap, moving further down the slope of her leg. I climb off the couch, never once losing my connection with her body, as my hands wrap around her ankles like human shackles.

She releases a surprised gasp of air when I snap my arms back, hauling her entire body forward so the arm of the over-stuffed couch cradles her mid back.

Logan's lips part as her expression turns from mild interest to uncontested lust.

"Did you say something about not wanting me to be gentle?" I snicker wickedly.

She nods her head in acknowledgement, giving me free rein to do as I please. So I do.

My sexual history is vast and wide. I'm not ashamed of that fact. What I'm finally realizing, however, is that it was all meaningless and held only one objective. Although physical, there were never any true connections. I had no time or interest in learning about what those girls wanted or developing a relationship.

But I want it with Logan. And it clouds my thoughts with uncertainty. I stare down at her, spread out like a king's banquet, and I wonder if I'll be able to leave her after I fuck her. Will this weekend be the last of us? What if I fuck her and I want more than this weekend can offer?

The world begins to spin too fast and I feel dizzy. My hands stall and my breath falters.

Logan's sultry voice prods me along, giving me the sarcastic prompting I need, "Do you need help with this part? Perhaps some instruction?"

Oh, it's on.

With lightning fast speed, I flip her over – ass up toward the ceiling, her surprised gasp muffled by the couch cushion. I'm so fucking turned on right now as my eyes drink in the perfectly round mounds of her ass cheeks. She's wearing a pink lacy thong, which disappears in the crack between her legs. My knees nearly buckle from the sight.

I take a deep intake of breath to calm myself so I don't go off the rails and let my baser instincts take over. But they're there, simmering beneath the surface, ready to take control and take what I want.

I palm one shapely curve, admiring the satiny smooth skin and the toned glute muscle. Gliding my thumb in a sweeping motion over the flesh – back and forth – as Logan's breath hitches every time I near her seam. Without warning, I smack the porcelain canvas.

It's anything but gentle.

Her reaction has me palming my hard cock, stroking it roughly, as it strains against the material of my briefs, calling for action.

"Yes," she cries out, like she's been waiting all her life for that swat. Like I'd just opened the door to a locked room, letting out her inner goddess.

Oh, fuck. She likes it.

I smack at her ass again, this time harder so the sting bites my own hand. I stare at the red mark of my handprint developing across her now rosy skin. I rub a hand across the heat wicking there and I bite back a groan. I want to rub my cock across this masterpiece.

"More," she moans, and my hand twitches with relief. I give her three quick snaps, all of varying intensity, and then once again run my palm over the mound to sooth away the sting.

"Fuck, baby. You look so good like this. Tell me...and don't lie to me...did it make you wet? If I press my thumb between your thighs right now, will I find you dripping for me?"

For added emphasis, I drop my thumb in the space between her cheeks, gliding it down, but not all the way to that secret place.

"Oh my God, Carver..."

"Tell me," I command.

I bite her reddened ass cheek and she bucks. Fuck me, I can smell her arousal. I know her pussy is flooded. Readying itself for my hard cock.

"Ye...yes..." she stammers, quivering underneath me.

Just like that, my restraint ends. Snaps like a tree limb in a winter storm.

My hands fly to my shorts and I unbuckle, unbutton and unzip, as I push the offending material down my legs and out of the way. I'm not sure I'll last very long. Everything about this is too intense.

My cock juts free – hitting me at the navel – and I take a moment to slide it up her seam. I ache to be inside her – to feel her wrapped around me, clenching me tight as she releases and as I come inside her.

But first I need protection. I bend down, grabbing the condom package out of my pocket, quickly covering my shaft. I could just slide in while she's on her stomach, but I want to see her. To watch her come undone.

Flipping her back over, my fingers inch underneath the waistband of her panties and tear them off. Her pussy is now exposed to me, pink and glistening. I salivate at the sight and can't resist, pushing at the insides of her thighs, and make a swipe up the center. I flick the tight bud at the top as I feel her thigh muscles tighten in my hands, the sounds of her moans hitting me like beautiful music.

Standing once again, I circle her clit with my thumbs, spreading the lips and the wetness there.

Logan squirms under my ministrations, soft whimpers along with strong thrusts.

"I want you inside of me."

Six words every guy wants to hear from a beautiful girl.

I comply without further ado, dropping one hand to my cock and dragging its heavy weight to her wet entrance. The sight is intoxicating. While Logan's position prevents her from seeing what I see, I have the perfect vantage point.

"Lo," I groan, as I push the first inch inside her wet warmth. I can feel the give of her inner walls and I close my eyes tight. This is heaven. I've been given an angel-on-earth to make all my dreams come true.

Her breath hitches when I push all the way into the hilt.

It's hard. It's fast. It's fucking glorious.

I have to square my legs to keep myself upright. I encircle the backs of her thighs with my fingers, right at her ass and I move them down toward her knees, gathering her in the crooks of my arms. This gives me more leverage, so as I plunge in, I can keep her from sliding down on the couch.

"Show me your tits." I command, frustrated with myself that I moved so fast that I didn't get to enjoy her breasts before the main course. But there's always dessert.

Logan quirks an eyebrow at me, her smile coy. She fingers the edge of her tank as she slowly slides it up to bare her mid-drift, exposing her nude-satin bra. It cups her C-sized breasts, boosting the soft mounds so the sweet curves pop at the top.

"So bossy," she teases, sensually playing with the edge of the cups. I lick my lips as I watch her work the material down, the firm globes exploding out. I stare in fascination, envying her fingertips as they trace the rosy-tips of her nipples, circling them; plucking them; pushing the soft-pillows of flesh together.

I'm stuck with a fantasy so hot, I nearly come at the thought. I wonder if she would let me pull out and come all over her tits? Would she like that? Would she allow me to defile her like that? Would she think it is as hot as I do?

I pump inside her harder, quick jabbing motions that elicit loud moans from her each time I hit the spot. My body needs to come so badly – it's been far too long since I've fucked a woman. My self-imposed moratorium since March.

Somewhere in the back of my mind, I anticipated this day. The opportunity to be back inside the girl of my dreams. The woman of my fantasies. How did I get so lucky to get this second chance?

"I've dreamed about you, Lo," I admit, as my eyes track the movement of Logan's hands as they squeeze, plump and pluck at her breasts.

"Oh yeah? Me, too."

"Wet dreams, where I had to get myself off because they were so damn hot. But it's nothing compared to this."

She moans when I must hit a sensitive spot deep within her. I want to get us off together so bad. I look down at her glistening pussy - her clit hard and swollen – and I know what I need to do.

Dragging my thumb down her smooth belly, I land at her center and begin working it in tight circles. Her response is immediate and needy – she begins to thrust her hips upward, trying to gain leverage with her shoulders against the couch.

"Right there...don't stop. Harder."

I do as she says, continuing to put pressure on the sensitive nub as I work us both to a climactic finish.

Logan's hair is spread out around her, some covering her face as she whips her head back and forth against the cushion.

"I'm close...Carver...I'm..."

I take that opportunity to press the pad of my thumb down hard, and it's like striking the match the leads to the explosion. She detonates on impact, her hips stilling, eyes shut tight and lips parting to extract the most exquisitely tortured sound I've ever heard.

"That's right, baby. Give it to me. Give me everything."

Logan blindly reaches out, grasping onto anything she can get her hands on. One hand goes above her head to reach for a blanket and the other to the top of the couch cushion, her fingers digging imprints into the material. It pushes her tits up further and brings me back to the idea of coming all over them.

Ah, fuck, not this time, no matter how much I'd love to do that. There's something so dirty about marking a woman. I just don't know how kinky she'll allow me to be.

My balls curl up into hard, tight stones, and I feel the orgasm barreling up my legs. All I can do is hold on and continue pumping inside her channel.

"Lo..." I bellow, my chin lifting to the ceiling as my head drops behind me. I come in long, hot spurts as the world spins in the most sensually and intense dance.

It takes a few minutes for me to come down from the high of my orgasm, but when I do, I'm hit with an emotion that I've never had after sex. Normally with a girl, I'm a hit-and-run kind of guy. Once we've achieved a mutually beneficial release, I find the fastest route out of there.

As I look down over Logan's satiated expression – her glorious tits still on display and her smile a playful come-on – all I want to do is wrap her naked body up in my arms and never let her go.

It scares the fucking hell out of me.

Schooling my expression, I reach for her arm and gently tug her up to a sitting position. She lazily drapes her arms over my shoulders, leaning her head into the side so her cheek rests against my chest. The scent of her hair captivates me. It's lavender and honey.

I have no desire to leave the comfort of her arms or the warmth of her body, but I need to go dispose of the condom, so I slide out as we both groan with discontentment.

"Where's your bathroom?" I ask, my hands cupping the sides of her cheek so she's looking up into my eyes. They sparkle with gratification and my ego soars. She nods down the hallway and I give her a peck on top of her head as I head in that direction.

I take care of business and stride back down the hall into the kitchen, where I find Logan at the sink, her hands massaging her lower back, her clothing now rumpled. I smile at her easy sexiness.

She's so fucking warm as I lean in, breathe her in, and replace her hands with mine.

"Are you okay?" I murmur in her ear, massaging at her lower back.

"Mm...yeah. I'm just sore from hiking today and that position on the couch was...well, I have to say, I've never..." she clears her throat like she's embarrassed by admitting this. "I've never had sex over the arm of my couch before."

I snicker, digging in my thumbs deep in her lower back so that she groans in pleasure. It's the type of sound that sends my dick back into overdrive, ready for another lap around the track.

"You're a vanilla girl, huh?"

She stiffens and turns in my arms so sharply my hands fly off her back. Her reply is full of outraged indignation. "No! I'm not vanilla...I just -"

I finish her sentence for her, offering my smug response. "Haven't been fucked by anyone quite like me before. I get it. I have that effect on you. I made you lose complete control and it was the time of your life."

I latch on to her hips and press her into my thickening cock before I take possession of her mouth, which is open wide with a response sitting at the tip of her tongue. The kiss doesn't last long, but it's gentle, as I pepper her lips and the corner of her lips with light touches.

"And," I add for good measure, "you just can't help yourself around me. I get it. I'm a pretty hot commodity."

"Argh! You're impossible," she wails, pushing at my chest, her small palms landing on my pecs. She tries to push me away but fails. It makes me laugh a little louder.

She gives up with a sigh, pressing her forehead to my breastbone.

"I forgot how arrogant you are. And annoying."

"Ah, but you love it. Admit it."

"Pfft. I'll do no such thing."

"Baby, by the end of the weekend, you'll be admitting to everything. You'll be on your knees begging for mercy, but dying for more of me. Just you wait."

I know this will bring a howl of indignation from her, because it's so outrageous. And as if right on cue, she huffs out an exasperated sigh.

The truth is, though, that I'll be the one begging for more. I'm not sure I'll be ready or willing to let her go when Monday comes around.

Even though I know it's the only choice I have.

CHAPTER 17

Logan

Except for an hour earlier this morning when Carver went back to Joel's place to pick up his clothes and toiletries, Carver and I spent the entire weekend together. Mostly wrapped up in each other's arms in my bed.

And just as sure as he promised, he cured me of my boring, vanilla sex life. Holy goodness, that man has an imagination and isn't afraid to try anything. I think he may have ruined me for anyone to come after him.

While sex with Jeff was never on the agenda, I can't imagine that he would ever do some of the things that Carver did to me. I checked a whole lot of kinky off my bucket list, things I only ever read about in Ali's smutty books.

Sixty-nine? Check.

Kitchen counter? Check. Check.

Ass play? Triple check.

When Carver's thumb found its way between my ass cheeks… like, *inside* my ass…sweet baby Jesus, I about freaked. But my, oh my...once I got over the initial shock of it, relaxed and became accustomed to the foreign feeling, I let go of my inhibitions and just rolled with it. All the while, Carver used his dirty words and erotic commentary to get me out of my head and into the moment. Enjoying all the naughty things he did to me.

I said a small prayer of thanks that Ali wasn't home this weekend, because I screamed so loud at one point, that our neighbor, Phong, knocked on my bedroom wall, yelling at me to *"shut the hell up"* in a very thick Vietnamese accent.

Carver takes dirty and raunchy to a whole new level, yet he remained careful and respectful of my emotional well-being. He never assumed anything and took it slow once I gave him the green light on anything new.

My sexual partner list isn't terribly long. Besides Carver, there have been three other guys. They were all decent – mostly acquaintances whom I'd dated a few times before sleeping with. Looking back now, I know Carver is right. None of those guys could do half of what Carver does to me.

And the spankings?

I. Never. Knew.

Sure, I've read all the well-known, made-into-movie BDSM books on the market. Every girl is curious about that. Most of the illicit, kinky stuff described in those pages turned me on, but I couldn't imagine doing it with anyone. The bend-her-over-his-lap-and-spank-her scenes were thrilling and hot, but not once had I considered that I would like it for myself.

And then it happened. Carver flipped me over and spanked my bare ass and I practically climaxed on a scream. In that moment, I wanted to dry hump the arm of the couch from how turned on I was by his dominance. As an independent and strong-willed woman who grew up with three older brothers, I would never fit into the submissive stereotype. In my mind, spanking is for disobedient children to remind them of who is in charge.

Sexually speaking? I had no clue how turned on it would make me. The ache grew exponentially between my legs and I was writhing for more in an instant. I actually *begged* him for more. Who the hell am I?

To say that Carver opened a whole new world to me is beyond an understatement. He's right. By the end of the weekend, there is a very large possibility that I'll be clutching his pant leg, on my knees, begging him not to leave. To give me more of what he's got.

And what he's got is aimed right at my mouth this very moment.

Long, thick and imposing. It's seven-thirty on Sunday morning and we've been in bed sleeping the last four hours, exhausted from wearing each other out all night long. I'd fallen asleep wrapped up in his arms and woke to the heat of his body next to mine.

I'd slipped out of bed to use the bathroom and padded back into the darkened room to find Carver laying on his back, one muscled arm flung over his eyes, the sheet resting at his knees to expose his glorious body. Even in sleep, his flaccid dick is impressive.

Carver's body is all sculpted lines, rolling hills of muscles and tattoos scattered in well-placed spots along his biceps, chest and back. I have to touch him.

And touch him, I do. I sink to my knees, the bed dipping, as I lean over the middle of his torso. My fingertips gently trace along his taut, smooth skin, over his ribs, across his pecs and then down the ridged valley of his stomach. I reach the light smattering of fuzz of his happy trail, and give in to the desire to lick it.

His breathing accelerates a notch, but when I peek up at his face, he appears to still be asleep. But the one thing that is wide awake is his cock, now completely erect and staring me in the face.

I've yet to taste him. I've fondled, stroked and petted him, for sure. But every time I tried to get my mouth near him, he'd distract me and end up fucking me in some far more adventurous position. Now in the dim light of morning, I've found an opportunity that I'm going to take.

I'm no porn star when it comes to my blowjob technique, but I'm not terrible at it, either. It's not always been on the top of my most favorite things to do list, but with Carver, my mouth waters with desire to suck him in deep.

Carver stirs slightly but continues to sleep as I lace my hand softly underneath his balls, cupping him, rolling him gently in my hands like Chinese Baoding balls. I marvel as his cock twitches and grows. My head hovers over him, my tongue tentatively drawing a line from the base of his shaft to the tip, swirling around the purplish-colored crown. This provokes a low groan from Carver and stops my movement, until I feel his hand on the top of my head.

I grin and continue lavishing my attention on his morning wood. His cock is so thick it's hard to wrap my entire hand around the girth, but I manage. Clasping him firmly in my palm, I stroke him as I center my mouth over the tip, slowly drawing him in. We both moan in unison when I take him in the back of my throat.

In order to accomplish this task, I lean over so my ass is head over teacup. I'm not surprised when I feel his large hand land on the soft flesh of my butt, his palm running along the curve – up and over, down and around.

And as if right on cue, I feel the biting sting of his hand when he paddles my cheek. I swallow a groan, effectively tightening my throat muscles around his dick.

"Oh fuck, Lo...yeah. Shit that feels good."

I hum at his compliment, as my world right now is centered solely on making Carver happy. To bring him fulfillment, because I know I'll receive the same in kind. He is the most unselfish lover I've ever had. He's made up for his oversight on the night we lost our virginity when I didn't climax. All is forgiven where that's concerned, because he's given me a multitude of orgasms the last two-days.

Continuing my ministrations of sucking, licking and swallowing around his large cock, his hand migrates between my legs, his thumb running along my wet center, dipping into my heat and then dragging my wetness over my clit. The lusty moan that emits from my mouth hardly sounds like it comes from me. It's thick and husky. Granted, I do have a dick in my mouth, so it's bound to come out a bit muffled at the moment.

When he hits a spot that has never been touched before, I cry out and thrust my hips backward. I've heard some women have a G-spot hidden somewhere inside them, but no one has ever found that buried treasure within me. Carver slips another finger inside and curls it upward, and sends me soaring. Flying over that cliff reserved for heavenly orgasmic flights.

My hand is still on his dick, and I'm practically strangling it as I come harder than I've ever come before. After the last and most intense wave of pleasure passes through me, I let out a deep sigh and begin stroking him again, ready to resume my mouth-to-dick loving.

"I want to feel you come on my cock."

I tilt my head to the side to look up at him, his eyes dark with desire and half-lidded.

I let him go to respond, "Well, I want to feel you come in my mouth."

He growls, "A sexual standoff. How inconvenient."

I grin widely and then take him back in my mouth, but before I can suck him in again, he's grabbed hold of my hair and yanked me back with a twist of his wrist. I startle a yelp and he loosens his hold.

"Put a condom on me and ride me."

He's holding an unwrapped condom out in his hand. When

did he get that? I don't remember hearing the crinkling sound as he unwrapped it.

I take it from him with a frown. "God, you're so bossy."

"I wasn't captain of the team for no reason."

I fit the rubber around his dick, but not before taking one last swipe of his head with my tongue. I'm awarded a taste of his precum and I smack my lips together in satisfaction. I'm about to straddle him facing forward, but he stops me.

"Nope. Turn around. Ride me reverse. I want to see your ass."

"I – *uh...*"

Now that it's a bit brighter in the room, I feel a little uncomfortable in my own skin. I'm not sure why, but it makes me feel vulnerable. We've done it doggie-style already, and that didn't bother me, but for some reason, this has me weirded out.

Carver shifts up into a sitting position, cupping my face in his hands, and then kisses me soundly. He gives such good kisses. His lips are perfect, commanding and pliable.

"Don't go shy on me now, Lo. I've already seen and tasted every inch of you. Trust me, baby. You'll like it this way. I promise."

Do I trust Carver? Yes. Yes, I do.

Yielding to his request, I swing my legs around in the other direction and face away from him, his long legs on display in front of me. Shifting forward, Carver's hands cup my bottom with a satisfied grunt. He's seemingly enjoying both the view and the touch of my butt based on the low, guttural and masculine growl. And then I feel him poised at my entrance, just as a wet thumb is gently nudging me in my other hole.

"Oh shit," I cry out, as he enters me with a hard push in both locations.

I may black out for a moment from the intense physical pleasure that explodes in my veins. Like firing out of a canon and flying a hundred miles per hour across the sky. It's freeing and beautiful.

The bite of his fingers as they grip me has me moaning, enjoying all the physical sensations assaulting my body all at once.

"That's it, baby. Ride me. Own me. Take us both there together."

I give in to his commands and do as he says.

And soon find out Carver Edwards was right.

I really did like it that way.

CHAPTER 18

CARVER

THE POST-COITAL BLISS covers us both like a warm, velvety blanket in middle of a raging snowstorm. I'm more content than I've ever been in my life.

Logan is cuddled up next to me in the crook of my arm, her cheek resting against my chest, the soft tendrils of her hair a waterfall of silk over my torso. From this vantage point, I can see the top of her pert nose, peppered with cutest little freckles. Her long eyelashes flutter, as she speaks softly, telling me a story about her friend Alison, who is an aspiring writer.

"I'm so jealous of Ali's imagination. She can create the most creative stories and characters. It's like they come alive on the page. I know once she submits her manuscript, she's going to hit it big."

"I don't doubt it if you're her biggest cheerleader. Speaking of cheerleader...you'd look really good in one of those tiny little outfits on the sidelines of my games. You don't have an old one lying around anywhere, do you?" I'm only half kidding because she'd look smoking hot in one of those uniforms.

She smacks at me playfully and I reach down and pinch her exposed nipple, extracting a little yelp from her. We've been lazily laying in her bed now for the last few hours. The perfect Sunday morning.

"I'm sure you have enough of your own cheerleaders that you don't need another one to add to your collection."

"Maybe," I admit honestly. "But you're the only one who makes me feel like I matter."

She shifts her weight across my body, flipping onto her stomach so her elbows are out and her chin rests on her hands that lay on my breastbone. Her eyes are light blue in the soft light cascading through the bedroom window, but they blaze with an intensity bigger than the ocean.

"I'm so proud of you, Carver. You set out to play in the NBA and you're so close to that goal. Most teenage boys say they want to play in the pros, but it never happens. They don't either have the drive or what it takes. But you've made it happen. Do you know where you'll be drafted?"

The unexpected compliment fills me up with pride. It means she paid attention when we were younger. I spouted off all my hopes and dreams as a sixteen-year-old boy. Dishing out dreams that I aspired to become. Hopefulness and arrogance that only the young can afford to extol.

I place a quick kiss on her nose, then her forehead, and then the top of her sexy, mussed-up hair.

"While I'm hopeful, it's still not a sure thing that I'll be drafted."

She gives a disgruntled huff. "Whatever. Don't get all humble now, Mr. Full-of-Himself."

I flick her nose with the tip of my finger and I laugh when she tries to bite it.

"Truthfully, I do think I'll get drafted, I'm just not sure in which round. My agent, Cristopher, has been working on the backend with the various team managers and owners to see where I might fit. It all depends on their current rosters and payroll. And even if I do get selected to a team, there's no guarantee that I'll actually play my first season, much less start. There's a strong possibility I could get a contract and then be waived the very next year. It's all a crapshoot."

This was the reason my dad was so adamant that I finish college with a degree, to ensure that my future was invested in something other than basketball. The exact reason he did what he did when it came to Logan's pregnancy. I'm old enough now to see the logic behind his actions, but not his tactics. Which reminds me about dinner tonight.

Logan interrupts before I can ask, "Where do you see yourself playing?"

My hand glides down her lower back, as I leisurely stroke the bare skin down the curve of her ass. The goosebumps that prickle over her flesh make me smile and I continue my sensual maneuvers.

I shrug my shoulder. "No preference, I guess. But I did give him a list of my top team picks. It really doesn't matter, though, because I don't control the outcome."

I continue, "Even if I get picked up by one team, they could work out a trade behind the scenes with another team – so I could end up somewhere else entirely. I really just have to wait and see and let the chips fall where they land."

Logan nods her head, scrunching her cute nose in worry. "That must be difficult, not knowing where you'll end up. Leaves so much up in the air right now, doesn't it? That's got to be stressful."

It doesn't surprise me that she's so intuitive and perceptive of my limbo. She's always been empathetic. "Yeah, I guess it is kind of stressful."

Especially now that I have someone here that I don't want to leave. This is exactly the reason I never wanted to get involved with a girl. The life on the road is not conducive to establishing a normal dating life.

"What do your parents think about all this?" she asks softly, with uncertainty threading through her words.

I crinkle my nose. "Honestly? I don't really care. They don't factor into my decision. I made them a promise when I went to college that I'd finish my degree, but after that, my life is mine. I choose to do what I want, with whom and where."

There's a quiet pause as she considers her next response. "I don't know what happened, but it's obvious you're angry with your father. For what he did. But Carver...you need to forgive him. He was looking out for your best interests. We were so young back then. Although I wish things had been different..." she hesitates, her voice now thick with emotion.

"Your father treated me with kindness both times I met with him. He helped me and helped figure out what was right for our child. I was still in high school and too young to be a mother. I don't regret giving him up so that he could have a better life...so you could have a life free of those burdens."

A current of anger bubbles up inside me from the bottom of my toes. I flip her on her back and hover over her so that she can see the truth within my eyes.

"Logan...you and our baby would never have been a burden to me. Just never."

A tear spills out from the corner of her eye and she glances away from me. Off into the distance.

"You don't know that. You..." I watch as her throat works in a swallow. Her eyes return to meet mine, locked with fiery intensity. "We would have failed each other. It would have been inevitable."

She squirms underneath me, trying to get up. I don't want to let her go, but it's obvious she needs space. I move to the side and she swings her legs over the edge of the bed, grabbing a t-shirt from the floor to cover her naked body.

The topic of conversation is naked enough. Honest, raw and painful to discuss.

The question I have on the tip of my tongue is scary as fuck, but I need to know the answer.

"Do you ever think about our son? Where he is? What he looks like?"

Logan's back is to me, but I see, more than hear, her entire body sob in response.

"All the time," she whispers with a sadness and despair that only a mother who's lost her child would know.

Her quiet sniffles ignite my movement, as I jump from the bed to wrap my arms around her. I hold her as she continues to cry, my own tears lodging in the back of my throat. They're tears of regret. Remorse and guilt. Unforgiven sins.

"Shh," I coo, holding her tight.

"Is there a way we could ever find out about him? Through the adoption agency or something?"

A deep gasp shakes her entire body. Shit, maybe I shouldn't have brought that up. But damn, I want to know. I need to know about the welfare of our baby boy.

Logan turns slowly in my arms so she's facing me, her eyes shiny and wet, rimmed with sadness and hope.

"I don't know. Your dad...he and his attorney handled everything. I don't know if it was an open or closed adoption. I know that makes me sound heartless, but..."

I squeeze her tightly, giving her a gentle shake. "Don't you ever think that way, okay? I know with every fiber of my being that you cared about our baby. You just weren't in a position, financially or emotionally, to handle it back then. But if you want to know now, then I say we do it. Together, this time."

Logan sighs and drops her head to the middle of my chest.

"We'll ask tonight at dinner."

Her head lifts suddenly, her face a question mark. "Tonight? What do you mean?"

"We're invited to my parents' house tonight."

She shakes her head back and forth, but I lock my arms behind her back and hug the shit out of her. She needs to know that I won't let her down this time. If I have a chance to make things right, I will do everything in my power to do it.

Whether I leave and never look back after this weekend – which is highly improbable with how much I feel for Logan – we share something that no one can ever change. Our lives are tethered by the secret of our past, and the possibility of uncovering the knowledge of our child's future.

"Yes. Tonight. We're going to dinner at my parents' house. And we'll learn the truth then."

CHAPTER 19

Logan

THE LAST TIME I met with Carver Edwards Senior was when I was dazed and exhausted from enduring thirteen hours of labor.

I remember I'd been lying in my private hospital bed (paid for by Mr. Edwards), looking into the angelic pink face of my son who was swaddled in my arms, cooing soft bubbles from his puckered mouth.

It was both a moment of serene beauty and of ugly loss.

His tall, imposing figure stood at the edge of my bed, in a fitted navy suit, holding out a manila envelope and pen while wearing a stern look etched across his face. It was like making a deal with the devil. Only that devil looked strikingly similar to the boy that I loved.

That boy is now grown and matured and stands towering next to me on the stoop outside his parents' waterfront home. The three-story structure overlooks Lake Washington, and features impeccably manicured grounds, a carriage-like garage, a cabana and guest house, and sweeping views of Lake Washington and Mount Rainier. I can't even fathom what it was like to grow up in a house like this. Nothing like the small shack of a rental home I grew up in.

Carver reaches for my hand as he rings the doorbell. I'm so nervous I'm shaking, my lips quivering with dread. I have no idea how Mr. Edwards will welcome me, but my guess is that he won't be pleased to see me with his son. I've never actually laid eyes on Mrs. Edwards.

Although Mr. Edwards helped me in the past, I know he regarded me as a money-hungry, gold-digging floozie. My guess is that his opinion won't have changed much. He'll still look down his nose at the poor, white-trash slut his son knocked up, who's now back in his life right before he enters the NBA.

The opulent double-doors open wide and we're greeted with a practiced smile from his mother. She's elegantly beautiful. Grace Kelly meets June Cleaver.

"Carver! I'm so happy you're home."

She leans in for what I think will be a hug, but instead she gives him air kisses on both cheeks. Who the hell gives their son air kisses?

"Hello, Mother. This is Logan Shaw. Logan, meet my mother, Althea Edwards."

His mother steps back and her eyes land on me for the first time, as if she hadn't even noticed me a second ago. I'm feeling a ton of awkward right now. It's in this moment that I have no earthly idea if she knows anything about me. To my knowledge, she was never aware of my "situation" or my past association with her son.

"Hello, my dear. It's a pleasure to make your acquaintance. Please, come in and make yourself at home."

I've been in their home once before. At the time, I was not made to feel comfortable or invited to stick around like I am now. I was a hen at a fox convention.

Carver's hand rests on my lower back, gently directing me

inside the large open foyer. Not much has changed in four years. Maybe some décor or wall coverings, but it's the same magnificent entryway with the grand staircase and gigantic chandelier hanging from the ceiling two floors up.

As the door closes behind us, we hear footsteps down the hallway as Mr. Edwards rounds the corner, a broad smile that quickly loses its emphasis. The moment he realizes it's me, his smile fades completely.

Except for the infinitesimal hitch in his step, he recovers so quickly you wouldn't know he was shocked to see me in his home. The smile is replaced with one that could put a campaigning politician to shame.

He strides toward us, heading right to Carver.

"Son, it's good to have you home." He gives a quick one-armed hug around Carver's shoulder before squaring his shoulders to me. "And you brought a *friend*."

I'm stunned by the venom in Carver's voice. "Cut the shit, Dad. There's no need to cover things up anymore. I know that you know, that she knows, we all know that you know Logan."

I give a tight-lipped smile and a small wave, glancing over to Althea's face, who is looking all too confused, her polished features turning a bit ghostly in appearance.

Althea turns on her brightest hostess smile. "Why don't we all come inside and take a seat in the sitting room. I'll get some drinks started for us. Logan, what can I get you, dear?"

If I'm going to get through this evening with my sanity intact, I need some liquid courage.

"Do you have some white wine, perhaps?"

She smiles graciously. "Of course, dear. Would you like a Pinot Gris or Chardonnay? I have both, whichever you prefer."

Carver and I sit down next to each other on a small plush couch. I smooth my sweaty palms over my knees, pressing down the hem of my dress.

"I'd love the Pinot Gris. Thank you, Mrs. Edwards."

A soft laugh, and a wave of her hand, admonishes me. "Logan, please call me Althea. And Carver, what would you like?"

"Just bring the whole bottle, Mother. I think we'll need it."

I snap my head and give him an icy glare. One that says, don't you dare fuck this up. Be nice or I'll punch you in the nuts.

Carver lifts his eyebrows, knowing exactly what I meant, before shrugging his shoulders.

Althea leaves the room to go after our drinks and we're left alone with Carver's dad. All the air gets sucked out of the room and the walls feel like they are closing in around us. Just like that scene in *Star Wars*, where the trash compactor begins to trap them in. Before that eel monster grabs hold of Luke and drags him underwater.

Mr. Edwards is the monster in this picture and Carver is my hero – ready to rescue his princess.

"This comes as a surprise, I must say," Mr. Edward admits quietly. At least he's being honest.

"Why's that, Dad? Because you practically ensured Logan and I would never see each other ever again? Because you made sure she would remain out of my life?"

The tension radiates from Carver's body, so I place my hand gently on his bicep, hoping to calm down his vitriol response. He physically relaxes as he takes a deep intake of breath and lets it go.

"Son, you know that's not what I meant to do." He looks to me, his eyes almost pleading for help. "We've gone over this before. I only did what I thought was right at the time. I'm sorry that you see it as some sinister plot to ruin your life."

Carver sighs with heavy exasperation, reaching for my hand and feathering his fingers through mine. My hand is swallowed by his, but it feels secure. Protective. Loving.

"Even so, aren't you the least bit concerned about the welfare of your only grandchild? The grandson that could've had our name, to carry on the Edwards lineage?"

A loud crash startles us all, as we follow the sound of breaking glass to find Althea standing in the doorway, wearing a look of heartbroken shock.

"Carver," she murmurs, her graceful hand covering her mouth as she glances between her son and her husband. Carver Sr. stands and begins to move into action toward his wife, but she thrusts out her hand in a universal sign for stop. "Did you just say our grandson? What in the world are you talking about?"

Everything happens in slow motion. Carver leans forward, dropping his head in his hands, and his father carefully shuttles his wife out of the broken glass mess with a gentle guiding of her shoulders. Althea sits in the loveseat directly across from us, still waiting for an answer to her question.

Her face registers grief and sorrow as if she already knows the truth inside her heart. It makes my heart break all over again.

"Yes, Mother. You have a grandson somewhere out there in this big wide world. One that was ripped out Logan's hands without thought or concern to what she wanted." Carver squeezes my hand. "And my loving father failed to let me know about any of it."

"Carver." His father's booming voice echoes against the wood-paneled, wainscoted walls. "Enough of your childish bullshit. You and I both know that it was never either one of our decisions. It was hers."

An accusatory finger is pointed at me and a pain so deep rips through me, slicing at my chest. It's obvious he blames me for everything.

"She made the final call. She was eighteen, no longer a minor. She got what she wanted. Money. I only facilitated the discussions. Don't you dare think that Logan wasn't the one who took that opportunity the moment it was availed to her."

I swallow down the tears that beg to let loose. But I stand firm. I will not cower or roll-over. His accusation deserves response. And I will give it.

Carver's face holds a myriad of pained emotion. He never knew about the money his dad gave me. I didn't take it to keep quiet. I took it to pay for my education. His head turns to me, his eyes searching mine for the answer.

"He's right, Carver. It was my choice whether I kept our baby or gave him up. It's not like your dad could just take him away without my consent. Your dad gave me the options I needed to conclude what was right for everyone involved. I did that on my own. It was the toughest decision I've ever made and I still cry every night over my loss. I let go of my flesh and blood. The baby I carried in my womb for nine months. A child that would undoubtedly grow up to look like you. To be like you. It gutted me. But it's not your father's burden to carry."

I stand, dropping Carver's hand from mine and face Mr. Edwards, who has his arm around his wife's shoulder. Althea is softly crying tears for a baby she just learned existed. She has a right to be hurt and angry with all of us.

I look back at Carver. "And as for the money. Your dad offered me something to go away. I accepted it only for one reason. I wasn't looking for handouts or charity. I wanted to go to school and it was the only way I could do it."

A flash of anger zings through Carver's eyes. He's upset because I never mentioned that before. I understand. He has a right to be mad. But it doesn't change where we're at now. Or who we are. Or what we need to accomplish.

"Mr. Edwards. I came here tonight for one reason. Carver and I would like to get the information you have on the adoption. We need to know what happened to our child. I can't go another day without knowing if he's happy and well-cared for."

His father stands, as if ready for battle against me.

"No."

I flinch at the strong force of that one syllable word.

"No?" I whisper, but don't get a chance to say anything else as Carver steps in.

"We don't need your permission, Dad. We can figure it out on our own, with or without you. But I know you have all the details locked away in your files since you arranged it all. It would save us a lot of time and difficulty if you'd just hand over the documents so we can move on from here."

Carver does a hard turn and heads to his father's mahogany desk that must contain all his legal documents. Carver Sr. takes one long stride and yanks on his son's arm. For a second, I'm scared that a fight will break out. Instead, his dad lets go and moves past Carver to his desk.

He opens a file drawer and pulls out the envelope, clutching it in his hands as if his life depends on keeping it secret.

"I want you to think long and hard before you proceed with this. Whatever you do at this point will change the course of your lives forever. You can never go back. You will never be able to retrieve the past or be a part of his life. It'll be like you're looking through a one-way window with a view into his life, unable to be present or involved. He'll not know you're there, and it will only make you desperate to reach him. Do you honestly want to put yourselves through that misery?"

Carver reaches out and grabs the file, yanking it from his father's grasp.

"Yes," he says, the agony pouring through his voice. "Because at least that misery will be accompanied by the knowledge that our son is living a full and happy life. That he's safe and loved."

My heart explodes with a reborn love for Carver Edwards.

A love that never left me, but was only hidden deep under the heartbreak of young love and a grief so great, I could scarcely breathe for the last four years.

CHAPTER 20

CARVER

THE DRIVE back to Logan's apartment is solemn, the light drizzle on the windshield echoing in the silent car like booming slaps across my face.

This evening did not go as planned. On the other hand, it went exactly how I thought it would go.

I'm mad at my dad and angry with Logan for not telling me about the money.

Logan's voice cuts through the gloom. "I'm sorry, Carver. I know you're upset."

"You have no idea how I feel," I snap, instantly regretful for my hostile response.

Out of the corner of my eye, I see her turn to look out her window and notice the glistening of tears against her cheek.

Fuck.

I reach over and swipe an errant tear from her cheek. Her profile is so beautiful, even when sad. Although I'm hurt that she left out such an important aspect of our situation, I don't blame her. I know she's suffered. If there was a way I could take away all the pain she suffered, I would. I'd give everything up – my future pro career, the fans, the money – everything. Just to see her happy.

"Your dad loves you, Carver. He only wanted what was best for you and doesn't want to see you hurt. And I'm sorry I made matters worse by not telling you about the money he gave me. It was wrong of me."

"It doesn't seem that way from where I'm sitting. He blamed you for everything that happened." I turn to face her, placing my hand on her shoulder. "Yes, I'm hurt that you didn't tell me about the money, because you didn't trust me to know the truth. But it's not your fault, baby. You were barely eighteen, alone and scared. I hate knowing you had to live through that and deal with this on your own."

"Carver." Her tone is resolved as she turns off the engine of the car and shifts to face me. "I do trust you, but I need time to process all of this. You've coming barreling back into my life and you're going to be busting right back out once you return to your new normal – whatever that looks like. I'm not sure I can handle learning about our child and losing him again. Losing you, too."

I can't argue with her because she's right. Once I'm drafted, it'll be off to whatever city I'm in and then I'll start training. Hard. Come fall, I'll begin traveling all over the country, never home longer than a few days. In fact, my agent recommended that once I know where I'll be, I shouldn't buy anything for the first year. It'll be a vagabond life and having ties anywhere will be relationship suicide.

Logically, I know this. But having just found Logan again and re-establishing our connection, I don't want to let that go.

I slide my hands across her cheekbones and through her hair, cupping her head gently in my palms. I touch my lips to hers – once. Twice. Three soft pecks of affection.

"I know my life will be different, but you've reminded me of what it's like to feel...to want and be wanted in return. I've been broken for so many years."

I take her hand in mine and bring it to my heart, covering it with our joined hands. "At the risk of sounding lame, and I will deny this to my dying breath if word ever gets out that I'm senti-mental...but you own me, Logan. You're the puzzle piece that locks my heart together. No matter where I am, you're my home. I want that with you."

Logan sucks in a raspy breath and turns away from me.

"No, I don't want that. I'm not going to follow you around like a groupie, living my life out of a suitcase so you can have me anytime you want."

"That's not what I meant - " I interject as our gazes lock for battle.

"Maybe not...but that's how it would feel to me. I have a life here. A job I love. This was a fun reunion that we both enjoyed – let's leave it at that. As for next steps, I'll contact you when I'm ready to proceed with the adoption investigation. Outside of that, we have one more night together. I want to be with you without this cloud hovering above us. Can you give me one more night?"

I drop my head, ready to protest that one night won't be enough.

Slipping my fingers through hers, I lift her hand to my mouth and kiss her palm. I wish I was a psychic so I could clearly see what the future looks like for us. So I'd have a clear path into the future to know for certain if walking away from her now is the right thing to do, or if I should stay and fight for her. To find a way to make this work between us.

Instead, I take the coward's way out.

"Okay, Lo. One more night. I want that with you."

~

MY DENTAL APPOINTMENT is scheduled for Tuesday morning at nine a.m. I'll be returning to Dr. Connell's office for the remaining two-hour session where they will replace my temporary bridge with the permanent structure that would hopefully be good for the next ten years. Barring any further incident or injury I sustain while playing, that is.

Logan and I spent the rest of Sunday night and a good part of Monday morning wrapped up in each other's arms. Talking, reminiscing and making love. I give myself an internal laugh for using that term. I've never made love to a girl before.

I've fucked lots of girls. But sometime in the middle of the night, I made love to Logan. She fell asleep afterwards, curled against my body, softly breathing as she slept, and my mind became aware of what my heart already knew.

I am in love with Logan and perhaps have never stopped loving her.

This love is not a childhood crush or a simple first-love sentiment. This is a connection between a man and a woman – the completion of two halves of the whole.

All the shit I've given Cade over the last year over Ainsley – his now fiancée – is finally biting me in the ass. Now I know what compels him to lay down his life, if need-be, for the woman he loves. I would, without a doubt, do the same thing for Logan.

A thought occurred to me while I was buried deep inside Logan yesterday, before I left her soft, warm body sleeping in her bed. Once dressed, I quickly typed out an urgent text to my agent to see if he could get the ball rolling. The idea would certainly take some finagling on his part – but he was a whiz with making deals and brokering trades. I was confident he could come up with a solution that worked out for me.

Crissy had called me around seven this morning, just as I getting up.

"Yeah," I greeted him brusquely. "Give it to me."

"Listen, we have a few balls up in the air right now – I've got some tugs and bites. I think this will pan out for you. But I don't want you to get your hopes up, either. There's still a lot of unknowns."

My body released a tense sigh. "That's cool, dude. I appreciate all your work on this one. I know it's kind of last minute, but if it works out...well, that'd be awesome."

He chuffs. "I don't get it, kid. You've done a complete one-eighty from where you were not even a week ago. Your change in direction is worse than my twelve-year-old daughter's weekly boy band craze. I swear, the minute I find out who she likes, she's on to someone new. Fickle. But whatever. It's what you want and I'll make it happen."

We said our good-byes and I sent off a few messages that I hadn't returned over the weekend before showering and dressing to head out to my appointment.

I step into the front entry of Dr. Connell's office just before nine a.m. and the girl behind the reception desk practically flies out of her seat. She must now know who I am.

I plaster on a smile and stride up to the desk, leaning over to casually lower my elbows to the counter.

"Good morning, gorgeous. I think you have me down for a nine o'clock this morning. Carver Edwards."

I give her a flirty wink, only to mess with her. My experience has proven that a good-looking guy like me can get a lot of life if I ham it up with the ladies.

She stammers a little, obviously flustered by my attention, "Hello...um, good morning...yes, you're Carver Edwards. Uh...let me see. I just need you to fill out these forms for your insurance and we'll get you back there shortly."

She hands me the clipboard and pen with shaky hands, which I take and plop down on the uncomfortable couch.

I'm finding it difficult to focus on the paperwork, knowing

I'm going to see Logan in a few minutes. I'm not even sure she knows I'm on the schedule this morning. I failed to mention it while we were together this weekend.

A thrill shoots through me, because now that I'm not doped up like I was the last time, I'll get to see exactly what she does in her job.

I have no idea if I completed all the forms correctly, but I walk them back over to the counter and hand them to the star-struck receptionist.

"Thank you, Carver. You can have a seat and Logan will be right with you." She says sweet-as-syrup. But then her tone changes – turning demeaning and snotty. "I'll need to go find her, though. She's never on time."

With a roll of her eyes, she gets up to turn toward the hallway, but I stop her.

"It's fine – I'm a little early and don't mind waiting. I'm sure Logan is busy with her other patients. She's very thorough and that's what makes her so good at what she does."

I give the girl – Bethany, her nametag says – a verbal smack-down. I know women, and it's clear that this chick is jealous of my girl. I'm not about to stand for her piss-poor and catty attitude toward her. Logan is leagues above this woman.

Bethany looks like the wide-eyed emoji, her round cheeks flaring red, her eyes bugging out like a caricature.

She backpedals quickly. "That's nice of you to say. Dr. Connell does hire the best."

That's more like it.

I'm about to return to my seat when the lobby door opens and Logan steps out looking fresh-faced and beautiful. Her hair is up in a messy knot, a medical mask pulled beneath her chin to reveal her pink lips, and her bright blue scrubs hang loosely over her slight frame. The uniform does nothing to hide the curves of her breasts and hips. Curves I had my hands all over the last seventy-two hours.

Shit, I have it bad for this girl.

"Good morning, Carver. I'm so sorry to have kept you waiting. We're already backed up due to the holiday closure yesterday. Please follow me and we can get started."

X-rated thoughts rush my head as I follow behind her, watching her ass swish in the cotton of her scrubs. My hands have a mind of their own, and on their own volition, I reach out and grab her butt. She startles, jumping forward, throwing her head over her shoulder to give me an evil glare. Her blue eyes mean business.

"Stop it, Carver. This is where I work."

"Sorry," I whine apologetically, raising my hands in surrender with a shoulder shrug. "My bad."

Hovering over her shoulder, I whisper in her ear. "How do you expect me to stop myself when I know exactly what that ass looks like naked? I had to touch it. It's been so long."

She giggles. "It's been less than four hours. I'm sure you'll survive."

"Doubtful," I mumble, lowering myself into the dental chair.

She busies herself at the medical counter behind me, but I can tell her breathing is heavier than normal. It's killing me not to touch her. Kiss her. Consume her.

The next two hours are going to be hell. And not because of the dental work.

CHAPTER 21

LOGAN

CARVER'S PRESENCE has me so flustered and nervous, I can hardly think straight. When I saw the schedule this morning, I did everything I could to prepare myself for this moment. Nothing is working, so I make a show of organizing the dental tools that will be used during his procedure, but my thoughts are scattered all over the place.

Mainly on the hot man lying in the chair two feet from me.

The one who did wicked, dirty things to me all weekend long. Whose masculine scent swirls around me and has my body amped up and fighting for air. The one I imagine straddling and fucking hard in that chair he's lounging in right now. I'd tilt him all the way back, unzip his jeans and stroke the steely bulge that I eyed earlier when he walked toward me in the lobby.

"Carver!" Dr. Connell exclaims, jolting me out of my erotic fantasy as he walks in to greet his patient. Holy crap, my cheeks are flaming red and must look like big red apples.

"Hey, Dr. C. Good to see you again. This time I hope to

remember our encounter." They both get a good chuckle out of Carver's self-deprecating humor.

Out of the corner of my eye, I watch Jeff drop his hand and give a pat of appreciation on top of Carver's shoulder.

"Sure wish we could have met under better circumstances, but hopefully this hasn't set you back too much. I hear you'll be heading into the NBA draft soon."

"Yep, that's true. Doesn't mean I'll get picked up, but we'll see where it goes."

It occurs to me that this encounter between the three of us should feel all kinds of awkward. My boss – a guy I've dated a few times and have even let kiss me – is having a casual conversation with my current love and former boyfriend.

I swallow the lump of uncomfortable and hand Carver's file over to Dr. Connell, who accepts it with a smile. Our eyes meet for a second before I look away, but not before I see a flash of something in Jeff's eyes that I can't quite make out. But it's gone in a moment as he opens the chart and begins reading through its contents.

"How has the temporary crown and replacement tooth been treating you? Had any sensitivity or pain with them?"

Carver shakes his head. "Nope. None at all, mostly thanks to your good work. And Logan offered me some very helpful after-care instructions that I followed to the letter. She's incredible."

I choke and drop the utensil I was prepping for the doctor. This garners looks from both men as I bend to pick it up. Carver gives me a flirty wink and Jeff with an inquisitive eyebrow quirk.

"Sorry," I mumble, jumping up to retrieve a replacement in the cupboard overhead.

My hands tremble and the full weight of this situation hits me with the force of a hurricane. I can't breathe. I'm afraid if Carver so much as implies that we've been sleeping together, I could easily lose my job. Even if I explained that we've known each other for years, I'm sure it's frowned upon. Especially if my boss acts out like a jilted lover and fires me out of spite.

When my eyes land on Carver, I glare at him, hoping he gets the message and shuts the hell up.

Jeff returns his attention to Carver. "Yes, Logan is definitely a keeper. She's one of the best assistants I've ever had."

Oh, Lordy. I can't believe my life right now. It'd be comical if it weren't so damn nerve-wracking. Now they both need to shut the hell up with the over-the-topo compliments before I run out of the room like a crazed lunatic.

"Speaking of which...Logan, would you mind stepping out with me for a moment so we can chat?"

Lovely. This isn't awkward at all.

"Sure," I respond, my voice wobbly with embarrassment.

I swivel out of my chair and walk around the corner, Jeff following closely behind. In a small dental clinic there isn't much privacy, unless we go to his office. Uncertainty plagues me. I'm freaked out he's about to fire me.

I take a large breath to steady my nerves and cross my arms in front of my chest, hoping to look both confident and calm. I keep my composure and watch as Jeff's gentle smile etches at the corners of his mouth.

"Logan," he says softly. Not like the tone a boss would take in firing their employee. I let out a sigh of relief.

His hand lands on my arm, his fingertips a little cold. "I know that this might be uncomfortable for you, seeing as what happened between us on Friday night. I just want you to know there are no hard feelings on my end. I've had a wonderful time getting to know you better. In fact, I've enjoyed every minute of it. You are a beautiful woman, inside and out. And in the future..." he clears his throat, talking in a hushed whisper.

Jeff smiles bashfully, the pink creeping up his throat and neck. "If you'd ever want to rekindle things, I'll be here. But for now, I'll honor your request to return things back to normal. I must admit, after seeing you again this morning, I think it's going to be harder on me than I thought."

He laughs, looking away from me and then squares his shoulders, as if to resolve himself in what he must do.

"But that's not your problem. It's all on me. I want you to know I won't treat you any differently than I did before. You have my word."

My mouth is dry and my stomach bottoms out. Even though I can't control my feelings toward him, guilt takes up residence in my conscience. I shouldn't have gone out with him to begin with, since I never liked Jeff in that way. Not in the way I feel about Carver.

He gives me a nod of assurance and my mouth curves into what I hope is a bright smile, even though I'm trembling on the inside.

"Thank you, Jeff. I'm sorry I can't return your affections, but you are a great boss. I appreciate your kindness."

He stuns me by leaning in and placing a swift kiss on my cheek, just as I hear a gasp come from behind him. My eyes pop wide when I see Bethany over Jeff's shoulder, seething with anger. Great. Now she has even more reason to despise me.

Jeff takes a gigantic step away from me, creating the more appropriate distance between doctor and employee. He turns and nods, acknowledging Bethany's appearance.

"Bethany. Can I help you with something?" His voice is clipped; a harsh tone I've never heard him use before. Huh, maybe Bethany grates on his nerves, too. The idea has me snickering with mirth.

She holds out a form in front of her, offering it up to Jeff. "Oh, yes. I just wanted to inform Carver that his insurance has covered the procedure in full, except for his deductible."

"Great," Jeff responds, plucking the sheet from her hands to hand it over to me. "Logan will let him know. If that's all, we'll get back to our patient now."

Bethany stands there for a minute, looking like she is biting back words she desperately wants to let out, but finally nods, giving one final disdainful glare at me before returning to the front. If I thought things were difficult between us before, I'd say it's going to get a helluva lot more unbearable.

Heading back into the exam room, I find Carver sitting rather rigidly in his seat, phone in his hands typing out a text, a frown displayed across his mouth.

Wonderful. The only thing that could make this morning any worse is if Carver heard any or all of that exchange between Jeff and me. Although we spoke in hushed whispers, there's not much ambient noise to drown out conversation. Unintentional eavesdropping can happen.

"Carver, I think we're all set to go. Logan will get things started with you and numb you up for the procedure. It'll take about fifteen minutes for the numbing to take effect, and then we'll begin. Do you have any questions for me?"

Carver's guarded expression changes, as he looks first at the doctor and then his gaze lands on me, a smirk replacing his frown. "None for you, Dr. Connell. Thanks."

It's easy to read between the lines if you know Carver. He clearly overheard our hallway conversation. Shit.

Not that it's any of Carver's business who I dated before spending the weekend with him. He didn't mention any of his previous relationships, so it shouldn't matter either way. For all I know, Carver's not even single. He might have a girlfriend back in Phoenix. I could have just been a weekend fling.

Jeff taps Carver on the shoulder and walks into the exam room down the hall, leaving Carver and me alone.

As I've already prepped the syringe and oral anesthetic, I pick up the cotton swab covered in Lidocaine and I'm about to apply it to the inside of his cheek when he speaks, his voice low with a tinge of anger.

"You failed to tell me you were dating someone."

I sigh. "It's not what you think. You don't know the whole story and this is not the time, nor the place, to discuss it." I wrench open his jaw and shove the swab deep into his cheek. "Close."

He snarls but does as I say, allowing me a few moments to compose myself and consider what I'm going to share with him.

Our eyes lock and I see the evidence of his emotions in his brown sugar gaze. It's ridiculous. This thing between us isn't even serious. Carver is set to leave tomorrow and I don't know when, or if, I might see him again, yet I feel compelled to tell him everything.

Although it's none of his business, I want him to know.

"Jeff and I never amounted to anything. I couldn't reciprocate his feelings. We went out three times since March, Carver. The last time was Friday evening when I ended things. Before I ran into you."

His sigh is as deep as the ocean and it swallows me whole.

"I know I have no right, Logan. No claim to you. But these feelings are here, none-the-less. And they run deep." Carver grasps my hand and places it above his heart.

I jerk my hand away and pick up the syringe, turning back to hold it in front of him. It's almost comical how he shrinks back into his seat, squirming uncomfortably as his eyes go wide with fear.

"Don't worry, Carver. It'll be over before you know it and you won't feel a thing."

I think we both know that it's not the sting of the needle I'm referring to.

CHAPTER 22

CARVER

IT WAS a lost cause trying to have any discernible conversation during or after my procedure. With a rubber dam in my mouth most of the time and my tongue swollen to the size of a grapefruit, everything I wanted to say to Logan was limited to simple head nods and blinking eyes.

And when my appointment was done, Logan quickly ushered me out the front and went right back to work on other patients. If I didn't know her better, and didn't know she wanted me out of there without making a scene, I'd assume she was just in a rush to get to her next client.

But I know she was doing her best to avoid me, using a busy schedule as her escape tactic.

Which is fine for now. Just as she said, we need our space. I need to wrap my head around everything that's happened this weekend. There's been a confusing barrage of emotions that I don't know how to handle. Being with Logan again; fucking her; spending time with her; figuring out what to do with the knowledge and whereabouts of our son. It's almost too much. And laid on that, my upcoming draft – well, it's a lot for one guy to manage.

And then come to find out she was dating someone – the dentist of all people – right before she spent the weekend with me. A streak of jealous anger I didn't know I possessed spiked through my veins when I heard them talking earlier. It pissed me off and I acted like a prick.

I really need a drink.

If I was back in Phoenix, I could grab a six-pack from my fridge and hang with my boys. Here in Seattle, I have my old high school friends – but even Joel is different now. We all went in opposite directions. I guess that's part of growing up – establishing new identities and lives that are influenced by our past, but no longer align.

I look down at my phone and notice it's only a little after eleven a.m. Probably too early to head to a bar. Plus, my mouth is still numb and swollen. Anything I'd drink would just dribble down my chin.

I've got time to kill. It's a nice summer morning – still cool and cloudy – so I decide to take a walk down by the waterfront. The streets have a fine sheen of dampness from the earlier drizzle, but the sun is making a valiant effort to peek out from the cloud cover.

It's weird how much I miss the crisp, damp air of the city. After spending four years in the arid desert, I'd expect to miss the heat. The only thing I do seem to miss is my friends. The guys who were with me through thick and thin.

I pull out my phone and decide to call Lance. I know he'll answer, even if he's still in bed.

He answers on the third ring. That's my boy.

"Yo, this better be the pizza delivery dude. I fucking called thirty minutes ago and I'm fucking starving."

I chuckle because some things never change. Lance is always hungry. He has a hollow leg.

"I'm way better than any pizza delivery, bruh. And you know it. I also know you miss me."

Lance snorts rudely. "Fuck man, you wish. But I do miss the extra female action you always seem to bring home with you. It's just been me and my hand lately, and that's just lame-ass boring."

"Ah, poor guy. You too lazy to go find some action on your own? You need my sloppy seconds to get laid?"

"Fuck you," he mumbles as I hear him open the door to the pizza delivery. He holds a brief conversation with the guy, seriously trying to broker a reduction in price because the guy was two minutes late over their thirty-minute promise. Yes, this is indeed one of my best friends, folks. And I couldn't love him more.

Lance finishes up his transaction and returns to our conversation.

He's already stuffing his face, chewing like a cow does on cud. Sloppy and disgusting. No wonder he's still single.

I hold the phone away from my ear as I step around a homeless guy sitting on the sidewalk begging for change.

"Now, what the hell was I saying? Oh yeah, I can get laid on my own, thank you very much."

"Sure," I snort incredulously. "Like you tried to get Mica? I'm pretty sure you crashed and burned there, bruh."

I know I hit a sore spot with that one.

Micaela Reyes, or Mica as she's called, is Ainsley's roommate. She's this petite, five-foot-nothing Hispanic girl whom I've honestly never heard say a word. But Lance has had it bad for her since they first met earlier in the school year.

Unfortunately for our Romeo, his Juliet won't go out with him and it frustrates Lance to no end. He relies heavily on his basketball status to get girls and can't figure out what Mica doesn't see in him.

From the sound of his annoyed growl, I know he'd punch me right now if I was there. I laugh out loud at the thought. Damn, I'm going to miss my college days. It feels like it was just yesterday when we all met each other at team orientation.

"Shut the fuck up, you twunt," Lance's made-up word has me rolling with laughter. "Mica will one day give in to me. I'm just wearing her down. She'll realize soon enough that I'm quite the catch."

"Good luck with that, dude. If you need any advice, just ask."

I don't know why I love getting under Lance's skin so badly. Maybe we both need this banter – the easy comradery that reminds us we're friends for life, even if we won't live together or see each other every day.

Lance just grumbles and smacks his food louder over the phone.

"So, how's it going up there, bro? You coming back before the draft? You still got all your shit here."

That was the original plan. To head back down, pack up all my belongings and then get ready to jet as soon as the draft happens so I can get to wherever the hell I'm going. Now that I have a good plan in place, I'm confident where I might end up. So I could just call a moving company and have it done without even being present.

"Yeah, man. I'll be back – probably later this week. I've got a thing to take care of up here before I leave."

"Will you still be heading to LA for draft day?"

Typically, new recruits and NBA hopefuls will attend the live event in the ballroom where the televised event happens. This year it's in LA. Now, with my change of plans, I may not be in attendance.

"Not sure yet. I'll let you know."

But before any of that happens, I need to take care of contacting the attorney and the adoption agency, to find out what rights Logan and I have regarding the adoption of our son, and then proceed from there.

It weighs like a heavy boulder on my heart. The whole process – learning about my son and his whereabouts – is a lot to consider. I'm at that pivotal fork-in-the-road in my life and I have no idea where either road will lead me.

Lance presses on, not realizing what can of worms he's opened by asking.

"What's so important there? I know it ain't your family, 'cause that door's been closed for years."

My friends know my relationship with my dad is strained but they have no clue what caused the riff. I've never once mentioned anything about Logan or the baby to any of my friends. Or my dad's interference in my life.

I'm literally standing at a corner in the road – overlooking the Puget Sound and Pike Place Market. People congregate on the sidewalks - next to me, in front of me and all around me. In fact, I've been bumped and shouldered by at least a half dozen passer-by's in the last minute while standing at this intersection. It's symbolic of where I'm at in life. If I make a move in the wrong direction, I could get mowed over.

Clearing my throat, I decide to come clean with my friend. "About that...the door got kicked wide open this weekend when I reconnected with my former girlfriend."

I hear something crash on the other end of the line and Lance sounds like he's choking on his slice of pizza.

"Dude...did you just say girlfriend? Holy shit, man. Why the hell have you never mentioned a girlfriend before? What the fuck, bro? When were you going to tell me about this? The guy I know was the king of pussy and never would have had a girlfriend."

I laugh over his confusion, but it lacks amusement.

"Hard to believe, I know. But it's true. Her name is Logan. I met her when I was fifteen at summer camp. She uh…got pregnant right before I started college. Gave it up for adoption at the urging of my dad. And I didn't know about it until well after it all happened."

"Holy fuck, dude. That's…crazy. Why didn't you ever tell me you were a dad?"

Good question.

It seems so strange to be called a dad. Especially by Lance.

"I don't know, man. The whole thing really fucked me in the head. So I tried to forget it ever happened."

I continue retelling the story of Logan and me, as he peppers me with questions. When I finally get to the part about reconnecting with Logan and our current circumstances, he whistles, long and loud.

"Bro, the way I see it, there's only one thing you can do," he says, full of wisdom and sage advice that only a single guy can dish out.

"Oh yeah?" I ask with an amused smile. It feels good to talk this through with someone who isn't directly involved. I know Lance has my back. "What's that?"

He laughs like I'm stupid as fuck.

"Find your motherfucking kid, dude. Otherwise it's gonna eat away at you and you'll regret not doing it. And then one day in the future you'll just be sitting there in a beat up recliner, fapping away at some porn streaming online, unable to keep it up. You'll look down at the limp dick in your hand and realize you should've done something when you had the chance."

Ah, Christ. This is how a serious conversation with Lance can turn sideways.

At very least, he gets me to laugh. And he actually makes sense, putting it into perspective the way only friends can do.

CHAPTER 23

Logan

I'VE HEARD nothing from Carver in two weeks, since the morning he left the dental office. It's the best thing for both of us. I know this but it still hurts.

It hurts that he can leave without looking back. Without at least saying goodbye. Without following through on his promise to help find out about our son.

Maybe I expected too much. I'd pinned my hopes on this man; on the memories we'd made together and the moments we'd shared. Apparently, that wasn't enough for him.

Outside of waiting to hear anything from Carver, my life went back to normal. Work, work and more work.

The only change was the level of hatred spewing from my co-worker Bethany's mouth. She was no longer subtle in her hostility toward me. It didn't bother me, and I never responded, except today, when a patient overheard her unkind words.

Mrs. Kline nearly stumbled and lost her footing when she overheard Bethany remark how if she knew what a slut I was, she wouldn't want me working around her mouth, in fear of what STD she might contract.

I have no idea why Bethany came to despise me so much and with such venom, but this time, it was also overheard by Dr. Connell, who fired her on the spot this morning. Good riddance.

As I finish cleaning my dinner plate, I plop down on the couch with a glass of Pinot and turn on the TV. This is the first evening I've had to myself in weeks, as Ali's scheduled changed and she's working more day shifts now. Tonight she's at the bar – which makes no sense as to why she'd spend her off-time back at the bar. She just said it was a special event that she and Troy were invited to attend.

Propping my feet up on the edge of the coffee table, I mind-lessly flip through the stations before I resign myself to watching one of the shows on the DVR. Just as I'm about to hit the button, I land on a sports network. It's broadcasting the NBA draft.

The remote shakes in my hand, as I hesitate with indecision. I leave the channel there. Excitement over the possibility of seeing Carver on TV tingles in my belly, like the taste of champagne on the tip of my tongue. Of course, I'm curious as to where he'll be drafted. He may have disappeared on me, but I still care for him.

Then the thought strikes me. He's moved on with his life. I was just a momentary blip in his soon-to-be celebrity life. Our weekend together meant nothing to him and now he's moved on to bigger and better things.

I thought I could handle it, but I was lying to myself. The pain of his loss is staggering. Maybe it's best that I don't know where he ends up. I take a quick peek, anyway, and see that they are on number five in the first round, but my attention is snapped away when I hear the text alert on my phone.

Ali: Come on down to Cal's. This event is off-the-hook.

Me: I'm in my pj's already. Not feeling it.

Ali: Don't be an old lady. Drinks are on me. And everyone wants to see you.

Me: How many drinks?

Ali: On the house. Now get your ass down here.

Me: Gee, you're so bossy.

Ali: I know. But you love me.

Me: Whatever. I'll see you in twenty.

I give one last look at the TV before I shuffle into my bedroom to change. I don't know anything about the televised event, but it looks like it's being held in some big ballroom – probably in New York or LA - with an announcer on the stage reading from a teleprompter each team's picks to an audience of suited men and women.

I wonder if Carver is there or if he's down in Phoenix surrounded by his friends – and girls. It makes me crazy wondering why he left things the way he did. He seemed genuinely jealous and upset when he found out I had dated Jeff, but obviously not enough, making it easy for him to leave me high and dry.

Maybe he just had a lot on his mind when he returned to Phoenix and hasn't had time to contact me. I suppose preparing for the draft could have taken much of his time and energy of the last few weeks. I'm sure it's been stressful on him.

It's stupid of me to think that our weekend reunion meant anything meaningful to Carver; I suppose I asked for it when I hurried him out the clinic after his procedure. Carver had just looked at me with soulful eyes as I shuttled him out the door. I practically slammed it on his way out.

But dammit, he could have called me later. Texted me. Stopped by. But he did none of those things. Instead, he left without saying goodbye. Like I'm just another notch in his belt.

Why did I let Ali sucker me into going out tonight? I have no energy or interest in hanging with Ali's friends, yet here I am, wiggling my ass into a tight pair of jeans. My mind goes blank as I stare into my closet looking for a top to wear, but my attention is drawn to the sounds of the TV from the other room. I run out of my bedroom, skidding to a stop in front of the couch, wearing only my jeans and a bra.

The camera is centered on the bald announcer, as he broadcasts the news.

"With the thirty-fourth pick in the NBA draft, the LA Clippers select Carver Edwards, from Arizona State University."

The tickertape at the bottom of the screen displays Carver's name and the camera pans out into the audience, but finds nothing. No sign of Carver. Then another faceless announcer from the network chimes in on the conversation.

"Carver Edwards is a leader and a winner. That's a good selection for the Clippers, who are in need of some fresh blood in their organization." There's a pause, and then another male voice joins in.

"That's right, Don. Coach Thorn and GM Malcolm Harrold will be looking to use Carver's leadership skills and his fantastic passing abilities as they rebuild their team."

I flip off the TV and struggle not to cry.

Carver's going to play in Los Angeles. My phone buzzes in the other room, jarring me from my stupor. I find myself back in my bedroom, pulling a tank on over my head and yanking a flannel from my closet to cover my bare arms. The phone pings again with a text message. I expect it's from Ali wondering where the hell I am.

But it's from Carver.

Carver: I have good news.

Carver: At least, I hope you think it's good news.

Carver: I was drafted #34. I'm pretty stoked.

Carver: I'm celebrating down at Cal's.

Carver: Come down and join the party.

I scroll through the series of texts, trying to comprehend what it means. It's the first time in over ten days that he's reached out to me. He's back in town – and not in LA – and is sharing this newsworthy information with me as if nothing has changed between us.

My thumbs work overtime as I quickly type out my response.

Me: Congrats. I'm proud of you. You've achieved your dream.

Carver: It's only a dream if I can share it with you.

Carver: I've missed you.

The words blur in front of me. I feel dizzy.

Carver: Are you coming down to Cal's?

I catch myself with my hand before falling over the side of the bed as I slide my foot in my shoes. Carver is at Cal's? He's in town? What the hell is he doing there? And why didn't he tell me before now?

This pisses me off because Ali must've known he was there, too. Some friend she is.

Stomping around my room like a two-year-old having a temper tantrum, I grab my keys and wallet from the bureau and head out the door, slamming it behind me for emphasis. I'm mad at Carver...but I don't know why exactly.

Oh, wait. Yes, I do. Because he failed to tell me he was in town. Forgot to invite me out to his draft party. Hasn't spoken to me in two freaking weeks. Is going to be moving to LA. You name it – it all makes me frenzied with righteous indignation.

By the time I reach the front door of Cal's, my blood boils even hotter, and then I hear a chorus of shouts and cheers from the back room.

"Carver! Carver! Carver!"

People are chanting his name in celebration. Cheering for the man-of-the-hour; their hometown hero who has made them all proud.

From a distance, I see Ali jumping up and down with a drink in her hand, hoisted over her head. And then, as if there's a parting of the Red Sea, the crowd opens and Carver stands in the center of the room with a bright smile on his face.

His gaze finds mine and he begins a swaggered walk toward me, working his way through the throngs of well-wishers, to meet me in the quiet part of the bar. I tip my chin up to get a good look at him as he stands in front of me, his head tilted downward.

I can't explain why I do what I do, but my hand acts on its own volition when it smacks Carver's smiling face with the force of a whip. All my anger, hurt, humiliation, shame – everything I've felt comes screaming out when my hand connects with his jaw.

He staggers back stunned, his hand clutching his cheek and a shocked expression registers across his face. It doesn't take him more than a second to recover, when a slow smile returns, blinding me with its capable power.

Without a single word, he grips the back of my neck and pulls me into a scorching hot kiss. We're lips and tongue, love and loss. Hunger and desire pour from the depths of our souls, mingling with a hint of desperation.

I place my hands on top his shoulders – either to bring him closer or to push him away – I'm not sure which. My grip is tight, digging into the solid mass of muscle, as it slides down the bulge of his bicep where I wrap my arms around his trim waist.

Carver loosens his hold on my head and releases my mouth.

"You slapped me," he states without malice or contempt, his voice holding a bit of amusement.

"You left me."

"I came back."

"You're not staying."

He takes my hand and tugs me toward the hallway near the restrooms, a dank corridor in the dark, hipster bar. When he stops, he presses my back up against the wall towering over me, one hand on my hipbone and the other above my head in a very alpha-like posture.

Carver's voice is low and tight. "It was never meant to be

permanent, Lo. I didn't want to leave you, but it seemed like you needed some time. So much happened between us that weekend. It was heavy. We needed time to figure things out."

I don't look at him. I can't. "It doesn't matter. It never did. We can't be together, now that you made it big."

"Bullshit," he snaps, startling me with the caustic censure as I stare at him with wide eyes. "We can be together. I want you, Lo. I want you in my life."

"That won't work. You're going to be in LA. I'm here."

Carver steps back and looks at me as if he's trying to figure out if I'm drunk. Or insane. Or possibly both.

"LA? What are you talking about? I'm going to be here. In Seattle. You're looking at the newest draft pick for the Puget Sound Pilots." He smiles proudly, confusing me even more.

"But...on TV, they said you were drafted by the Clippers. I don't understand." I shake my head in confusion.

Carver leans down, crowding me against the back wall. His breath is warm and has a faint scent of beer.

"Yes," he confirms, his voice hot liquid, melting my cold body. "But a trade was brokered right afterward. It's a common occurrence during draft day. The Clipper's wanted Zeke Aldridge, the Pilots' current point guard, and the Pilots get rookie sensation, me. I'm moving back home."

When I remain silent, Carver presses on.

"Aren't you happy?"

I can't help it when a bubble of hysteria bursts from my lungs. I'm laughing so hard I have to lean over and place my hands on my knees to catch my breath. Carver just stares at me like I'm a raving lunatic.

Maybe I am. But I'm ecstatic right now and a little delirious.

He rolls his eyes once I've stopped laughing, stepping in toward me again, a lazy grin growing at the edge of his lips. "I'm not sure what's so funny about this, but I'm glad you can have a good laugh at my expense."

"I'm sorry. It's just really good news. And yes, I'm very happy for you, Carver."

His lips find the side of my neck, flicking the soft wisps of hair away and sucking lightly as my belly swells with the flapping of butterfly wings.

"I think I can make you even happier."

"Mm," I hum, an ache building between my legs that I know he'll be able to take away. "How do you plan on doing that?"

"Let's get out of here," he mumbles against my sensitive flesh. "And I'll show you."

I tilt my head away to get his attention. "Don't you have to stay? This is your own draft party. I think your fans would be disappointed if the star left so early."

His groan sounds like he's ill with a fever.

"Fine. But you're joining me back there. I'll introduce you to my agent and some of my friends who came up for the party and then we're getting the fuck out of here. I'm taking you back to my hotel where I plan to make you a very happy woman, all night long."

He gives me a peck on my mouth and my tummy shimmies and flips, as he takes my hand and leads me back to his party.

CHAPTER 24

CARVER

To watch Logan interact so effortlessly with Crissy and my former teammates made me the happiest guy alive. And turned me the fuck on.

She's always had an easy-going style, but her natural effervescence was illuminated tonight amongst the crowd. She wasn't even ruffled when the guys shared some embarrassing stories about my sexual prowess in school. She just laughed, joined in on mocking me and took it all in stride.

She also got along with my friends, which is always a good indicator about a potential girlfriend. Cade, Lance and Van all made it up to my draft party, showering me with congratulations and 'atta boys all night long. It was a night I won't forget anytime soon.

The draft aside, having Logan back in my life is cause for even further celebration.

The circumstances that kept us apart over the last four years sucked. I wish I could go back in time and make a better effort at finding her. I would have cleared the air and found a way to work our way back to good. All those moments that could've been, but don't exist now because of how things ended between us.

Shoulda, coulda, woulda.

On the other hand, maybe it's what needed to happen. For us to be apart. To learn who we are as individuals. To grow the hell up.

I was deadly serious when I told her we'd leave in thirty minutes. I was ready to take her back to my hotel room within ten, but she was right – I needed to be there to celebrate my big day. It's not every day you get drafted into the pros.

But when the time came and I found her talking with Cade and Ainsley, I didn't hesitate to throw her over my shoulder in a fireman's hold and drag her ass out of that bar. To a lot of wolf whistles and catcalls, I might add.

As I met Crissy in the hallway toward the exit, he gave me a congratulatory pat on the back and quirked a bushy eyebrow at me, presumably for my caveman behavior.

"Do try to save a little strength for your faithful viewers and fans tomorrow at the press conference," Crissy said with a lewd grin as I walked by.

"I hope I'll be a withering mess, but I'll be there. You can count on it." I wiggled my eyebrows, as Logan kicked and giggled when I patted her ass.

We Ubered it to the Four Seasons, where Crissy had booked me a room when I told him we'd not be going to LA but Seattle instead. I'm glad Cris is my agent. He's a decent guy and has been looking out for my best interests since day one. But even more so when he went to bat to get me a spot on the Pilots' roster.

While I'm now a name on the roster, things are still up in the air as to my longevity and career with the Pilots. I could get cut within the first two weeks of training. Or could stay the length of my NBA career. It's a crapshoot but I'm determined not to worry about all that right now. Not when Logan's body is stretched out beautifully naked on the fluffy down comforter of the hotel bed.

The minute we walked in the room – well, after she got over the shock of the ornate and luxurious suite I had – I began divesting her of her clothes. One piece at a time, starting with the red flannel shirt she wore.

It took every ounce of restraint to avoid ripping off her clothes, throwing her down on the floor – or maybe up against the wall – and fucking her fast. My balls ached and my cock pressed painfully hard against my jeans – dying to be inside her again.

And here I am, still painfully hard, my jeans pulled down to my ankles, as I grip my cock in my palm, stroking it leisurely while I'm on my knees over my beautiful girl. Logan watches with heated interest, her fingers wandering over her taut belly, teasing me with her seductive movements.

"I've had a lot of time to think about what I'd do with you the next time we fucked."

Her voice is raspy. Low. Sexy. "Oh yeah? Like what?"

"I could tell you…or I can show you. Which one do you want?"

I bend forward and suck in her tight, rosy nipple into my mouth, biting it with just enough force to send her body jerking with a yelp.

My tongue laves across the rosy flesh, soothing away the pain, as she pants and squirms below me. Her moans grow louder. Needier. Just like I want her.

Every part of me yearns to spread her legs open and go fucking wild inside her. Lose myself until I can't even say my name from the pleasure that consumes me.

"Both," she says breathlessly.

I take even breaths through my nose, calming my revving engines to avoid rutting her like a dog. I flip her over with hands on her hips, her sharp gasp garnering a devious smile from me.

She's now on her knees facing the headboard, shoulders and head pinned to the mattress, ass in the air. She moans lustfully because she knows what's coming. She wants what's coming. And what's coming will soon have *her* coming all over my face.

"I'll give you both...or maybe not," I tease, one finger coasting down her spine. "Arms overhead."

She yields to my demand, the slope of her back bowing in front of me.

I place my hands on the insides of her thighs, pushing them out and lifting her ass higher. Because of our height difference, I scoot her toward the edge of bed as I land on my knees behind her, the canvas of her pussy at eye level.

My fingers feather lightly over her smooth, apple-bottom ass, gently caressing a path down between her cheeks.

She stills...she's waiting for it. Her body quivers in anticipation of the smack that usually comes.

But I make her wait, teasing her while I palm both cheeks and spread her open. The sight is so incredible I have to drop one hand and squeeze my cock to keep from releasing.

Logan is wet and glistening. And it's beautiful.

"You expect a spanking, don't you, naughty girl?"

She moans her response, her nostrils flaring.

"I'm not sure what a spanking would accomplish. You're already wet, aren't you?"

I trail my thumb down between the globes, pressing into the folds of her hot seam. She's gloriously wet. Her hips push back, yearning for more.

I give her more. She'll always get the most from me. The best of me.

It's unfair of me to say this to her when I have her trapped in this compromising position, but I'm a jealous prick. And I need her honesty while she's drunk with lust.

"Tell me, Logan. Tell me I'm the only one. That there's no others. That it's only me you want to be with."

Dipping my tongue in between her sweet folds, I lick upwards, tasting the sweetest part of her. She's trembling and I can tell only a few more swipes will get her off.

I swipe again, circling my tongue against her clit as she screams out my name.

"Oh, God, Carver! Yes...it's you. Only you...always you."

This right here is everything I could ever want. Her body needing me. Needing what I can give her. What no one else could ever give.

Her sweet, tangy flavor explodes across my tongue as I continue to lick and suck greedily between her legs. My hands grip her hips hard and I smile perversely knowing that she'll have dark bruises there when I'm done with her.

She's writhing and grinding against my face now, and I know she's close. Ready to give into the pleasure that's building within her. I know how to take her to the edge using all the weapons in my arsenal. There's no resistance when I slide two fingers inside, the wet heat and the friction unleashing the storm within her.

Just like that – she's coming with a low-pitched mewl. Her body clamps down around my fingers and her body tremors beautifully. I want that vice-like grip around my dick.

I give her a few moments to recover and then stand up behind her. Her hands still grip the comforter above her head and my smile widens knowing I've created such a lingering response. But I won't rest. I'm not done with her. Not even close.

I reach out with one hand and lightly feather up the curve of her back until I reach the front of her neck. With just the right amount of pressure, I wrap my fingers around her exposed throat, pulling her body toward me so she's flush against my chest.

The sensation of her throat swallowing – opening and closing – induces a volcanic response within me. The tip of my cock is pressed against her lower back.

"How bad do you want me, Lo? How much do you need me?"

I emphasize my question with a slide of my arousal across her entrance.

I do this a few times, as it glides easily over her slick folds and she whimpers breathlessly, bucking unabashedly against my straining dick.

She manages to turn her head to look over her shoulder, her lips parted, eyes closed. My lips capture hers, my tongue sweeping through her mouth. I know she can taste herself on my lips and the thrill shoots down my spine.

"Carver," she rasps, pulling her mouth from mine. "Give it to me. I want you inside me now."

Before I can pick up the condom package I'd laid on the bed, Logan reaches underneath her legs, latches a tight fist on to my cock, and lines me up at her entrance. All her heat – her wetness – make me crazy. Lost in the sensation of oblivion.

My body wants to push in. Sink deep into her wetness. Relish everything she's offering me. But I hesitate. My mind questions this insanity. Because we've been down this road before.

Logan is the only girl I've ever fucked without a condom. I've never trusted any other girl. I'd learned from my past mistakes.

"Lo."

"I'm good, Carver. I'm covered. Are you?"

Hell yes, never been better. I'm clean. Was just tested in my physical. I want this with Logan again. I want it all.

Instead of a verbal answer, I take another pass at her entrance and then sink into her wet heat in one fluid motion. The hand I have wrapped around her throat tightens, the other roams latches on to her breast, plumping and plucking at her nipples.

Logan squirms underneath my ministrations, her ass jutting up against my pelvis as I move inside her. I've never felt a more exquisite body. She's developed in all the right places since the first time we had sex. Back then, she was still stick straight, with hips like a boy. Now she has the curves of a woman.

"Goddamn, Lo. You feel so fucking good."

She hums when I place open-mouthed kisses at her shoulder, sucking greedily at her powder scented flesh.

Coasting my hand down her torso, my fingers snake over the soft swell of her belly until I reach the promise land. I caress the insides of her thighs, enjoying the sounds of her raspy breaths. The anticipation builds as I toy with her, lightly brushing over her soft mound. Each time I make a pass, flicking the swollen bud, she tenses up and grips me like a vice.

I groan when her hands circle behind me and she grabs my ass. My balls begin to tighten in a telltale sign that I'm getting ready to unload. But before I do, I need to know what she wants from me. If we're on the same page.

My voice is thick, barely recognizable. "Am I coming inside? Or pulling out to mark what's mine?"

She surprises me when she flattens her chest down to the bed, exposing her back. My canvas.

"Mark me," she moans.

"Ah, fuck."

Hottest thing ever.

She's not only beautiful, but willing. Allowing me freedom to be dirty. Without condemnation. She likes it as much as I do.

Grabbing a fistful of hair, I yank with just enough force so she feels it, but not enough to injure. Her head tips back so I can see the tip of her freckled nose and her forehead. And then glance down to where our bodies are joined. Her heart-shaped ass fully exposed to me, begging me to spank it. To redden those creamy cheeks. But I'll save that for another time.

With my other hand, I grip her hip and increase the pace of my thrusts. Each time I do, those firm cheeks jiggle with the force of my momentum and I know I'm hitting her deep. She gasps and whimpers, and with each sound, I get closer and closer to losing myself.

The familiar tingling begins crawling up my spine, uncoiling like the rope on the anchor, as my body readies itself to let loose.

I pull my dick out in one quick motion, gripping my slick length and jerking it in long hard pulls. And then my head hangs back in ecstasy and I come all over her back.

Momentarily dazed, I let it all sink in as my breath begins to calm and my body recovers from the incredible high it just experienced. When my gaze floats to Logan's face, which is turned to the side against the bed, I notice her eyes are closed and her lips are drawn into a serene smile.

"God, you are so beautiful it hurts."

One of her eyes pops open, her forehead wrinkled. "Ha. I bet you say that to all your girls."

What the actual fuck?

I flop on my side to face her, cupping a cheek, still flushed from her orgasm. She may just be joking, but I want her to know the truth.

"There's only one woman I've ever called beautiful. She's the same one I fell for when I was just a boy. She's the only one I've ever loved."

Logan's lashes flutter, her lips part and I take the opportunity to plant a kiss on them. Gentle. Soft. Barely a breeze.

"I love you, Logan. I don't think I ever stopped."

CHAPTER 25

Logan

THIS IS dangerous being with Carver again this way.

I've never been a weak woman. I couldn't with three older brothers and a father who didn't want an emotional girl in the house. But the pain I felt when Carver broke my heart and left me to face the consequences of our love on my own was too much to bare. It took me years to overcome it. To stand on my own again without falling.

Since then, with the exception of the tears I cried the day I gave birth and relinquished the rights to my baby boy, I haven't wept or shown emotion over anything since. My heart became an empty vessel, left wounded and broken all over the hospital floor that day. I vowed never to get attached to another human being again. All they do is break your heart and abandon you.

Letting Carver back in is just so damn risky.

He's officially a pro basketball player in the NBA.

He's going to be traveling the country, making money, becoming famous.

How in the world will I be able to handle that?

Carver says he loves me. But how long will that last before he succumbs to the temptations of the road? To the female fans who will do anything to get in his bed?

I'm not a jealous person by nature, but I've read enough celebrity mags to know about the unfaithfulness of professional athletes. The women they keep at home must know what's going on while their boyfriend or spouse is on the road, right? Those women must either have really open minds or be completely clueless to their man's infidelities.

That's not me. I'm too independent to just pick up my life and travel with him wherever he goes. And I respect myself too much to turn a blind eye to the possibility that there will be women in his bed.

I can't and I won't.

So, I plan to end things with Carver today. After we meet with the lawyer and the adoption agency today and determine our next steps, that is. That way, we'll be able to find resolution from our past, and move on with our future – and hearts – intact.

It will hurt like hell, but at least we can move forward and not get trapped into holding onto something that we shouldn't.

I keep telling myself it's the only way.

After last night, when he told me he loved me, I knew I had to end things. I love him, too, but I couldn't return the sentiment. Instead, I made a sarcastic comment to lighten the mood.

"Oh, come on, Carver," I said, feeling the wet stickiness of his release on my back begin to turn cold. "You just love me because I let you defile me. And because I liked it."

A flash of disappointment appeared in his eyes, but quickly vanished as he got up to get me a towel. When he returned, he gently wiped the remnants from my body, making my heart clench so hard I thought it would hammer right through my ribs.

"You know that's not true," he said quietly. "I do love how dirty you let me be. But that's not the reason I love you."

And then he went on to list all the reasons he loved me, placing soft butterfly kisses all over my body, nibbling on my earlobes and various other sensitive spots, until it turned into another round of hot sex.

"Ahem. Don't let me interrupt your sexy daydream, but it's getting me hot over here," Ali cackles from the hallway as she enters the kitchen.

My head jerks up to find her standing on the other side of the kitchen counter, filling her coffee cup with her favorite coffee blend from the pot I made earlier this morning.

My high-pitched refute is obvious admission of guilt. But that doesn't stop me. "I was not daydreaming about sex..."

"Ha!" she exclaims giddily as if she's caught me with one hand in the cookie jar. "I didn't say you were dreaming about sex, but you just admitted to it! So, tell me, how pornographic was it? Give me all the details."

I roll my eyes and take another sip of my coffee that's already grown cold as she sits down in the chair next to me at the table.

"You're blushing, so I know you were thinking about Carver. Just admit it."

"No," I respond haughtily. "You can't make me. So there."

She tries to slap my tongue that I've stuck out at her but I quickly suck it back between my lips.

"Fine. Don't tell me. But where is your hot pro-baller this morning? I heard you come in early this morning all stealthy-like. As if I was going to bust you for breaking curfew. Carver's not here with you?"

Ali scans the room, like he might be hiding in the corner somewhere. I shake my head, remembering how I left him asleep in his comfy hotel bed as I tiptoed out the door at five a.m.

I tap an imaginary tune on the countertop with my fingers, looking anywhere but at her. I can feel her inquisitive gaze burning a hole in my head.

"Nah. He needed his rest."

"Mm-hm. I see..."

"Really? Just what exactly do you see? Are you clairvoyant now?"

"Well," she drawls. "The word on the street is that Mr. NBA draft had his agent work out a deal so he could play here in Seattle. Any guesses why it would be so important for him to live here?"

She lifts her cup to her lips, smirking as she does.

I shrug innocently. "How should I know? Maybe because he grew up here and it's his hometown?"

"*Riiiight.* You mean the hometown where the love of his life currently resides?"

I wave her off like she's full of shit. But it does make me wonder. I mean, what are the chances that Carver would get drafted and then immediately traded to Seattle? Although he never mentioned wanting to move back here, maybe the rumors are true.

Whatever. It doesn't matter. This is a big enough city for the both of us to live and not bump into each other. He'll be gone half the year, anyway. NBA seasons are long, I think. His travel schedule will be grueling and relentless, so there should be no concern over running into each other by accident.

I feign disinterest. "Whatever. Carver and I are not a long-term thing. So, don't go romanticizing the reasons he's playing for Seattle. Carver told me last night that the Clippers needed the other player, and the Pilots needed his talents and that's where he ended up. End of story."

"You are so oblivious, Logan. You were blind to Mr. Potato Head's interest and devotion, and now you're absolutely clueless when it comes to Carver. I saw how he looked at you last night. That boy is in *lurhv.*"

I cock an eyebrow at her.

She heaves a big dramatic sigh. "Like you were the tiered cake on the dessert buffet table and he was in desperate need of a sugar fix."

I spit out my coffee. "So, now I'm just something to satisfy his sweet tooth craving? Is that what you're saying?"

I don't know why I'm even debating this with Ali. She always wins arguments. Maybe that's why she's an aspiring writer, because she's really good at twisting words to ensure her perfect outcome.

"Girl, what I'm saying is that whatever you think this is with Carver, it's a whole helluva lot bigger for him."

"Ali," I admonish, glaring at her as if she is a petulant child. "You know nothing about Carver. He's not looking to settle down. He's a young, hot pro-athlete and he's ready to capitalize on that fame. He's not looking for a girlfriend experience. We're just having fun."

I wash out my coffee cup and place it in the dishrack to dry. All this talk about him makes me antsy. I don't know where he expects things to go from here. Sure, he thinks he loves me, but that's just residual feelings and emotions coming into play from opening up Pandora's Box. They'll soon pass and he'll move on.

We just need to get through this meeting with the attorney today and then I can part ways with Carver. We can both shut the door on the past and move forward in our respective lives with no hard feelings and no past regrets.

As I head back toward the bathroom to jump in the shower, there's a knock on the door.

Ali scurries over in her stocking feet, peering through the peephole before she wiggles like she has to pee.

"Ooh...looks like lover boy misses his sweetie already!"

She swings open the door, as Carver appears in the hallway, looking absolutely devastating in a charcoal gray suit and white collared shirt open at the neck. But the most beautiful thing he wears is the bright smile on his face. He also has with him a bag of Top Pot donuts in his hand.

Ali turns her head over her shoulder, staring wide-eyed at me, giggling at her inside secret. "Mm-hm. As I mentioned, Lo. Carver here has a hankering for the sweet stuff."

CHAPTER 26

CARVER

LOGAN SEEMED WEIRDLY DISTRACTED this morning when I stopped by her apartment with breakfast. Although she claimed she was just nervous about our meeting with the lawyer this afternoon, it felt like something else entirely.

I stayed only thirty minutes before I had to dash off to meet Crissy for my press conference with the Pilots. I had dressed up in a suit before stopping at Logan's and teased her a little for the way she gawked at me when I strode through her front door.

Not gonna lie. I know women have a thing for me in suits and I've gotten a lot of action when I've worn them in the past. But seeing the admiration in Logan's eyes this morning filled my chest with warmth and smugness. If I'd have had the time, I would've let her undress me and do wicked things to me. But alas, I didn't want to be late for my first official media session.

The press conference was a breeze. Nothing I hadn't dealt with in the past at ASU. This time, however, the questions weren't just about play, or the team, or even my physical abilities.

They pressed with questions about my contract and salary and whether I felt I was deserving of the weighty paycheck I'd been promised.

There were already some rather pointed questions – all thankfully diverted by Crissy and my publicist – about my personal life. One day into my pro-career, and someone has already captured a video of Logan and I making out in the back corner of the bar last night, as well as pictures of me carrying her out the door over my shoulder.

I have nothing to be ashamed of over my burgeoning relationship with Logan. She's not some chick I just happened to pick up and bang for a night; and she's not a gold-digging skank who's out to get notoriety and a pay day. We have shared history together, and hopefully a future.

My concern, though over those photos and video, is that they'll end up plastered all over the internet, infringing on Logan's privacy. She didn't sign up for this crazy, media-frenzied life.

The minute our press meeting ended, I asked Crissy and the publicist to get those images removed before they ended up splashed all over the headlines. It didn't matter that I was exposed, but I'm one hundred percent certain Logan wouldn't want the attention.

With all those items checked off my list, I return to Logan's apartment around three to pick her up for our four o'clock appointment with the attorney. I'm waiting for her outside her building. She texted me fifteen minutes ago to say she's running a bit behind because of a patient. I laughed out loud, because that's so typical of her.

While I wait, I decide to text my dad to tell him what's going on. He and my mom stopped by the party last night, but we didn't get a chance to talk much. I figured since he put me in touch with the attorney, I should update him on our progress.

Me: Hey dad. Just want you to know that Logan and I meet

today with the attorney and the Ashfords. The couple who adopted our son.

I see the three dots pop up immediately.

Dad: That's good to hear. How do you think it'll go? Do you think you'll be able to walk away if they deny your request?

Well, fuck. I hadn't thought that far in advance. Maybe I've been living in a dream world, imagining only a happy ending where the adoptive parents introduce us to their son and we get to know him. I didn't even consider that they might be fearful of this reunion and not want to give us this chance.

Me: Well, thanks for putting a damper on this for me.

Dad: Just being realistic, son. You have to be prepared if it doesn't go smoothly. I want the best for you.

Me: Sure. I know.

And I do. After I returned to Phoenix and before returning to Seattle for the draft, my dad and I spent an hour on the phone talking about everything that had gone down during my visit. My mom was finally coming to terms with the situation and had forgiven my father for keeping her in the dark so long. And I was willing to concede that my father had only done what he felt was best for everyone involved, even though it still pissed me off the way he went about it.

But all of that was now water under the bridge. Today was the reckoning day. At the very least, we'd get to meet our son's parents and maybe even have a chance to see pictures of him.

God, how many times have I wondered what he looked like? Whether he had my skin tone? Logan's cute nose? My eye color? If he would grow up to be tall and play sports like me?

I jump when there's a knock on my car window. Logan's wearing a strange look.

I roll down my window and smile.

"You look lost in thought."

"I was. Sorry, you startled me."

I reach over the center console and open the door for her to slide in. I don't move, crowding in her personal space. Her eyes pop open in surprise as I place a brief kiss on her cheek, her hair flowing over her shoulder, providing me a whiff of her shampoo.

I want to bury myself in her neck and not come back up for air.

"How was your day, babe?"

"Good."

"You look beautiful."

"Carver." I hear the disapproval in her tone and I shrug.

"What? I'm just stating a fact."

My need to touch her is overwhelming, so I reach for her hand, entwining my fingers with hers. She seems to relax infinitesimally when I give her a reassuring squeeze.

"There's nothing to be nervous about."

Not exactly true, but I can tell she needs to know things will be okay. Even if it doesn't go as planned, things between us shouldn't change. We're good.

"I know. It's not that."

My ears perk up, curious as to what could be troubling her if it's not our upcoming meeting.

"What is it, then?"

Nothing like Logan's bluntness. "You."

"Um, okay. Care to elaborate? You make it seem like I'm a problem. And there were no problems last night when I made you come three times."

I know she's staring at me so I wiggle my eyebrows suggestively. I'd heard no complaints from her last night. There's no doubt she left my hotel this morning one satisfied woman. So, I'm confused what happened between now and then.

Through my sidelong glance, I get a peek at her blush, creeping up her neck to her rosy cheeks.

She scoffs and tries pulling her hand free from mine, but I don't let go. She's stuck until she comes clean.

Sighing heavily, Logan drops her chin to her chest. "This isn't going to work between us."

I practically swerve into oncoming traffic. "What the fuck? What do you mean, Lo? I just moved up here for..." I stop before I can blurt out the real reason I'm playing for Seattle. She doesn't need to know that I came here specifically for her.

Swallowing my bitterness and confusion, I continue with a softer tone this time. "We've just reconnected and spent a fan-fucking-tastic night together. What part of this" – I point to the space between us – "isn't going to work?"

She stares out the passenger window, lost in thought until she speaks.

"There's too much history between us. And after today – I know it's going to be even more difficult. Meeting the Ashfords and learning about our child's life is going to destroy me."

I want to stop her before she says more. I pull her hand to my lips and kiss her palm.

"Logan, I'll be here with you. I won't let it destroy you."

She shakes her head. "You don't understand what it was like to have to give him up. To let him go. You were long gone and I was left to suffer with this shame that nearly wrecked me. All of that will be ripped wide open again today."

Logan hides her sniffles, but I know she's close to tears. It's gut-wrenching to hear the pain of her loss. I felt it too, but as she says, not nearly as acutely and intensely as she did.

I pull into the underground parking lot of the large Seattle skyscraper and find a space. The minute I turn off the engine, the silence engulfs us, highlighting the distance she's created with her words. I can't let it become emotional. I need her to share her baggage with me so I can make it right. Once and for all.

I shift toward her in my seat, wrapping my hand behind her head and forcing her to look at me.

"Logan, all I can say is that I'm so sorry the way things turned out. Please believe me that if I'd have had a choice, I would have been right by your side the entire way. I could have deferred school until you had the baby. You wouldn't have been alone."

A sob escapes her chest as I lay my palm across her cheek, lightly stroking her jaw with my thumb.

"I know it's impossible to undo the past. So here we are, at this fork in the road. We can either go upstairs, meet the parents of our son and see where things go from there. Or, we can just walk away and never look back. It's up to you, babe. You choose."

I stare into her reddened eyes, her lashes wet from the unshed tears, and know in that instant that I would do anything for this girl. I'd lay down my life for her. Give her the moon and the stars if she wants them.

I just can't give her back the past.

Her eyes close in anguish, but when they open again, they stare at me with resolve.

"I have to do this, Carver. We need to know. I won't be able to live another minute without knowing he's okay. And if that's all there is, and they don't allow us access into his life, then that's that. I won't push it. It'll have to be enough."

My smile is wan and tight, but it's there for her. I'm here for her.

"Okay then. Let's do this. Whatever you need, I'll be here for you. For as long as you want."

I just hope she'll want me by her side forever. Because that's where I want to be.

CHAPTER 27

Logan

My hands shake as we walk into the foyer of the attorney's office. The room is decorated in a modern style and is framed in windows overlooking the Puget Sound and the Olympic Mountains. It's warm and welcoming, even though I don't feel particularly warm as we wait.

My body trembles with nerves. With fear. Anticipation that this meeting could go horribly wrong and we never get the chance to meet our son.

"Mr. Edwards. Miss Shaw. Don will see you now."

Don Simmons is the lawyer that Carver's dad worked with to draw up the legal adoption paperwork four years ago. He specializes in domestic and international adoptions. I never met him in person back then. Carver Sr. was the one who handled everything and hand delivered the documents to my hospital room for me to sign.

As we follow the young secretary down the hallway and into a conference room, she inquires politely of our refreshment needs.

"Please take a seat anywhere. May I get either of you anything to drink? I have coffee, teas, water, soda."

Carver looks to me and I nod. "Just water is fine."

"For me, as well. Thank you."

Carver pulls out a leather conference table chair for me to take a seat and I do, crossing my feet at the ankles and folding my hands on the table in front of me. He takes a chair next to me and covers my knuckles with his large palm. The warmth envelopes my icy-cold fingers.

"God, maybe you should get some hot tea. You're freezing."

"I'll be fine."

The lady returns with our waters and shuffles out just as fast. The door remains open and we hear some quiet murmurs from down the hallway. Glancing behind me, I see a man in a dark suit, with salt and pepper hair who's probably in his early sixties. He's followed by a younger couple, maybe in their early thirties. The Ashfords.

My breath stalls and I forget how to breathe. All the air is trapped in my lungs, fighting to get out. Only when Carver's arm finds its way around my shoulders do I release the breath that I've been holding onto.

I can't stand up because my legs will give out. I think Carver knows this, so he stands for both of us and introduces all of us to everyone as they find their seats across the table. Don takes the head seat.

The Ashford's – Jared and Karina – are soft spoken, polite and mild-mannered people. Dressed casually and comfortably, not overdressed or underdressed, representing a hard-working couple. Through introductions, we learn that Jared is a store manager with a large pet care retail chain and she is an accountant, who works from home so she can stay at home to raise their son.

Their son. My son. *Our* son.

His name is Jeremy. Jeremy Foster Ashford.

Foster after Karina's maiden family name.

I reach for the box of tissue and dab my eyes. It's almost too much, but I know there's more to come.

Don directs our conversation with professional courtesy and efficiency.

"Mr. and Mrs. Ashford...Mr. Edwards. Miss Shaw. As you know, the adoption contract and agreement you entered into four years ago states that it is an open adoption and was handled privately through the third-party agency, Whole Family, Inc. Regardless, there are certain laws specifically enacted to protect the rights of all parties involved, but first and foremost, the rights of the adoptee, Jeremy. All decisions made then, and now, must account for the well-being and best interests of the child."

He clears his throat and I take the opportunity to wipe my clammy hands against my lightweight pant leg.

"This adoption was contracted with a form of openness – an open adoption clause – that allows for certain liberties, if you will, of establishing open communication between the adoptive and birth parents. As we are engaged in together today."

My eyes flicker over to Karina, who happens to be staring right at me. Her light-brown hair is pulled back in a low ponytail, exposing her long neck and tiny-diamond studded ears. Our gazes collide and her lips form a soft, sympathetic smile. I return it with my own, a little tremble vibrating over my lips.

Don continues discussing the legalese and finally stops to take a breath before opening it up with a question.

"Mr. Edwards and Miss Shaw. Since the two of you called this meeting, what would you like to accomplish today? Let's get that out on the table so we can begin to determine next steps and come to some consensus or compromise, if possible."

I turn to Carver who takes a deep breath and then speaks, directing his response to the couple in front of us.

"We – Logan and I – have recently, um, reunited. And together, we've concluded that it's important for both of us to know a little bit about our son – um, I mean, the boy we gave birth to...or um, well, that Logan gave birth to."

The way Carver stumbles over his words is enough to break the tension amongst everyone and quiet laughter filters through the room. I reach for his hand and squeeze him tight – letting him know he's doing great.

"Sorry," he apologizes. "I'm nervous. Anyway, we'd like to find out how he is. Learn a little about him. Maybe see some pictures. And if all goes well, maybe at some point be able to write him letters or maybe even meet him personally, if you'd let us."

He lowers his eyes to the table as if embarrassed by his desire to meet his son. I glance back across the table to see how Jared and Karina respond to his question. They both nod at each other and Karina bends down to the floor next to her chair. I can't see what she's doing, but my guess is she is reaching for her purse by her side.

Jared speaks on her behalf, "We thought this day might come. And although it's something that Karina and I are extremely nervous about because we only want to protect our son – we also know that at some point in Jeremy's life, he'll want to know about his birth parents. We would never prevent him from finding out about the people that gave him life. Who loved him enough to give him up so that we could raise and love him as our own."

I can't help the loud sob that bursts from my chest. I've tried so hard to keep my tears at bay, but I can't any longer. They flood my eyes and burn a path down my cheeks. Carver pulls a wad of tissue from the box and begins dabbing at my face, practically poking my eyes out. I laugh through the tears and push him away.

"I'm good. I'm sorry." I raise my hand to wave him away.

Hearing Jared mention Jeremy's life and the hopeful love that exists within this couple makes me so very grateful to them. They seem so loving toward their son.

Karina leans over the table, pushing an unsealed envelope in our direction.

"These are for you. We want you to have them. They are pictures of Jeremy at various ages over the last five years. Up to his kindergarten graduation last month."

Carver accepts the envelope and pulls out the contents. Inside are over twenty photos of our son. Bald and naked in the sink being given his firth bath; the roly-poly chubbiness of a six-month-old Michelin baby; his first birthday party where his hands, face and hair are covered in vanilla frosting; his first haircut – blonde tuffs of curls scattered on the floor around him; a snaggle-toothed grin of a toddler with his first tooth; on a swing at a park.

Every single picture displays a beautiful boy smiling a broad, happy grin. His sandy blonde hair at different lengths through the years, with a cute wavy cowlick. The spitting image of Carver.

Carver's mini-me.

Had I never given him up, I would have spent every day with a smaller version of Carver.

Carver's voice is shaky and full of emotion. "Does Jeremy play sports yet?"

It's sweet that he wants to know if his son will follow in his footsteps.

Jared laughs a booming sound. "Well, Jeremy tried T-ball last summer for the first time, but wasn't too into it. He does like riding his scooter and kicking a soccer ball around, so we've signed him up for a soccer team this fall."

Jared's eyes move between Carver's and mine, a smile forming on his face. "And of course, we'll give basketball a try when he gets a little older. At five, his hand-eye-coordination isn't quite there yet."

Jared's comment means that he knows who Carver is. That

he's a basketball player. I check with Carver to see how he feels about this, and the smile tells me it means a lot to him.

Carver nods. "Yeah, I don't think I started to get the hang of dribbling and running until I was in third grade."

Karina clears her throat, sharing a brief look with her husband before turning back to Carver. "We thought…maybe… perhaps someday you might want to play some one-on-one with him. Teach him some skills."

"Wow. Yeah, I'd like that. A lot."

Everything from here is exactly what I'd hoped would happen. They continued to regale stories about Jeremy, sharing with us about the boy he is – how smart and sweet. It makes my heart swell to the size of a boulder and frees my soul from the burden of knowing whether I did the right thing all those years ago.

Jeremy Foster Ashford is in good hands and was blessed with wonderful adoptive parents.

And the shackles of shame and despair that had bound my life for so very long are finally broken, as I walk out of our first meeting a free woman.

CHAPTER 28

CARVER

IT's easy to see that Logan and I are in different places right now. She seems to have retreated into herself after our meeting the other day and hasn't answered my phone calls or texts.

I thought this would bring us closer together. But instead, I've had to give her space. Again. It's hard as fuck to do, but I'm not about to force myself into her life if she doesn't want it. So, I bide my time, spending the last few days in search of an apartment and getting back into my regular workout routines in preparation for training camp.

I understand that Logan has legitimate concerns about dating a professional athlete, but I would never let her down. Logan's just scared to give it a try. To put herself out there after everything she's had to deal with.

I've leased a nice loft apartment in Bell Town, just a short distance from Logan's place, that will work fine for me for the next year. I don't need a lot of space and don't have much, anyhow. Some furniture that I ordered won't be in for another week, so right now the only things I have are a king size mattress and box spring, a chair from a local furniture store, a flat screen TV and some framed photos.

One of those picture frames hold the side-by-side baby pictures of my son and me.

I'd gone over to my parents' house yesterday for dinner and brought with me the pictures of Jeremy. As expected, my mother cried when she saw them and promptly brought out my baby album. And fuck me – the resemblance between Jeremy and me was mind blowing. I couldn't believe how similar we looked as babies. It made me so happy I nearly cried.

So now I have them in a dark photo frame with our pictures side-by-side.

I'm staring at the photos now as my phone blows up with texts and calls. Grabbing it from the kitchen counter where I left it, I notice a series of texts from Crissy, and then others from the new publicist, Meredith.

Crissy: Got issue. Need you to call me. Or Mer. I think you have her number.

Meredith: Carver, please contact me ASAP. PR issue. <<<<URGENT>>>>

I can't possibly imagine what the hell this is about. I've done nothing to cause a stir in the media since the draft was announced. Where many other players go out and have a field day, cavorting and partying like fucking rock stars, I've laid low. Kept to myself. Dealt with some pretty life-changing shit. Not what I would've done a year ago.

But this thing with Logan and Jeremy has changed me. I'm seeing things – my life – differently now. What my life could be in the future, with the right woman. With a family. With Logan.

I hit the number from my Contacts list and the phone rings. I call Crissy first since I know him better than my new publicist.

He answers on the first ring.

"Carver. We need to pow-wow."

"Uh, okay. What's going on? Did I get dropped already?"

He snorts and I hear him opening and closing his car door and starting his engine. "No, that would be easier to remedy. Have you read anything online today? Any news reports? Gossip blogs?"

I shake my head. "Nah. Been busy. What's up, bro?"

"You have a kid?"

The question feels like a bomb just exploded in my ear.

"Excuse me? What the fuck kind of question is that?"

"It's a fair question. If it's just salacious gossip, then we need to decide how to respond to. But I first have to know...do you or do you not have a child?"

"*How*...I mean, nobody knows about this. It's a private matter. No one else knows."

My ears ring and a hundred things run through my head. First and foremost is Jeremy and Logan's privacy.

"Just answer the goddamn question, Carver." The biting force of his reply is unsettling.

This can't be good. Oh shit. Logan. Karina and Jared. Jeremy's privacy is going to be compromised.

Fuckity, fuck, fuck, fuck.

"Shit, Cris. We've got to stop this. You've got to take care of this right the fuck now. My son's life and privacy are at stake."

Crissy heaves a long breath over the line. "Start from the beginning...no wait, let me get Mer on the line and then you talk. We'll get it handled from there."

LOGAN

The banging on my front door is loud enough to wake the dead. Which was how I was sleeping until a few moments ago.

Prying my eyes open, I try to focus on the digital numbers on the iHome docking station next to my bed. It's eight-fifteen a.m. on Saturday morning. I throw the covers off my bed, grab the light-weight robe off my chair and throw it on as I walk out to the front room.

Ali's door is open and but she's not in there, so maybe she left early for a jog or something and forgot her keys.

I snort in laughter at the silly thought. She never runs. And no way in hell would she be up this early on a Saturday morning. I don't even think she made it home last night because her shoes aren't in their normal spot – in the middle of the hallway where she usually leaves them.

I place my eye in the peep hole and suck in a sharp breath. Didn't I tell him it was over? What is he doing here?

Instead of opening the door, I talk through the barrier.

"What do you want, Carver? I was sleeping. And I'm grumpy when I'm tired. So why don't you go away."

I peer through the hole again and see him running a hand through his disheveled hair, head down, eyes averted with a grimace on his face.

"Sorry, Lo. No can do. We need to talk like right now. Please let me in. And I know you're grumpy in the mornings before your coffee."

He lifts his head and his sexy smirk knocks me back a few feet.

Grumbling about his appearance and the rude awakening, I unlock the door and let it swing open, turning to walk back down the hallway to the kitchen. I know he'll follow me in.

Without glancing back, I hear the door slam shut and I feel the weight of his eyes on my back. I begin the chore of making my coffee before I finally acknowledge him.

"What's so important that you couldn't wait until a decent hour to come bursting into my home?"

"We've been outed. Or at least, Jeremy has."

The coffee cup I'm holding in my hand goes crashing to the floor, shattering and sending large ceramic pieces scattering around my feet.

My eyes are wide in alarm. "What? How?"

I lean my weight against the counter and rub my eyes with the heel of my palm. "Oh, God," I whisper, more as a plea than anything.

Carver bends down and begins cleaning up the mess, and then stands, looking around for a garbage. I point under the sink, where he disposes the broken pieces and returns to stand in front of me. Placing large hands on my shoulders, he squeezes gently.

"I don't know. But once word got out about the adoption, the leak spread and research was done. *Fast.* And most of it is scarily accurate. I always thought those fucking magazines were trash." He yanks at his hair in frustration.

My knees give out and I reach behind me to grab the edge of the counter to keep myself from falling.

"Shit. Have you contacted..." I don't finish, as Carver interjects.

"Yes. I called Don's office and called Jared. My publicist is handling things from here."

Thankfully, when we parted company the other day, Jared and Karina had been amenable to exchanging numbers. They'd promised to send us regular updates and photos of Jeremy. Carver had also promised they would receive tickets to one of his upcoming home games so they could bring Jeremy to watch him play.

"It's not good, Lo. I'm so, so sorry. I never thought this would get out."

For some reason, I direct my anger at Carver. Logically, I know he's not to blame for the situation, but it's his newfound celebrity status that prompted any interest in his life to begin with.

I fear the ramifications – not for us, but for our son. He's still too young to understand any of this. Jared and Karina shouldn't have to be forced to divulge anything about his adoption this soon. He's so young. My heart breaks all over again.

Instead of the broken cup on the floor, it feels more like the pieces of my own shattered heart.

I push against Carver's chest. Hard. My balled fists begin beating on his pecs, damning him with every word that comes out of my mouth.

"It's all your fault! I hate you."

My voice breaks and sputters with emotion, "Damn you, Carver. Damn you for moving here. Damn you for being drafted. Damn you for getting me pregnant in the first place. Damn you for entering my life again. Just get out! Get out of my life for good!"

His tone is soft and apologetic. Nakedly hurt. He clasps his hands around my wrists and holds me steady, the brown-warmth of his eyes filled with anguish.

"I know, Lo. I'm sorry. It is my fault. Maybe we should've left well enough alone."

He drops my hands and steps away, leaving a foot of space between us. It might as well be a mile, with no bridge sturdy or long enough to cover the distance and repair the damage that's been done.

His eyes linger on my face, his mouth in a tight line, jaw clenched hard. I watch as indecision turns to resolve and he slowly backs out of my kitchen.

I should move. Run to him and tell him I didn't mean any of it. That it's not his fault. That I do still love him. That I don't want him to leave me.

But my feet remain firmly planted and I'm unable to make myself any more vulnerable than I already am. Just as he opens the door, he turns back to stare at me, his expression unreadable.

"I'm truly sorry, Lo," he whispers a broken apology, his forehead pressed against the doorframe. "But I don't regret my time with you. I only regret that it's ended like this. I'll love you forever, Logan. I'll never stop."

And then he's gone and I fall to the floor in a broken, shattered heap.

CHAPTER 29

CARVER

"You want a brat or a burger?"

Lance is the grill master today, flipping meat between swigs of beer over the last hour. I'm hosting my first party at my new loft apartment. Just a few of my friends to celebrate the summer before I head off to training camp.

It's an unusually warm and sunny July Fourth in Seattle. The rain and gloom of June has moved off to make way for the summer sun. I just wish the same could be said for me. The gloom has lingered since the moment I left Logan's apartment two weeks ago.

The sting of metal against my bare leg has me jerking up from my lounger on my deck overlooking the Sound. "Ow. Fuck dude, what'd you do that for?"

Lance stands over me with a perturbed stare, the offending grill flipper in his hand. "Bro, I asked you a question. Your fucking head is stuck somewhere up in the top of the Space Needle. Come back down earth."

"Oh, uh. Brat's good. Thanks."

Lance has been staying at my place for the last few days and we've done all the touristy things around town. Last night we went to Cal's and hung out, played pool, discussed basketball and the likely standings for the upcoming season. Just like old times, except it's not.

Touring the city just reminded me of Logan. I couldn't even walk by the Great Wheel without flashes of us up there together.

I didn't want to go to Cal's, either, because that would remind me of running into Logan again – although I'd hoped she would be there. She wasn't. Her friend, Ali, was though. It was her idea that I hold a BBQ this weekend.

Which meant that Lance invited enough women to start at a whole new cheer squad for the Pilots. A few have already propossitioned me, making very compelling offers. But I've declined. Uninterested and unaffected.

I'm so fucked.

A loud, angsty, guitar riff by the band *Royal Blood* blares through my speaker system and the sounds of people singing and having a good time can be heard wafting from the living room. I notice my beer is empty and I get up to grab another one from the kitchen.

"Yo, grab me one, too, man," Lance says, handing me his empty bottle.

I step inside my new apartment and come face-to-face with Alison, Logan's roommate. She gives a little wave and I stand there hopeful. I not so subtly lean to the side to peer behind her, in the event Logan is hiding in plain sight.

Ali laughs. "She's coming. Just bringing up some drinks from the car."

She gives me a brief kiss on the cheek and then whispers into my ear, "Logan doesn't know this is your place. So, be chill, okay? And nice shirt, by the way. Keeping it classy, Edwards." She gives me a two-gun salute with her thumbs.

My stomach gurgles with nervous energy as I glance down at the decal on my rumpled t-shirt. It's one of my favorites. It's a picture of a roll of toothpaste being squeezed over a toothbrush. The caption says, "*Everyone needs fresh breath. Now put me in your mouth.*"

"What can I say? Oral health is very important."

Ali waves me off and heads into the kitchen to grab a drink. That's where I should be heading, but instead, I work my way toward the front door, which is slightly ajar to allow people to come and go. I hear Lance in the background yelling after me, knowing he's not going to get a beer from me.

"Asshole." I hear him gripe in the background.

My breath catches in my lungs when I step into the hallway and see Logan heading my way. She doesn't notice me because her head is down as she adjusts the bag in her arms. It gives me a moment to take in her beauty.

Her hair is pulled back in a high ponytail, but the sides are braided around the crown of her head. No make-up from what I can tell, but her long lashes are darkened with some sort of eyeliner or mascara. She's wearing a tank top and a pair of shorts, and flip-flops on her feet that remind me of our summers by the lake.

By the time she's an arm length away, I reach out and remove the bag from her hands as she startles in surprise.

"Hi," I say, cracking a small smile.

For just a second, I think she might turn and run in the other direction. It's obvious she's mulling it over, but then answers my greeting.

"Hey," she responds, giving me a small—but none-the-less beautiful smile—before looking around the room for Ali. "I didn't realize…um. Ali didn't tell me whose party this is."

She glances around nervously as we enter my apartment, the noise drowning out anything else she was about to say.

We move into the kitchen and I place the bag on the already

full countertop. Pulling two beers out of the ice chest, I pop off the caps and hand her one. Then I raise a finger as a signal for her to wait.

"Just a second. Don't move. I need to run this out to Lance."

While I'm risking it by leaving her on her own with the chance she might leave, the grin that forms on her mouth is a good indication I'll find her here when I return. Sprinting out the slider, I throw the bottle at a surprised Lance and run back into the kitchen before he can even say thanks.

Logan's already talking to someone; a guy. But I can't have that. Although I'd deny it if anyone ever asks, I cut in abruptly and protectively, snaking my hands around her waist and pulling her to my side.

"Excuse me, but she's with me," I snarl, the guy giving me a double take before lifting his shoulder, as I pull her down the hallway toward my bedroom. She lets out a little yipe of protest. I count my blessings she doesn't kick and scream as if it were some sort of abduction.

I take my chances in hopes she'll give me the chance to listen to me.

Shutting the door behind us, I snap the lock and turn to face her. Her expression is unreadable as we stare at each other like it's a face-off. I'm not sure anymore what's going on in her mind, but I'm wondering if it would be considered kidnapping if I kept her in this room with me for the next ten years.

The air gets sucked out of my lungs when she looks around and then smiles.

"Nice place you got here."

I try to see my bedroom through her eyes. It's pretty sparsely decorated, but I put some money into the furnishings.

"Thanks. I'm not the most skilled decorator."

She nods and then takes a seat at the corner of the bed, covered in a basic gray comforter. I remain standing, uncertain as to whether I should move or not. I decide the best tactic is to let her have her space.

"I've been wanting to talk to you, but I didn't know what to say. Things got ugly."

I lean back against the door and cross one foot over an ankle, crossing my arms in front of my chest and nod.

"Yeah, they did."

Logan drops her head down to her hands, her elbows on her knees. She takes a big breath and exhales slowly.

"Carver, I've missed you," she says softly, her eyes shifting to mine. "I said a lot of hurtful things to you – things I didn't mean, but at the time just came out because I was just so angry at the situation. At how the news so callously got reported about Jeremy, without a thought to his privacy. I took it out on you and I'm very sorry."

Those words mean more to me than anything I've ever heard in my life. I take this as my cue to continue our conversation and I sit down next to her on the bed. The six inches of distance feels more like a thousand miles and all I long to do is wrap her in my arms and hold her on my lap.

Her scent surrounds me, engulfing me in awareness that we're locked in my bedroom together, while the party continues to rage outside my door. Even in her remorse, she's so beautiful.

"Logan," I whisper as I place my hand behind her back, caressing her softly. "There's nothing to forgive. And I've missed you, too. So fucking much. Nothing seemed right without you. I kept hoping this would blow over and you'd come back to me. I was waiting for you to come back, baby."

She drops her hands from her knees and sits upright, as I cover her cheeks with my palms, staring down into the face that takes my breath away every single time I look at it. The face I know I want to see every day for the rest of my life.

The kiss we share as our lips touch is one full of promise. It's a reminder that we can exhale the regrets of our past and inhale the beauty of our future together.

The pain we experienced – the things we lost, yet also found together – is buried within the touch between us. It'll always be there but will be overcome by the joy that pours out of the love we share because we're in this life together.

It's an extension of our sweet summers of love – the endless moments that took our breath away. The moments that shaped who we are individually and who we became together.

And from the bottom of my heart, I know that someday we will be able to share those memories with our son.

Logan pulls back, leaving room for her question. "Where do we go from here?"

I scoot closer, closing the gap between us, twisting at my waist so I can lock my hands around her hips, lifting her off the bed and onto my lap. She straddles my legs and places her hands on top of my shoulders.

Her long blonde hair is loose and wavy, cascading down her back as I thread my fingers through the strands, holding onto her like she's my anchor.

"Wherever you want us to go. I'm yours, Lo. Yesterday, today, tomorrow and always."

She smiles and throws her arms around my neck, wiggling over my now very eager cock.

"Well," she whispers into my ear, pushing me down onto my back against my new comforter. "I know one place where we could start."

EPILOGUE

WHEN YOUR BOYFRIEND IS ONE OF THE HOTTEST NBA ROOKIES, you get your fair share of evil glances and stink eyes from his female fans.

But you also get treated like a rock star, with your choice of hanging with the other WAGs in the team suite or sitting in center court seats to watch your man play.

Tonight, there was no question of where I'd be viewing the game. Sitting next to me is Jared and Karina, and on my lap a wiggling, squirming, overly-sugared and excitable five-year-old.

My heart swells to epic proportions as he turns his head to look up at me, smiling as he points and says in his cute little boy voice, "Dat my fren, Cava."

Jeremy can't pronounce his R's yet and everything he says is just pure cuteness.

I nod my head and point at Carver out on the court, who has his left hand in the air, calling out a play to his teammates as he dribbles the ball down toward the basket.

"Yep, it sure is. Now watch what Carver's doing, Jeremy. He might either pass the ball to one of the other players or he might post up and take a shot."

Jeremy turns his attention back to the game, his sticky hand reaching in once again to the popcorn bucket on our laps and shoving his face full of buttery goodness. We both watch Carver intently, excited to see him play. I've learned a lot about basketball over the last six months, more than I ever thought I would.

I've also learned a lot about how active and rambunctious little boys this age can be.

It turns out, the media fiasco that occurred earlier in the summer ended up being a blessing in disguise. While it didn't happen the way any of us wanted, especially for Karina and Jared, it did force our hands in making a decision on how we'd play a part in Jeremy's life. With it being unveiled to the general public, it didn't make sense to hide us from Jeremy any longer.

It also proved rather advantageous to Carver in his paid sponsorships, who is now a national spokesperson for a new condom brand – reminding the sexually active youth to always use backup protection, because you just never know when one of those buggars will slip by and score a shot.

But in all seriousness, Carver was also asked to be a spokesperson for the International Adoption Association, shedding light on the reasons adoption is a blessing for families around the world. It's one of his most rewarding roles.

I thought being in a relationship with a young, hot superstar athlete would be difficult. And honestly, there are times it's a drag – especially when he's out on the road for days at a time. But he always makes it up to me when he returns home. In multiple ways.

Carver and I don't live together. Not yet, at least. And he hasn't popped the question, yet, either. Although I did hear rumors that he'd been ring shopping downtown. The thought of us getting engaged and then married fills me with so much hope and love I could just burst.

But until then, I still live on my own. Mostly because I don't like being alone at his loft when he's on the road for away games.

When he is in town, we spend most of our time together, but I like having my own space and spending time with Ali and my friends. All of them adore Carver – and who wouldn't? He's the biggest flirt and charmer there is.

Once the news got out that I was Carver's girlfriend – and that we shared a past that would forever bind us together – it got a smidge uncomfortable at work between Jeff and me. But things soon smoothed over when he began dating this lovely South African woman whom he met at a symphony gala this fall. It makes me happy that he's happy, because he deserves it.

My brother, Leo, the youngest of my brothers, reached out to me recently. He'd heard that I was dating Carver and asked if he could come down and meet him. He said he felt bad for the way I was treated by the family and the way Dad kicked me out. He said he didn't have the courage at the time to stand up to Dad, but he wasn't scared any longer and he wanted to make amends.

I'm still mulling that over. There's still a lot of pain that resides in my heart over how my brothers and father treated me. The way they turned their backs on me when I needed them most. Carver hasn't pushed me to reconcile but considering how well things mended between him and his parents, it does offer me hope that someday my family can be whole again, too.

Until then, I love my life. It's not easy. There are times, like now, when I hold my young son in my arms and wonder what would have happened if I hadn't given him up when I did. What would our lives be like now had none of that happened the way it did?

I shake off the thought as Jeremy wiggles off my lap and hops up and down in the stands as Carver leaps into the air and makes a slam dunk, sending the crowd roaring in excitement, all chanting his name.

It's surreal to watch my man play in front of thousands and to see his mini-me try to be just like him. Jeremy is so precious, with so much energy, and has so much of Carver in him that it fills me with an unbelievable amount of love and pride.

Jeremy is mine – he was born from my body and out of love for his father. Yet, he'll never be my son. He's a part of us and will always have my heart. It made me sad for a long time and it's taken a lot of self-reflection for me to come to terms with that.

And I'm finally okay now with the choice I made at the time to give Jeremy up for adoption. I've had to learn to pivot. To go where that decision took me. And how ironic that when I finally let go, it brought me right back here.

And until the day Carver and I get married and expand our family, I'm so thankful for the life we already brought into the world. Together.

THE END

MORE FROM THE COURTING LOVE SERIES

DID YOU ENJOY LOGAN AND CARVER'S SECOND CHANCE ROMANCE? Your recommendation is the highest compliment I could receive. Please feel free to share your feedback by posting a review.

And, keep reading on in the **Courting Love Series**. All the players will make appearances in all of the remaining books in the series.

Courting Love (A College Sports Series)
Read about them all here:
Full Court Press
The Rebound
Pivot
Fast Break
Jump Shot

And, there's more!

You can find out what's happening with Carver and Logan five years later when they pop up in a new spin-off series coming in the fall of 2021. **The Girlfriend Game** is a brand new sports romance coming soon.

Excerpt from *The Girlfriend Game*
Releasing September 2021

PROLOGUE

"Zeke? Can you hear me? Open your eyes, man. Open your goddamn eyes."

I can hear the panicked words spoken from my teammate, Carver Edwards, who kneels over me, the bright lights of the arena shining so bright that I keep my eyes closed and the world dark. I hear his voice and understand the words, but I can't respond. They sound like it's coming from the far end of a mile-long train tunnel. They're muted and overlapping with the blare of train whistles whooshing through my ears.

The silence of the crowd, mixed with the hushed whispers of my teammates, creates an even louder presence inside my head, competing with the massive cacophony of noise that's deafeningly loud, drowning out all thought and ability to speak.

Carver shakes my shoulders, my body jerking with the motion, and my eyes pop open on their own accord. Carver sags with relief as Marek Talbert, the team's GM and Coach Green run to my side, all shouting questions at me all at once. I stare up at them, gripped with paralyzing and uncontrollable fear, restraining and imprisoning my mind and body. I'm unable to move or respond. I open my mouth, but nothing comes out. I try to move my arms, my head, my legs. Nothing.

I blink and blink again, trapped in a world turning hazy as I quickly lose focus. I don't know what's happening to me. All I know is it can't be good.

"Zeke. Are you okay? Talk to us. Tell us what's going on."

Marek asks me the question and the muddled words get lodged in the back of my throat. I feel my eyes rolling inside my head and then everything goes black.

And I don't remember a thing after that.

When I wake up in a hospital sometime later, I'm surrounded by beeping machines and a medical staff of people in and out of my room, checking my vitals, poking, and prodding and asking me questions I don't have answers for. All I want is for them to tell me what the fuck is wrong with me.

"You're awake," comes a soft voice from the right of my bed. I slowly turn my head against the pillow, which reeks of the harsh concoction of bleach and Lysol, to peer at a nurse at my side. "Hi Zeke. I'm Carla, the nurse on duty. You're safe now and we've given you a sedative, so you're probably feeling groggy. That's normal. But the doctor wanted me to tell you he'll be in on his next rounds to speak with you."

My mouth feels gritty, and I lick around my lips, the arid texture like sandpaper against my parched tongue.

Nurse Carla seems to anticipate my needs and hands me a tiny cup and straw. "Here you go. I'll move your bed up so you can take a few sips."

The motion of the bed has my head spinning and my eyes rolling back. I catch myself with a hand against the cold metal siderail of the hospital bed, to avoid slumping forward and off the bed. The nurse throws a hand out and catches me, boosting me back upright.

My vision clears, the white spots dissipating, and I glance down at the end of the bed for a place to focus. My feet poke up underneath the hospital blanket, which app apparently isn't made for six-foot-seven basketball players.

Nurse Carla giggles lightly as she notices what I'm looking at and reaches down to tug the sheet over my toes, shrugging apologetically just as the doctor strides confidently into the room. My head swivels toward the door to find an older gentleman with salt and pepper hair, glasses on top of his head, and a full beard walking toward my bed with a tablet in his hands. He gives me a head nod of greeting, and his eyes glide over me, before he flips his glasses down on his nose and his eyes land on my face.

"Good evening, Mr. Forester. Sounds like you had quite a night out on the court."

I squint, screwing up my forehead at his comment. "I guess... but I can't remember a thing."

"Hmm..." he adds, tapping some notes into the tablet before looking back at me with concern etched into his brows. "I see...we'll continue to run some more tests, but so far the ones we've done have all been negative and inconclusive. The EKG shows nothing with your heart. That's in great shape. The blood panels indicate no signs of elevated white blood cells, so that eliminates the possibility of cancer...which narrows things down significantly. Although we will still need to do a scan to check on any signs of neurological trauma. You haven't had a concussion or hit your head recently, have you?"

I shake my head. "Not that I recall."

I try to remember the past few weeks. It's all a blur. My stress levels have been through the roof as our team has been working to get into the conference playoffs and hopefully the NBA finals this year. The pinnacle of my basketball career.

"What if it's not my brain? Does that mean I'm okay?" I ask optimistically, hanging onto some hope that it's an easy fix and I can get back out on the road to help my team in the playoffs and to clinch a conference title. I've never missed a game or had a significant injury of any sort in my ten-year NBA career. I really don't want to start now. "What do you think happened to me out there, Doctor?"

His name tag says Harmon, MD.

He strums a hand along his trim beard, reading over the notepad thoughtfully. "That's a very good question. We don't often see such healthy young men in their early thirties without some sort of predisposed condition or head trauma. Which leads me to believe it's nothing physical, per se."

I perk up. "That's good, right?"

"Well, we'll see. I'm going to send in another doctor to have him conduct his own assessment. And if he agrees with me, we may have a diagnosis and can get you discharged. But it may require medication and regular treatment."

My brows furrow indignantly. "What? You just said it's not physical..."

He tucks the tablet against his chest inside his crossed arms, the gaps in his lab coat sleeves flapping to imitate angel wings. "Mr. Forester...Zeke... I don't believe your collapse tonight was a result of any physical ailment or injury. Based on what I saw in the video footage and what you described feeling before the collapse, the heaviness in your chest, the dizzy spell, the trouble breathing. I think it's possible you may have suffered a severe anxiety attack that caused you to lose consciousness and black out."

He smiles tightly as I gape at him in horror.

"What? Are you literally saying it's all in my head?"

Dr. Harmon chuckles and shakes his head. "Well, to some extent yes, it's your mental health I'm referring to. But it's treatable with anti-anxiety medication and therapy. You'll be fine."

With a condescending pat on my hand, he nods his head and strides out of the room, leaving me with more questions and a seething anger brewing inside me.

No...no, no, no...absolutely not.

That's impossible. I, Zeke Forester, professional basketball player and NBA All-Star *do not* suffer from anxiety.

And I certainly don't need therapy.

ACKNOWLEDGMENTS

Nicole Kim – my beautiful and brilliant cousin! I'm so proud of all you've accomplished in your career – from working to obtain your MA in Counseling, to the work you performed as advocate for adoptees rights. Thank you for taking the time to answer my questions on the adoption process. Love you, Nic!

To my faithful readers and followers – thank you for reading and loving these books as much as I do. I hope you'll continue reading as I have lots more books to come.

Thank you to my beta reader, Cristina Neese, for your invaluable feedback and the amazing support you've given me.

ABOUT THE AUTHOR

Sierra Hill is a *2020 RONE Award-Winning* author of *Game Changer*, as well as over 30 novels, including the award-winning college sports series, *Courting Love*, and the twice award-finalist erotic ménage serial, *Reckless – The Smoky Mountain Trio*.

Subscribe to her email list and download a FREE book here: www.sierrahillbooks.com

And don't forget to look for me on one of these socials:

ALSO BY SIERRA HILL

Change of Hearts (A College Campus Series)

Game Changer (Book #1)

Change in Strategy (Book #2)

Change of Course (Book #3)

Courting Love (College Sports)

Full Court Press

The Rebound

Pivot

Fast Break

Jump Shot

The Boy Next Door (All American Boy Series)

Stuck-Up Big Shot (A Cocky Hero Club Novel)

The Physical Series (New Adult Erotic Contemporary)

Physical Touch

More Than Physical

Physical Distraction

Physical Connection

Physical Desires (3 Book Boxset)

Standalones and Short Stories

One More Minute With You

The Reunion

Character Flaws

His Fairytale Princess

Made in the USA
Columbia, SC
16 August 2021

43081125R00143